Pr

THE CELLAR

"[A] ripped-from-the-headlines novel."

—*School Library Journal*

"Fans of realistic horror like *Living Dead Girl* (2008) may appreciate this."

—*Booklist Online*

"A well-written, completely absorbing nail-biter of a book…[with] a powerful, suffocating atmosphere of dread and uncertainty."

—*Bookish*

"Like watching an episode of *Law & Order: SVU*… I honestly could not tear myself away."

—*Chapter by Chapter*

"A real treat for avid mystery and thriller fans; the story line pulls you inside the world of a madman and the women he preys on… Never a dull moment."

—*Teen Reads*

YOU WILL
BE MINE

YOU WILL BE MINE

Natasha Preston

sourcebooks
fire

Published by Sourcebooks Fire, an imprint of Sourcebooks, Inc.
P.O. Box 4410, Naperville, Illinois 60567-4410
(630) 961-3900
Fax: (630) 961-2168
sourcebooks.com

Library of Congress Cataloging-in-Publication data is on file with the publisher.

Printed and bound in the United States of America.
WOZ 10 9 8 7 6 5 4

Alice, you share a birthday with Valentine's Day,
so I thought it was fitting to dedicate my Valentine's book to you.

Sorry you have to share again!

ROSES ARE RED,

VIOLETS ARE BLUE,

WATCH YOUR

BACK,

I'M COMING FOR

YOU.

I

Thursday
February 1

Valentine's Day. *Ugh*. Of all the holidays, this one is my least favorite.

I give the paper hearts Charlotte decorated our living room with a mental eye roll. Two of my roommates, Sienna and Charlotte, are *super* into Valentine's Day.

Fourteen days until all of social media is swarmed with cutesy couple photos and declarations of love, and I'm already living in an explosion of pink and red do-it-yourself crafts.

Puke.

The theater students put on a show every year about the story of Saint Valentine. Only they use dramatic license to make it sexier and bloodier. Last year was amazing, and this year is supposed to be better.

Plus there's an after-party.

My housemates—Chace, Sonny, Isaac, Charlotte—and I are

lounging in the living room waiting for Sienna to be ready so we can head out. There is just enough space for us all in the modest room.

"Turn it up, Lylah," Sonny orders. Sonny is from London and speaks like he's a gangster. He's far too soft to be one though.

I stand and dip in a sarcastic curtsy before adjusting the volume on the speakers that are paired with Sonny's iPhone. Puff Daddy's *I'll Be Missing You* blasts through the room.

Sonny is the oldest and, like a child, thinks that gives him the right to order everyone around. He's not all bad, but I don't think he heard the word *no* his entire childhood.

He ignores me and taps on his phone, likely lining up tonight's hookup.

Chace, who is a media student like me, smirks. I stick out my tongue at him. We met on our first day at college when we got lost on campus together and then stuck together in an attempt to look like we knew where we were going. Since then, we've spent countless hours watching movies, working on projects, and hanging out. Besides Sienna, Chace is my best friend. It didn't take long after meeting him to start having feelings for him—actually, it was about three minutes. I don't think he feels the same way though, because he treats me like one of the guys. But recently he's been finding more and more reasons for us to spend time alone together. I'm definitely not imagining it. Well, I don't *think* I'm imagining it.

Sienna appears in the doorway. "Lylah, are you sure this is the one?" she asks, running her hands down the sides of her blood-red dress.

Raising an eyebrow, I reply, "No, you look awful." She doesn't and she knows it.

Sienna is stunning. Born in Korea, she and her family moved to the United Kingdom when she was two years old. Her hair is unfairly sleek and shiny, and she wouldn't be out of place on the catwalk, though she's probably a bit short for that.

"Shut up. Tonight is my night with Nathan. I'm going to make him fall in love with me if it kills me."

Two weeks until Valentine's Day, and everyone is supposed to be coupled up. Chace doesn't seem to hate the day, so maybe he'll surprise me. Maybe I wouldn't dislike Valentine's Day as much if he had feelings for me too. "Sie, don't give it away, babe," Isaac says, throwing an arm around her shoulders. "Make him work for it."

Isaac is a brave, stupid man.

Sienna's black eyes darken as she shoots Isaac a look that could kill. "Thanks for that," she replies, sarcasm dripping from each word.

Taking a step back, he drops his arm and runs his hand through his short, black hair.

"Only trying to help," he defends.

Charlotte watches our interaction with interest. She's the quiet one who came to live with us by pure chance. Over the last five months, since we've all been living together, she and I have become friends. But she's still a bit of an outsider, preferring to stay in and keep to herself, rather than joining in activities with us.

"You okay, Charlotte?" Chace asks, sensing her tension.

"Maybe I'll stay here tonight," she replies. "It doesn't exactly sound like my thing."

Charlotte is dressed in a long denim skirt and a coral T-shirt. Her pale blond hair is pulled back in a high ponytail. She doesn't look like she's going out, but I know she'll enjoy it. Every time we've managed to drag her with us, she's had a good time.

I lay back against the cushions on the sofa. "No way. You're coming."

She leans in. "I know I said I wanted more of the university experience, but I'm pretty sure a play about martyrdom isn't it."

"It's not only about the play. You know we're going for the after-party."

"Now I *know* I won't enjoy that."

"What did you do before Lylah adopted you, Charlotte? Stay home and play chess against yourself?" Sonny asks, laughing at his own comment.

I grit my teeth.

"Don't be a dick, Sonny," Chace says, backhanding Sonny's chest.

Charlotte ducks her head to avoid Sonny's gaze, and I glare at him.

Sonny sighs. "You're right. That was mean. Char, I'm sorry."

She nods, but I don't think she forgives him. I wouldn't if I were her.

"Can we move on and have a good night tonight, please?" Sonny asks. "We're all single, and since everyone"—he stops and looks pointedly at me—"well, *almost* everyone loves Valentine's Day and doesn't want to be alone, hooking up is practically a guarantee."

Sonny doesn't have a problem getting girls, but if every woman on campus could hear how he usually speaks, I don't think he would be as popular.

Charlotte looks up and nods. "It's forgotten."

Sonny's gaze meets mine. "Lylah?"

I shrug. It's really not for me to forgive him. "Sure. I just want to have a fun night." *And for Chace to realize he's in love with me.* Having fun at the party might make this time of year a little more bearable. "No more breaking hearts this year, Lylah," Isaac teases.

Here we go again...

I harrumph and point at him. "Shut up, you. I didn't break anything."

"Please. Jake left school because you rejected him."

Jake, one of our other friends, tried to kiss me last year. It was right before I went home to spend Valentine's Day, the anniversary of my parents' death, with my brother, Riley. Jake knew that I was upset and still thought it was appropriate to kiss me. *Er, no.* I pushed him away and told him he could go to hell.

Looking back, I could have been a tad more diplomatic telling him I didn't like him, but I was emotional. My anxiety was raging, and I was dreading going home. It still felt—feels—so fresh that they are gone.

He could have chosen a better time to get rejected.

"Jake did not leave because of me. He left *five months* after that happened."

"Because even after all that time he couldn't get over you," Sonny adds, winking at me.

Chace stands up. "Guys, cool it."

He's always there to tell everyone to back off when they're teasing me. I can handle myself, but they're relentless with the Jake thing, so it's nice to have Chace backing me up.

"Mate, we're only joking," Sonny says to Chace.

I'm about to jump in when the doorbell rings.

"Want to wager who's out there?" Chace asks.

"I bet it's one of Sonny's ex's who can't take no for an answer," I guess.

Sienna laughs. "I bet it's the girl who keeps following Isaac around like a lost puppy. She's a total weirdo."

"Nah," Isaac says. "I bet it's Nora trying to be Lylah's BFF."

I roll my eyes and walk to the hallway.

Nora lives in a house across the street. She's nice, and we've studied together a few times, but she's been forcefully trying to insert herself into my circle of friends. It's not that I don't like her, but we have nothing in common besides our classes.

I tug open the front door, and am greeted by an empty porch. "Guys, it's just a prank ring and run!" I call.

I'm about to shut the door when I see an envelope on the doormat. It's cream and addressed to Sonny in typed letters. There is no return address or postmark, so it must have been hand-delivered.

Bending down, I grab it and take it inside.

"Who the hell plays ding-dong-ditch after the age of twelve?" Sonny asks.

I hand him the envelope. "Must be one of your friends. This was left on the doorstep."

With a frown, Sonny rips open the envelope and pulls out a piece of paper. The next words out of his mouth are wholly unpleasant. His glare is so intense, it's like he could set the paper on fire.

"What is it, man?" Chace asks, looking over his shoulder. "Secret admirer?"

"Probably. Whoever it is, they're dead when I find them out."

I share a look with Sienna, silently asking if she's in on whatever prank has been pulled on Sonny. She shakes her head.

"Show us," Isaac orders, and Sonny turns the note so we can see.

My eyes widen as I read what's on the paper. Each letter has been cut from a magazine or newspaper. It reads:

"That's creepy. Who would send that?" I ask. Students around here hit pranking pretty hard, like any college. But it's usually stuff like replacing ketchup with hot chili sauce in the dining hall or filling communal areas on campus with pink and red balloons. People don't usually write personal notes, not that I'm aware of anyway. Usually they stick to big, public pranks with a large audience and a large laugh.

"Do you think it was one of your castoffs?" Charlotte asks, her blue eyes glistening. She's enjoying Sonny's discomfort.

"I don't think I've done anyone *that* clingy," he replies.

Lovely.

"Whatever, it's only a prank," Chace says. "Is everyone ready? Let's go."

Sienna and Isaac head out first, Sienna practically glowing with excitement. Charlotte follows Sonny out, looking like she'd rather do anything else. Chace waits for me and holds out his arm. I loop my arm around his.

It's pitch-black outside and bloody freezing. I shudder at the chill.

I should have put on a heavier coat. I look up and down the block as we walk the short path from the door to the gate. The area is eerily quiet. The houses look the same on both sides of the road, all Victorian town houses, most of them occupied by students. Our place is nestled in the middle, so there is usually noise of some sort, though living off campus is significantly quieter than the dorms. I love having the independence being away from home, especially my brother, brings. But I still hate doing laundry.

Ahead, Sonny opens the trash bin by the street and throws the note inside, swearing as he slams the lid shut.

I lick my dry lips and look out to the street. Between the sidewalk and road is a stretch of grass with large oak trees, which have grown tall and wide, blocking out the glow from the streetlights. At the end of the row, one of the lights flickers. It's the perfect setting for a stalker; they could come and go easily without being seen. Could whoever left the note be waiting in the shadows?

"Do you think we should be concerned about Sonny's note?" I ask quietly.

Chace drops my arm so I can go out of the gate first. "What do you mean?"

"Well, it's definitely not a love note, and it's not a fun prank either. Could it be a real threat?"

He stops outside the gate and folds his arms. "I think you're letting that imagination of yours run wild."

"But a prank is supposed to be funny. No one laughed. A creepy note cut from magazines is—"

"Someone's twisted idea of a prank," Chace cuts in. "Forget about it, Lylah. Sonny clearly has. You know today is the start of all the Valentine's madness, and apparently people are stepping it up this year."

I open my mouth to object. He's not getting it. We're all friends, we all live together. If someone is messing with Sonny, it affects all of us.

Chace dips his head and smiles. "Lylah, relax. You watch too many horror movies. We're going to have a good night, and you're going to forget that note. No one is threatening Sonny. Okay?"

I nod, returning Chace's smile. It must not be convincing though, because he grabs my hand and squeezes it.

Inside, my heart is racing. But I can't tell if it's from being close to Chace or from worry about who's messing with Sonny.

2

Thursday
February 1

We arrive at the theater a little early, but the ushers are allowing people to go in. I flash my ticket and follow my friends inside. The large room is filled with round tables, chairs all arranged to face the stage.

"We're unlucky table thirteen," Isaac says, looking around. "Where the hell is that?"

Chace smirks. "You're standing next to the table plan, man."

Isaac turns his head and makes an *O* with his mouth. Idiot.

"We're over there," he says, pointing to a table near the left side of the stage. Second row from the front. Looks like we'll have a good view, and each table is spaced out well.

Included in our ticket prices are some kind of finger food, which wasn't specified when we ordered them, so I have no clue what's on the menu.

Servers dressed in black slacks and red shirts mill around the edges of the room, directing the audience to tables, food nowhere in sight. I guess they're waiting for everyone to be seated before bringing it out. I take a seat between Charlotte and Chace. Sienna and I made a secret pact to ensure that Char has a great night and maybe even help her meet a nice guy. Since we've known her—which, to be fair, isn't that long—she hasn't been on any dates or even shown interest in anyone. She said her last boyfriend was when she was in high school.

"When's the food coming? I'm starving," Sonny mutters, grabbing a drink menu from the table.

"The show doesn't start for another twenty minutes, so after that probably," Sienna replies. She scans the room, probably looking for her crush, Nathan, the reason for her outfit, to arrive with his friends.

"You okay?" I ask her.

Her mouth twitches in a fake smile. "I bet he's decided not to come."

"Sie…" I try to say in sympathy.

Air hits my face as she flicks her hand, cutting me off and pretending she's fine with him backing out.

Slowly, the room starts to fill as we talk, and before long, the lights flicker on and off—our cue to get our drinks and take our seats for the show.

"I'll go to the bar," I say, pushing my chair out to stand.

Chace mirrors my action. "I'll come with you."

I knew he would. He's always a gentleman, saving me from carrying a whole tray of drinks on my own. He hangs back a step, letting me go ahead, and puts his hand on my lower back as I walk past him. With my heart racing in my chest, we work our way to the bar area.

The bar smells like lemons, as if it's just been cleaned. I lean on the dark wood next to Chace, who is flagging down a bartender.

The guy, who's very tall, dark, and covered in tattoos, frowns. His green eyes look between me and Chace and his eyebrow raises like he's trying to figure out where he knows us from. He bends down and picks up a polaroid from behind the bar. The way he's holding it, I can only see it's black backing and white border.

"Everything all right, man?" Chace asks. "We were just after some drinks."

He grins. "I thought it was you. Your first round has been paid for."

"Nice!" Chace says. "Who bought the drinks?"

The bartender flicks his wrist, tossing the photo to him.

My mouth falls open and my spine stiffens as I see it. The photo is of the six of us sitting around the table. It must have been taken in the last ten minutes. Someone was watching us?

The bartender shrugs. "No idea, bud. Some dude who looked built to hell. Wearing a dark hoodie. He left cash."

A muscular person in a hoodie? I know plenty of guys who work out, and most of the population owns a dark hoodie since the school colors are black and yellow. I think I have three.

"Huh," Chace replies. "Okay, we'll have three Coronas, two white wines, and a vodka soda."

Is he for real? He's reeling off our order while my heart is racing.

"Chace!" I snap, tugging on the shirt sleeve he has rolled up to his elbow. "What are you doing?"

"What do you mean?"

"We don't know who's buying our drinks."

"They're free drinks, Lylah."

"First someone leaves that note and now this?" I gesture to the photograph. "Are you not at all concerned they could be related?"

"Concerned that Sonny has *another* girl following him around? Concerned that we don't have to pay for drinks?"

"We don't know who bought them."

"Who cares! The bartender's making them now, so it's not as if they've been tampered with. Anyway, it's probably Nora trying to wedge her way in."

Tilting my head to the side, I give him a side-eye. "So you think I'm overreacting?"

"A little bit, yeah. Look, I know it seems a bit sketchy, but you know how campus gets around holidays. There are going to be tons more pranks, and they never have ulterior motives other than to amuse people." He steps closer, and the scent of his aftershave wraps around me. Like a drug, I'm instantly hooked, and I lean in. "Please don't worry and enjoy tonight."

"Are you celebrating Valentine's Day this year? You weren't that into it last year." My voice is barely a whisper, but I'm too transfixed to care.

Chace's deep-green eyes stare into my soul, and I can feel my cheeks redden. "I've never had a reason to like it before," he replies as he closes the distance between us.

Do you have a reason now? Please elaborate.

"Here you go, guys," the bartender says. *This bartender has the worst timing ever*, I think. Chace breaks our gaze, looking instead to the bartender, and nods at him.

No! Chace, what's your damn reason?

Our moment is over.

Chace drops a tip on the counter and picks up the tray. I want to throw a full-on tantrum. He might have been getting ready to confess he has feelings for me, or he might have kissed me. I've been waiting for this for so long, and then we get interrupted.

Smirking over his shoulder as he walks away, Chace asks, "Are you coming or not?"

I grab the photo off the bar and follow him back to our table, where he sets down the tray. I slap the photo next to the drinks.

"That was left behind the bar, along with money for a free round," I blurt.

Chace might not be worried, but surely one of my friends will make the connection. I can count on Sienna and Charlotte…I think.

"That's us," Isaac states.

"Congratulations, Sherlock," Chace mutters sarcastically.

Sonny picks up his drink and raises it. "Well, thanks to the mystery drink fairy."

"Why would someone take our photo?" Charlotte asks.

"Exactly!" I exclaim.

"So the bartender would know who to give the drinks to," Isaac replies with an eye roll. "Obviously."

But I'm not buying it. "Why keep it a secret?"

Isaac shrugs. "I don't know, Lylah. Drink up. The show's about to start."

I don't understand why no one is taking this seriously. It doesn't make sense.

"What's that on the back of the photo?" Sienna asks.

"Huh?" Chace says.

"The edge is peeling." She picks it up and pulls at the black shiny backing.

What the hell?

When the backing peels off, Sienna looks at the photo, then drops it on the table like it's burned her. The small black square looks like the note Sonny received earlier with cut-out letters.

3

Thursday
February 1

No one says a word as we stare at the note.

"This is more than a prank," I say.

Sonny's lip curls in disgust. "I'm being stalked. I've always been straight-up with women. I don't want anything serious, and I damn well hate it when one of them conveniently forgets or thinks she can change my mind."

"Dude, do you have any idea who it could be?" Isaac asks.

He picks up the note and turns it over. "Not a clue. She clearly doesn't know me if she thinks a free drink is going to win me over."

"Should we leave?" I ask, scanning the crowd. The place is packed; each table has at least four people around it. A handful of others are at the bar waiting for drinks. No one is looking our way. If the person responsible for this is here, wouldn't they be watching for our reaction?

"No, we're not going anywhere," Sonny spits. "Some asshole isn't going to ruin my night."

Chace leans closer to me. "Look, you were excited to come here, and you haven't been excited for much recently."

The lead-up to the anniversary of your parents' death will do that.

My hand instinctively reaches for the heart-shaped necklace my parents bought me for my sixteenth birthday.

"Chace, I—"

The pad of his index finger covers my mouth, and he shakes his head. "Nope. I'm going make sure you enjoy yourself if it kills me, Lylah." He drops his hand. "Forget the notes for tonight. We'll figure it out tomorrow. Sonny can report it to the police or campus security or something."

I sit back and bite my lip. My stomach is bubbling with unease for Sonny, but there's little I can do right now. Nodding, I turn my attention to the stage as the lights cut out altogether.

The show is starting.

I shift in my seat and watch. The drama students are incredible, but I can't get into their performance. My mind is on the notes and the fact that whoever sent them doesn't want anyone to know who they are. Surely if it's a girl who wants Sonny, she would make herself known? Right?

It doesn't make sense.

If I'd gone straight to the door earlier, I might have caught whoever it was. Now the person who bought us drinks is probably somewhere in this room. Watching the show. Or watching us. The hairs on the back of my neck stand on end.

Once the show is over and the lights flick back on, I'm on my feet. "Are you guys ready to go?" I ask.

Chace chuckles. "Whoa, Lylah, where's the fire? Are you that eager to get to the after-party?"

Crap. With everything that happened tonight, I forgot about the party. "Actually, I'm tired. I was going to go home."

"Whatever. I'm going to love and leave you guys. Places to be and all that," Sonny says.

Sienna grabs his arm. "Wait, Sonny! Do you think you should go alone with a stalker out there?"

I don't know if she's being sarcastic or not, but Sonny laughs.

"Hilarious, Sie. Don't wait up."

Sonny jogs off, probably to some prearranged location to meet whomever he's seeing tonight.

I watch him disappear in the crowd. "Do you think he's actually in danger?"

"He'll be fine," Charlotte says. She walks beside me as we head toward the exit. "Thanks for making me come tonight. I really did enjoy it."

"I'm glad," I reply. At least someone had fun. I'm not sure I did.

"I think I'm going to head home with you too, if that's okay," she adds.

"Me too," Sienna chimes in. "Nathan is a no-show, and there'll be more parties this weekend. I'm gonna call it a night and get my beauty sleep."

Chace and Isaac look a little disappointed, but they insist on walking us back. "We came as a group, we should leave as a group," Chace says. "Well, except for Sonny."

I flash Chace a smile, but I'm only partly paying attention as the audience trickles out of the theater. I'm looking for someone in a hoodie. I start chewing my lip, anxious to get out of the crowded space. *Come on, come on.* I don't want to be in the same room as a person who takes our photo rather than coming over to buy us drinks.

Chace stays close, his chest almost against my back, as if he senses I'm on edge. Two bouncers on either side of the door stand with their arms folded, making sure the drunk students keep moving. They're both about the size of a house so I can't see many people starting trouble.

Outside, it's even colder than it was earlier. The temperature has dropped, and ice starts to glisten on the concrete. The bitter wind bites into my skin through my coat. I wrap my arms around my stomach and huddle closer to Chace. At least I can blame it on the cold if he asks why I'm creeping closer to him.

Chace's arm lands heavy over my shoulders, and I bump against his side as he pulls me close.

Result.

"Cold, Lylah?"

"Yes. I don't like winter."

"You're living in the wrong country."

Don't I know it.

"Oh my God!" Sienna shrieks, her voice so high-pitched it makes me wince.

"Jesus, Sie. Only dogs can hear you," Isaac grumbles.

I follow her line of sight. On the side of the library is a massive, artistically styled piece of graffiti. Red words, which look like they're dripping blood, read *YOU WILL BE MINE*. The artist has used blacks and grays to shade each letter, making the words pop.

It's creepy, but it looks good.

"He's talented," Isaac says.

"How do you know it's a guy?" I ask.

He raises his hands. "Or she."

Smiling, I reply, "Thank you."

"It wasn't you, was it, Lylah?" Isaac jokes.

"Yeah, we all know her artist talent begins and ends with stick people," Chace teases, squeezing his arm around me.

I'd snap something sarcastic in reply, but I am *really* horrible at drawing.

We head toward our rented town house, which is about five minutes away. As we cross campus, we pass two guys running around dressed as cupids—all they have on is what looks like a sheet wrapped around their arses. I hope they get frostbite. *Idiots.*

Laughing, I roll my eyes. "People are crazy."

We turn the corner, passing the Coffee House—a favorite among us college students—and we're officially off campus. It's darker here, those tall trees shrouding the light as usual, which always makes me nervous when walking alone at night. Not that anything ever happens. I think there has been one mugging in the entire time I've been at college, and it doesn't even count because the mugger was shit-faced on Southern Comfort and robbed his own wallet from his girlfriend.

Sienna walks in front of us, swaying her tiny hips. Isaac is right behind her, laughing at something she's said. On the opposite side of the road, walking toward us, is a guy in a hoodie. The guy from the club?

I tug my lip between my teeth. It's something I've always done when I'm anxious. After my parents died I almost chewed the damn thing off.

Chace chuckles. "Do you want the whole path there, Lylah?"

"Huh?" I say, looking up at him. He's almost on the road where I've veered over, obviously not paying attention to where I'm walking and taking up most of the sidewalk. "Oh."

He opens his mouth, but before he can speak, there's a loud *crack* as something hard hits the concrete. Chace tugs me to him as I whip my head in the direction of the noise. Red smoke billows from the middle of the street.

"God!" Chace says, laughing. "That was impressive. I actually jumped."

Sienna and Isaac are practically cheering, but I'm rooted to the ground, watching the hooded figure run away from us.

The smoke slowly thins, fading pink before it disappears into the night.

"What was it?" I ask.

"Smoke bomb," Chace replies. "Pretty good trick. I probably would have held off for a bigger crowd."

"Yeah," Isaac says. "If everyone is stepping up the prank game this year, we may need to do some planning after all."

Chace smirks. "If you can't beat 'em, join 'em, right?"

I frown into the distance where the man took off.

I guess.

• • •

We crash in the living room, slouching on the sofas. Chace joins me on the love seat, and Charlotte, Sienna, and Isaac occupy the couch.

"Want to talk about it?" Chace whispers, leaning his whole body closer to mine.

I lay back and look up at him. "Talk about what?"

"Whatever is making you so tense. I notice you, Lylah. Always have."

Always?

"I just can't stop thinking about the notes, the drinks, the graffiti, the smoke bomb. It's a lot to take in."

"We saw a smoke bomb and graffiti last year," he points out.

"Yeah, but they weren't linked. That graffiti read almost identically to Sonny's note. You can't seriously think this is all coincidental?"

"Maybe not, but it's probably someone trying to mess with his head. Please don't let it mess with yours. I know it's a sensitive time for you."

"I won't. I'm fine." I force my mouth to smile when I feel like screaming at him to stop rationalizing away my fears. And bringing up my parents. Chace has asked me a few questions about them since we met, but he respects that I don't want to talk about what happened. I can't. It's taken such a long time to be able to function normally, to breathe without feeling like I'm going to suffocate. I don't want to do anything that could take me back to a time that was so bleak I wasn't sure I'd survive it.

Besides, talking doesn't always help, especially when you've had to confront the loss as many times as I have in therapy.

I want to forget how it hurts to miss someone so bad that you want to die.

"*Nothing* is going to drive me crazy," I say, a little stronger this time. Chace's shoulder bumps mine, and he smiles. "Glad to hear it."

"Do you think we should call the cops about these?" Sienna asks, holding up the letter and picture. Sonny didn't care enough to take the photo with him, but Sie picked it up before we left the performance. I would have if she hadn't grabbed it. She was also the one who rummaged for the note after Sonny tossed it in the trash. At least it was on top of the bin.

"Yes," I reply. "We should *definitely* call the police."

"They're not going to do anything though. I mean, what *can* they do?" Chace says.

"Fingerprints? You know, other than ours. There are probably other identifying clues. Don't you watch any detective shows on TV? Even if it started as a joke, Sonny needs to know who this is and the cops need to make sure she—or he—stops."

"I wish we knew who sent them *now*. I have a great idea for a payback prank," Isaac says. "We buy those bugs they sell in pet shots for lizards and let them loose in their room."

I shudder, the very thought making my skin feel like bugs are crawling all over it.

"I just want Valentine's Day over with," I say.

"Still feel awkward about the Jake thing?" Isaac asks. He laughs and ducks as Chace's arm flies out to punch him. Chace shakes his head and mouths something I can't read, but my guess is that it's a swear word.

Literally this is *all* the material Isaac has to tease me with.

"No, I don't feel awkward about Jake," I reply. It's been almost two years and the anniversary of my parents' death is still as painful as when my brother and I were first told we were orphans. But it's a massive lie to tell my friends that Jake didn't make me hate the day even more.

Although it was mega-awkward with Jake for a while, we were cool before he left school. Or I think we were. Neither of us brought up the kiss again. And I haven't heard from him since he dropped out, besides exchanging brief Merry Christmas texts in December.

"She has nothing to feel awkward about," Sienna defends me.

Isaac holds up his hands. "I was kidding. You may have broken the poor guy's heart, but that doesn't mean you have to feel bad about it."

I narrow my eyes to show him I'm not falling for whatever he's trying. "You're being dramatic, it was one almost kiss, and he was fine after. It's not like he proposed or something."

Isaac scowls. "Fine. You're no fun."

I give him a fleeting smile. "Sorry to disappoint. Now, if we can stop discussing my tragic love life, we can talk about pranks."

Chace chuckles. "Lylah wants to join in this year."

"Really? You usually don't want anything to do with them," Sienna says.

"But now I have motivation. I really hope we prank the person stalking Sonny."

"Baby powder inside the girls' swim team's hair dryers," Isaac says. "I volunteer to go in the changing room!"

Sienna rolls her dark eyes. "Good one."

"I want to do something like…burn a pile of cupid dolls in the middle of campus with fake blood all around them," I suggest.

Chace laughs. "Jesus, Lylah. You sound like you'd enjoy that a little too much."

I think I might. What does that say about me?

Isaac smirks. "You really don't like this holiday, do you?"

"Nope." I really don't. If my parents hadn't been on their way to a romantic celebration at a swanky hotel, they would still be here. They wouldn't be dead. My brother and I didn't even hear about the accident until hours after it happened. Riley and I arrived at the hospital to be told both our parents would be fine, don't worry, but they died minutes after the clock ticked past midnight into the fourteenth.

"Anyway," I continue, switching the subject. "I'm tired and need my bed. Tomorrow we shop for baby powder, fake blood, and cupids."

I say good night to my housemates, brush my teeth, and go to my room. Closing my door, I pad across the carpet. My dress comes off easily over my head, and I chuck it on the chair in the corner of my room. I'm usually tidy, but when I'm tired, I don't care. I pick up my pajamas that I left crumpled on my bed. They'll do for tonight. My eyes are heavy, and my legs ache. I can't be bothered to find another set.

I slip on the fleece pajamas and instantly feel warm and cozy. They're lilac and fluffy with a unicorn pattern. I would *never* let Chace see these. When I leave my room in my pajamas, it's in one of the silk pairs.

Gripping the edge of my quilt, I slide it back, and something stabs my thumb. My fingers part instinctively, and I yank my hand away. There's a small bead of blood on the pad of my thumb and a red rose lying on the floor between my feet.

What the hell?

Sonny.

I press my lips over my thumb. Sonny has history of leaving surprises in other people's beds, like spiders or women's underwear in his friend's bed.

Bending down, I pick up the rose by its stem and chuck it on my bedside table. Tomorrow I'm going to put something in his bed, and it won't be as pretty as a flower. Maybe I'll buy some prawns or fish heads or something that will really stink. If I were brave enough I would steal Isaac's bug idea.

Whatever happens, Sonny is going down.

4

Friday
February 2

I wake up to the rain gently patting against my window.

Despite my annoyance at being damp when I'm out and about, I actually love the rain. There's something about the sound that's deeply calming. My Fitbit vibrates on my wrist, the silent alarm telling me it's 6:00 a.m. and time to get up.

Raising my arms above my head, I stretch them out as far as I can and arch my back. Before my parents died, I would sleep in as long as I could and roll my eyes whenever Mom told me I should be making the most of each day and not sleeping my life away.

Now no matter how much I don't want to get out of bed, I do it anyway. Mom will never get that chance again.

Right. Get up.

I grip a fistful of my quilt and throw it off my body. The cool air from the old house immediately makes goose bumps rise on my skin, so I sit up before I change my mind, snuggle back under the covers, and drift back to sleep.

I leave my bedroom and move across the hall to the bathroom. It's warmer in here; the radiator was installed last year and it kicks out a lot of heat.

When I'm finished showering and getting dressed, I tiptoe downstairs, stepping over the creaky floorboards so I don't wake anyone.

Sonny and Sienna are the only ones who get up around the same time I do. Everyone else is bloody lazy. The kitchen is quiet as I creep toward it. Charlotte and Isaac both have bedrooms downstairs, so we keep the noise down until 7:00 a.m. when they surface.

"Morning," I say to Sienna, who's already perched on a seat in the kitchen. Her sleek hair is sticking out all over the place. "Bad night?"

She doesn't even look up from her massive cup of black coffee. "Ugh. Couldn't sleep. Tired," she mumbles.

"We don't usually beat Sonny. Has he been down yet?"

"He wasn't in his room," she mutters in a monotone voice that makes her sound like she's prerecorded the sentence.

"How do you know?" I ask, grabbing a mug for my own coffee.

"His door was open. No idea where he is."

I turn to face her. "That's weird. He doesn't stay out. Ever." Sonny's a massive ladies' man. I doubt I can count high enough to number his "conquests," as he calls them, but not once has he stayed over with anyone. He would never risk the awkward morning walk of shame or morning-after conversation.

Sienna shrugs. "I thought so too. Maybe he's changing his ways." She pauses, and a small, low-pitched laugh bubbles out of her throat involuntarily. "Or maybe not."

I pour my coffee and join Sienna at the table, waiting for everyone else to get up.

Logically, I know worrying about a grown guy who's probably decided to stay out all night is ridiculous, but something is wrong. I can *feel* it. I'm unsettled; my stomach is full of lead. Since my parents' death, I've always prepared for the worst. When they arrived at hospital after the accident, they were both expected to make a full recovery. Mom died on the operating table, and Dad died less than forty minutes later after massive internal bleeding.

"Have you heard from Sonny?" I ask when Charlotte and Isaac walk in the room an hour later. Once I know where he is, I'll be able to settle.

Charlotte raises her eyebrows. Her expression says it all: *He wouldn't call me if I were the last human on Earth.* And fair point; he wouldn't.

Isaac lifts one shoulder in a half-hearted shrug. "Nope."

"He hasn't come home yet," I explain.

"Really?" Isaac asks. "He's probably fallen asleep in some girl's bed by accident. Likely had too much to drink."

"Hmm, maybe," I murmur.

"Should we worry?" Sienna asks, now more awake after her second caffeine hit. "This really is unlike him."

My stomach tilts with unease. Sonny is *always* here in the morning—especially when he has class. His family doesn't live nearby either, so he rarely goes home even when we're on a break. He's always here.

I push my chair out and stand up. "I'm going to ask Chace if he knows anything."

"Ask Chace if he knows anything about what?" Chace's voice is like a volt of electricity to my heart. Every. Bloody. Time.

Look at his face, not at how incredible his toned arms look in his gray T-shirt.

"Sonny's missing," Isaac says.

"Whoa. Missing? So we're definitely saying he's missing?" I ask. My heart starts to race. Isaac's words give my worst fears life, and, suddenly, they grow from a nagging worry in the back of my mind to an overwhelming apprehension.

Were those notes serious threats?

"He's not here, and we don't know where he is. I think that's the exact definition of missing," Isaac counters.

Chace shakes his head, causing his messy blond hair to ruffle. It's beyond cute. "Don't overreact. Maybe he decided to take up running again. Maybe he's gone to the shop. Maybe he accidentally fell asleep at some girl's place?"

Chace's explanations are all possible…if you don't know Sonny.

"I'm going to try his cell again," I say, jabbing my finger at his name on the screen.

"We're all worried, Lylah, but you seem paranoid," Chace replies. As he walks past me, his arm brushes against my back. I'm not sure if was intentional or accidental, but I'm not going to complain. Also, I'm not paranoid; I'm being a concerned friend. A good friend.

I put the phone to my ear and wait. When Sonny's voicemail message begins, I hang up. "It's not even ringing."

"He's fine, Lylah. Are you ready to go?" Chace asks, pouring coffee into a travel mug. We have so much editing to do for our advertising campaign class project, but that's not really what I'm worrying about right now.

"Er, yeah. I'm ready." I turn to Isaac, Sienna, and Charlotte. "Will you guys text me when you hear from him?"

"Yeah. I'll swing by the coffee house and library on my way to the gym and see if he's there," Isaac offers. "To be honest though, this whole situation seems like something he'd pull. You know how he loves a show. The notes, the picture, the drinks. It was probably all him."

Sienna stands and brushes her hair back with her fingers. "I'll join you at the gym before class, Isaac. You do have a point though. If anyone is going to orchestrate a prank like this, it's him."

He *did* leave a rose in my bed. Is this Sonny's idea of a joke? While it wouldn't surprise me, I would be seriously pissed off if he was playing with us.

Chace's hand circles my wrist, catching my attention and sending my stomach free falling. Why couldn't he have left me the rose? It's really unhealthy to have a crush this big. "See? Sonny's probably pranking himself for attention. I don't know why I didn't think of that. Let's forget him for a bit and concentrate on our assignment, yeah?"

Smiling, I dip my head. "Sure."

Isaac and Sienna gather their things, then head out the back door to the gym they joined off campus. Neither of them likes the one on campus—it's always full of male students grunting in the mirror as they pose with weights. I'm impressed they go at all. I don't mind running, but the gym is definitely not for me.

A few minutes later, Chace and I head out the front door. It's not as cold as yesterday, but cold enough to send a shiver rocketing down my spine.

Chace chucks his arm around my shoulders and we head along the sidewalk, then cut to a path through a wooded area that is a shortcut to campus. The bare branches above us sway in the wind, and the frost-covered grass crunches beneath my feet.

Then we pass the shops and restaurants, all decorated with glitter and hearts for Valentine's Day, Chace smirking at me the whole time. I want to be lighthearted and mess around with him like we usually do, but it feels like there's a dark cloud following me around. My parents were worriers, and I guess it's rubbed off on me.

Like always, when we arrive at the media building, Chace reaches for the door to let me go first. His gesture is enough to put a smile on my face. "Thank you."

"You're welcome, ma'am," he replies with a really bad American accent.

"That was awful. You should be ashamed."

His beautiful green eyes roll. "Let's just get this done, yeah?"

The halls are surprisingly silent as we walk toward the editing suites. Chace and I are both hoping a degree in film and television production will land us jobs working on movies. Or TV at least. Living in LA would be nice, but I'm scared of emigrating in case I end up working in a restaurant forever, never being able to get a job in my field. Plus Americans drive on the wrong side of the road.

"Why is it so quiet?" I whisper to Chace.

"It's seven thirty in the morning, Lylah. Most university students don't like early morning classes and projects," he says sarcastically.

We've booked an editing room for the earliest time possible because I've left my assignment to the last minute. I've had so many papers to write this semester, I can hardly keep up. Chace is thankfully further along than me, so he offered to help. I could use another perspective, and I trust Chace to be honest and offer decent feedback.

"Whatever," I mutter, knowing he's right. I'm always up early, but I've never been on campus to work *this* early, and if I weren't on the verge of failure on this ad, I wouldn't be here before 8:00 a.m.

We head into the room, and Chace begins switching on the equipment while I check my phone. I hold my breath in hope. *Please let there be a message from Sonny.*

Nothing from him, but I do have a text from Isaac letting me know that he hasn't seen Sonny yet and one from Riley asking me to reconsider coming home over Valentine's Day. I can't go home, and I can't deal with him right now. Not if I'm going to get good marks on this assignment.

"Still nothing," I say, biting my lip as the uneasy feeling settles lower in my stomach.

"That doesn't mean anything is wrong, Lylah."

"I know. I just wish he would get in touch."

"He will soon." Chace's eyes flick away from mine too quickly. He's worried. That makes me feel worse. Of all of us, Chace is the one with a level head. If he's concerned, then we all should be. And that thought is terrifying. I can feel anxiety creeping up on me.

"Do you think… Do you think we should report him missing?" I ask, running my finger along the computer keyboard nervously.

"Lylah," Chace says.

I can't bear to look at him for fear I'll fall apart. Using his index finger, he gently turns my head and gazes into my eyes reassuringly. "There's nothing the police will do until it's been twenty-four hours, but we'll speak to campus security and see if they'll keep an eye out for him. Okay?"

"A lot can happen in twenty-four hours, Chace." Two years ago, my life upended in an even shorter period of time.

"I know, but there's nothing we can do about police protocol. Let's focus on getting your ad sorted. We need to try different music if you're still not sure. We'll work on that until ten, and then we'll leave."

"Yeah." I nod. "Okay. Thank you."

He gives me a smile that makes his cheek indent with the cutest dimple, but his eyes are flat.

"So," he says, clicking the mouse and bringing me back to task. "Work, or you'll fail."

He wouldn't be a very good motivational speaker. But I do as I'm told.

5

Friday
February 2

A gainst all odds, I work really well at this ungodly hour of the morning. So when our time is up, Chace books the suite for the same time tomorrow. It'll be Saturday, so I'm already planning on bringing my own travel mug—or bucket—of coffee.

We were really productive and made great progress on my media project, yet as we walk home together, I can't help but grumble. "Ugh, pink and red paper hearts *everywhere*." I flick my hand toward the love-themed window at the café I now plan to avoid until it's decorated for St. Patrick's Day. "In two weeks they're going to be in the bin."

Chace rolls his perfect emerald eyes, and my insides turn to mush. "Lylah, try to be more optimistic."

Maybe if things with Chace were going the way I've been hoping for the last year and a half, I would be more enthusiastic. It would be nice to have a distraction, something to look forward to this time of year. "I think you'll find that I'm a *realist*," I reply.

Okay, that's probably a stretch. I do sound like a miserable, single grump. Valentine's Day doubly sucks when it marks a family tragedy *and* you're painfully in love with someone who doesn't know you're in love with him.

I still remember when I first met Chace. He looked like he belonged in a Calvin Klein advertising campaign. His dark blond hair, muscular physique, and outgoing personality turned me into a blubbering mess when he introduced himself.

Then there's me. I'm petite with light blond hair, dark brown eyes, and a slightly socially awkward personality. Or maybe I'm only awkward around him.

Regardless, we don't match, and the sooner my heart gets that memo, the better. But so far I've not had much success on that front.

Chace launches into describing a trailer he saw for a new movie, and I can't help imagining us both in the theater, snuggled up next to each other, sharing popcorn. *Totally inappropriate, Lylah. Focus.*

As we turn the corner onto our street, I almost collide with someone tall. He's wearing a long, black leather coat. Underneath is a dark gray hoodie, the top of it pulled down low over the person's face.

"Sorry," I say to the only part of his face that is visible—dark-brown stubble that completely hides his chin.

"Right," the guy mumbles, stepping aside. His voice is very deep, but it sounds like he's trying to disguise it. But why would he? His head turns as I walk past, watching me from his shroud like I'm prey.

Chace raises his eyebrows, seemingly also uneasy.

I glance behind me. The man has disappeared.

Chace and I continue walking, but my chest tightens with nervousness.

"I guess it's not just Halloween that brings out the crazies," I say.

"Huh. He was kind of dressed like the grim reaper," Chace replies.

"It wasn't only the way he was dressed. His whole vibe was creepy. Intimidating."

"He probably couldn't see you with his hood that low."

I roll my eyes. Sure seemed like he could. "Yeah, what's up with that?"

"Hey, not everyone is blessed with quality hair like this," he teases, running his hand through his locks.

Whipping my hand out of my pocket, I slap Chace on the arm. Laughing, he bats my hand away. "Sorry. Forget it, babe. He's gone."

I don't think I'll ever get tired of hearing him call me *babe*.

Chace starts walking again. I follow, pushing my legs faster to catch up with his long strides. At the moment, I don't want to be left behind.

"Lylah, I can hear you thinking. What has you freaked out?"

I shake my head, and my hair falls in my face. Brushing it back, I reply, "Nothing. I guess that guy startled me."

"I don't know how you get through April Fools' Day or Halloween."

"Well, those I like. You're *supposed* to scare people then."

"You're confusing."

So are you.

Chace and I make it home, and I dip my hand into my bag to grab the key. He stands behind me, and the close proximity makes my mind cloud. His warm breath blows through my hair and against my ear. *Concentrate. Key. Lock. Now, Lylah.*

With an unsteady hand, I turn the key, and the green door creaks open.

"Sonny?" I call as I tentatively walk through. There's no answer. My throat constricts. I just want to know that Sonny is safe. It's been more than twelve hours since we last saw him.

"You here, bro?" Chace calls.

We're met with complete silence. No one is home.

Turning to Chace with my bottom lip wedged between my teeth, I shrug my shoulders, at a loss.

Chace glances at his phone. "Wait—doesn't he have a class now?"

"Yes!" I exclaim. "He's always complaining that he has more classes on Fridays than any other day."

"So, he's probably there. Why don't we head back to campus and see if we can find him?" Chace shrugs his shoulder. "I know we just came from there, but at least it'll stop us from worrying."

"I don't care that we have to go straight back, but you want to peek into his classroom? Like stalkers?"

Chace's lips kick up in a smile. "But we'll know he's safe, so who cares if we look a bit creepy doing it?"

"Yeah, I guess." He could go for lunch in town or hang out with a friend afterward, and we'd still be worrying. I can't wait for him to show up somewhere. "No, you're right. We need to look for him."

He takes a step back out the door. "Let's go. It's getting closer to the end of class. We'll have to hurry."

I lock the house back up and then check my phone. There's only a message from Sienna saying she and Isaac haven't seen Sonny. Charlotte will be looking too, but she and Sonny don't usually cross paths. She's strictly a class, library, and home kind of girl. The only time she goes out is if Sienna and I drag her. And the only time Sonny goes to the library is to cram for finals.

On a new mission, Chace and I race back to campus, with no time to stop and exchange pleasantries with anyone. Sonny's class will let out soon, and we could miss him. We pass people we know with a brief wave, but I don't care about being rude. There's a tenseness in my stomach that won't allow me to relax, and I know it won't disappear until I've seen or heard from Sonny.

Sonny's math building is up ahead. "Please be in there. Please be in there," I mutter, trying to calm the acid churning in my stomach.

"Lylah, I'm sure he's fine," Chace says. His eyes darken with worry as he stares at me like I'm a fragile child.

He doesn't fully know this side of you.

I don't want him to know everything about me. Chace is protective enough without seeing me at my worst. I think it would scare him.

"I'm just worried," I say, giving him the best smile I can muster. "I hate not knowing if he's okay. But you're right, he's probably sitting in that classroom, head bowed over his notebook, battling the worst hangover."

Except I don't believe the words that pour from my mouth any more than Chace does. He returns my smile, but it's weak and unconvincing.

As we approach the classroom, Chace takes my hand. I hold on to him. I peer through the large windows. My throat is so dry I feel like I could choke.

"He's not there," I whisper. Three rows of students stare at their professor as he lectures. None of them are Sonny. "Are you sure this is the right room?"

"I've walked over with him before," Chace says, "and there is only one empty seat."

"What do we do now?"

Chace replies in a low voice. "We go to security."

I nod my head and take a bracing breath. "Okay."

"Campus security will know what to do before we can go to the police and officially report Sonny as missing. They might even have him on camera somewhere," he adds.

God, I hope so.

I will never forget what it was like to wait in limbo for news about my parents. When things took a turn for the worse, every second felt like an eternity. It was excruciating, and now the feeling's back.

Chace turns, tugging my arm, but I'm still rooted in place.

"Sorry," I say, and I fall in step beside him. Even holding his hand doesn't anchor me.

We head toward the student union, where campus security has its main office. A man the size of a tank greets us from behind a reception desk. His eyes are friendly, and he smiles. I recognize him. Security officers are always walking the grounds, but I've never really paid much attention to them before. I've never needed to.

"Everything all right?" the officer asks.

"No," I reply, my voice shaking, betraying how worried I am. "Our friend is missing. We haven't seen him since last night—it's totally unlike him. He never stays out. Never."

The security officer frowns. "Come inside a minute." He comes out from behind the desk and opens the door to a small conference room.

"I'm Paul," he says after he closes the door and we all sit down. He takes a notebook and a pen from his pocket. "What's your friend's name?"

"Sonny James," I reply.

"When and where were you the last time you saw him?"

"Last night, around ten thirty." Then Chace and I launch into the story of the notes.

Officer Paul frowns, the creases on his forehead rolling. "And you don't know who sent these notes?"

"Not a clue. They weren't signed," Chace says.

"Where was Sonny going last night?"

I shrug. "He decided to meet up with some girl rather than going to the after-party, so just into town I think."

Chace clears his throat. "He could have gone home with someone. He's known for that, but he never stays out all night."

The security officer nods. "Okay, let me take some more details, and I'll have a word with a friend at the police station."

My shoulders sag. I was hoping he would have a more immediate solution. "Thank you."

We give him our address and answer everything else we can for him to relay to the police.

"Okay," Paul says. "I'll have last night's footage from the theater building checked out, but if your friend went into town after, it's unlikely we'll see anything useful. Take my number and leave yours. If he comes home, let me know immediately. Meanwhile, I'll get his photo out to the rest of the team."

"Thank you so much." My breath comes a bit easier. I'm so glad he's taking over. He's probably handled situations like this before. And they've probably turned out fine.

Paul reassures us that he will do everything in his power to find Sonny. In the meantime, with me having no classes on Fridays, there is nothing I can do but wait. I hate waiting; it's always been unbearable. But it looks like we're in for a really long evening.

6

Saturday
February 3

t's 5:45 a.m. I think I got about three hours of sleep. None of my other housemates seem to have slept better, as we're all sitting in the kitchen, eyes glazed over. Our table seats six, so the empty chair for Sonny is obvious.

Around nine o'clock last night, a police officer came to take our statements. They agreed that given the circumstances, the fact that it's completely out of character for Sonny to stay out and not get in contact and to miss class, they should look into his disappearance sooner. We're all still pretty unsettled. The situation became even more real when the police talked about contacting Sonny's parents—and the university administrators. "How long before you think we'll have news?" I ask.

Chace shrugs.

Sonny wasn't caught on any of the university's cameras the last night we saw him, and we searched everywhere we could think he might go.

"Do you think we should be out there?" Sienna asks. "You know… looking for him? He could be in trouble. He could be hurt."

Isaac shakes his head. "We were told to stay here. I think we should wait to hear from the cops this morning before we do anything."

I voice the question no one wants to put out there. "What if something bad has happened to him?"

"Don't, Lylah," Chace says, averting his eyes.

"Should we not discuss what could happen? Prepare ourselves? I mean, we all know this isn't nothing," I say in a rush, my anxiety taking over.

No one says anything.

Our last hope is the police tracking him down. They're contacting his family and friends back home. It's unlikely he'll be there though.

I press my fingers against my temples and shut my eyes. When my brother and I were waiting for news on our parents, we sat in silence. It was suffocating. I felt so alone. Instead of facing reality and giving each other support, we said nothing. And when the doctor told us Mom was gone, I couldn't bear to talk. I didn't have the words. I could only wail.

Sitting there out of my mind with worry isn't helpful. "I'm going to shower." I dash out of the room before anyone can stop me, not that anyone seems to try.

My friends know that my parents died. But they don't know about my mental state and what I went through afterward. Riley is the only one who truly knows how affected I was. I'm not exactly ashamed of how much I struggled—how much I *still* struggle—but I don't want to talk about it. I'm stronger now, and I like who I've become. But now that Sonny is missing, I feel like I'm reliving part of that experience.

After my shower, I spend the next hour practicing deep breathing exercises in my room.

Chace comes to get me when it's time to leave for the media lab. If my grade wasn't on the line, I'd cancel. But I need to keep my mind busy, so Chace and I head back to the editing suite. We probably have two more sessions, and then I'll be finished.

I wrap my arms around my body as we walk against the cutting wind. It's even colder today, and I can't wait to be in the warm again. "When we're done with our session, let's go back to security," I tell Chace. "Maybe they'll have new updates from the police by then. Or should we stop there first?"

Chace gives me a side-glance, his lips thinning. The longer Sonny is missing, the more I can tell he's letting himself think something bad has happened. When an officer tried to get ahold of Sonny's family last night while the police were at our place, she was met with only voicemail. Apparently that wasn't an immediate cause for concern—and doesn't mean that Sonny *wasn't* with his family. It's concerning to me, but I really hope Sonny had to go home and simply forgot to let us know.

But that doesn't explain why he's not answering his calls or texts.

"We'll go and see what's going on as soon as you're done. More time likely means more news. Otherwise, you'll lose your session and be even more distracted. Focus on what you can control: finishing this project."

I sigh. He's right.

We turn down the hallway with the editing suites, and I push open the door to room nine. A rancid smell attacks my nose and then hits the back of my throat, making me gag. I slam my hand over my nose and mouth so hard it'll probably leave a mark. "What the hell is that?" I murmur against my palm.

Chace spits out an unintelligible reply through his covered face and flicks on the light. My world stops.

Oh, God.

Sonny.

He's slumped against a wall in the corner, mouth is open, as if he's drifted to sleep. But he's not asleep.

Dark-red blood covers his chest. There's something wrong with his shirt.

My legs give way. It's like I suddenly weigh too much and they bend until I land on the floor in a heap. I jut my hands out to brace myself and stare in shock. Sonny's shirt looks strange because it's cut open—no, his *chest* is cut open. The dark, crusted blood disguises the full horror at first glance. But now there is no mistaking the long, deep gash running down the center of his torso.

Chace backs up, and his heel bumps into my knee. Gasping, he startles and looks down, surprised that I'm on the floor. His green eyes are wide like saucers.

He lowers himself, crouching in front of me. With a shaking hand, he cups my cheek. "Lylah," he whispers. His voice is breathy, like he's hopping up and down while trying to talk.

"He's…dead." My heart stops. "He's dead," I say again. It's all I can think to say. *He's dead and we're here with his body!* My heart jump-starts again. I need to get out of here. "Oh, God. He's *dead*, Chace! He's dead!"

"Lylah." Chace tenderly grips my upper arms and hauls me to my feet. His gaze flits around wildly like he's completely unsure of what to do.

Our friend is dead!

"I can't be in here, Chace." I burst into tears. I can feel my blood pumping through my veins. The smell of Sonny's blood is so strong it burns my nose. This is all too much to take in, too much to process. We need help. "Sonny's dead."

No matter how many times I say the words, I can't quite bring myself to comprehend it. *Am I asleep? Is this a nightmare?*

Chace nods robotically, his eyes fixed on mine as he helps me up and backs toward the doorway. I want to look at Sonny again, to prove to myself that I'm wrong, to prove that he's not dead, but Chace is like a magnet. I can't look away from him.

In the hallway, Chace closes the door behind us. Without taking his eyes off me, he pulls his phone from his pocket.

"Right," I whisper. "We need the cops." *Is this actually happening?*

I lean against the wall. Chace lets me go, and I slide down until I hit the floor.

I bring my knees into my chest and wrap my arms around my legs. *Sonny is dead. Sonny's dead. And not just dead.* Murdered. *Sonny was murdered.*

My vision starts to blur, and I feel like I'm falling. Nothing makes sense. Reality becomes fantasy. *This can't be happening.* Sure, Sonny wasn't always likable, but no one would want to *kill* him.

Around me, I hear footsteps and voices. I'm sure Chace is talking, but I'm stuck in an alternate universe trying to make sense of something so senseless.

Someone kneels in front of me, blocking the light above. The sudden darkness is enough to snap me out of my trance. I sit taller, my heart hammering.

"I'm sorry if I startled you. I'm Detective Ewelina Saunders, but you can call me Lina. I'm going to take you and your friend with me to a room down the hall. Let's get you a drink, okay?"

"You have questions," I say.

"Yes, but let's get you some water or tea first."

Chace holds out his hand. I've never been so grateful for his help before. The second we touch I feel more grounded. He helps me to my feet again and doesn't let go when I'm standing.

"You okay?" he asks.

I shake my head, practically collapsing into his arms. My feet are still planted in the same place, so I almost knock him over. Chace steadies us and holds me close. "You will be, Lylah. I promise."

I wish I could be as sure. Our friend has been murdered. Mutilated. I can never un-see the horrific image of his hacked-open chest.

My legs are moving forward now. I'm aware of that much, but I can't feel anything. I'm numb. We will have to talk about Sonny. We will have to explain what we found, even though the detective has seen him too.

I don't want to talk about it.

Lina opens the door to a room I haven't been in before. There's a small kitchen and seating area. It must be a lounge for staff, but it's empty today. *Today is Saturday*, I remind myself.

Chace stops in front of the bright blue sofa. "Lylah, sit down," he says softly, like I'm a baby. His forehead is wrinkled from his frown, and he looks a bit scared. Scared for me.

"Sorry," I murmur, following his instructions but still not letting go of his arm, pulling him down to the couch with me. "I'm okay. I'll snap out of it."

The corner of his mouth curls in a sympathetic smile. "It's okay. We're both in shock, I guess."

"Sorry to worry you."

"Stop apologizing."

Sorry.

"Chace, Lylah, can I get either of you a drink?" the detective asks.

"Coffee, please," Chace and I say at the same time.

I need a strong hit of caffeine to make it through this.

"I think there is only instant. Is that okay?" she asks.

We both nod. It is so strange to think about beverages when Sonny is in the editing suite with his chest cut open. Dead. Tears start to fall again. Why would someone do that? Why would someone hurt Sonny?

In the distance, I hear the electric kettle start to boil, getting louder and louder. Lina clangs around with mugs and spoons. Beside me, Chace stares at a spot on the floor. Nothing is there.

"Chace, are you okay?" I whisper.

He shrugs. "I don't really know."

Yeah, me either.

Detective Lina comes back with a white tray and puts it on the table in front of us. She picks up a mug of milky tea and sits down. I reach for my coffee. It's too hot to drink, but I need to hold something. Suddenly I feel fidgety.

Chace and I sit still, waiting for her to start. She bends down, reaching for a pen and notepad from her bag, and she pulls out something else too. It's a recorder. Of course she's going to want to record our conversation. That's what the cops have to do.

They'll replay it and listen—over and over and over—to how we found our friend dead.

She presses a button, and a tiny red light flicks on.

She asks us to state our names, then asks, "How are you two doing?" Chace shrugs his shoulders again.

"I'm not sure," I reply. "I don't understand it. How could someone kill Sonny? Why would they cut him like that?"

"Hold on," Lina says, raising her free hand. "Let's start at the beginning, and we'll work on figuring out the answers to your questions after that."

I nod.

"I'm told Sonny was reported missing late last night by security here?" she continues.

"Yeah," Chace says. "He went out Thursday night and wasn't home Friday morning. He always comes home. We spoke to security, and the guy we talked to, Paul, said he'd report it to the station. Sonny had gotten a few threatening notes before, so the police came by our house and filed a missing person report last night."

She nods. Putting down her mug, Detective Lina looks at her notepad. "Right. I have read those statements. And this morning, what happened?"

I sit up. "Chace and I were going to work on my ad project in the editing suite. When we arrived...I knew something was wrong as soon as we opened the door. There was a smell. Chace turned on the light, we walked into the room, and that's when we saw Sonny in the corner."

"Do you know anyone who would want to harm Sonny? Does he have any enemies?"

"No," Chace says. "Sonny's direct. Sometimes that pisses people off, but he doesn't have enemies. He wouldn't intentionally hurt anyone. There's nothing for anyone to hate him for."

I add, "He's a good person. *Was* a good person..." I pause. "I can't think of anyone who would have wanted to hurt him or send those notes."

Lina nods. "Sonny didn't use this building for class, am I correct? According to the university, he was studying engineering."

"Yeah. Of our housemates, it's only me and Lylah who come here..." Chace glances at me, and it finally clicks why she's asking that. Why leave Sonny in the editing suite Chace and I booked?

My jaw drops. "Whoever killed Sonny wanted us to find him here, didn't they?"

"Who knew you would be here?" Detective Lina asks, avoiding my question.

That's not a no.

I shake my head. "Um, we had to book the room, so it wouldn't be hard to get that information. But why was he left for us to find?"

Detective Lina doesn't have that answer, but I need it. My mind is spinning, and it is hard to catch my breath.

"We will do all we can to find that out, Lylah. Where were you two last night?"

Does she think we could have done this? They have to eliminate the people closest to the victim first—everyone knows that. I take a quick glance at Chace; he's staring at Lina with a prominent frown.

"After reporting Sonny missing to security, we went home to wait for Sonny. The police came by to take our statements after that," I say.

"Our housemates were there too. We all stayed in all night," Chace adds, making it crystal-clear that we have an alibi. And *witnesses*.

The detective offers a smile. "All right."

Chace puts his elbows on his knees and rests his head in his hands. After a few moments, he looks back up and clears his throat. "Are *we* in danger?" His question is directed to the detective, but his eyes are trained on me.

Oh, God. I hadn't thought about that.

"Let's not get ahead of ourselves, Chace. We should all absolutely exercise caution, but right now there is no evidence to suggest you're at risk."

"What?" Chace snaps. "Sonny was left in our editing suite!"

"He was, but it's also the room closest to the back entrance. It's the first room you see when you come in that way, and the building backs onto the street and the rear door is concealed by trees. Sonny had also received notes only for him, not any of you."

"So you think it's coincidental?" I ask, hoping for reassurance.

"I'm not saying that, but it's possible. We'll need reporting from the forensics team, but given that the blood is only around Sonny, not all over the suite, and there are no signs of a scuffle, he was likely killed elsewhere and put in the suite afterward. I don't want to create panic that this might become a series of incidents. Unless we find any evidence to the contrary, this was an isolated incident. An independent crime," Detective Lina says calmly. "Now, I'll take you through some safety precautions that would be wise for you to follow. But there are *no* signs the perpetrator has multiple targets."

I swallow sand. "Okay."

We listen to the detective. She's essentially telling us to continue our lives as normal. But how do you do that when you've seen what we have? I'm not sure I can do normal again.

Chace frowns, and his left eye narrows. It's what he does when he's frustrated or stressed. It's like he doesn't think Lina is taking this as seriously as he wants her to be, but what can she do? Sonny is already dead. There's no saving him. And if there's nothing to suggest whoever killed Sonny wants to hurt us, then she's stuck. What is she supposed to do? Order us all into the police's protective custody?

"So we do nothing? Just pretend it is a regular day?" Chace asks.

"We'll go through what you can do to help our investigation, such as not talking to the media or publicizing any details on any social media sites, but I see no reason why you can't carry on as normal. I can put you in touch with a wonderful grief counselor—"

"I don't need that," Chace says, cutting off the detective midsentence and standing abruptly. "And I'm hardly about to sell our story, so are we done here? I need some air. I want to go home."

The detective offers to have an officer drive us home, as they will be going to speak with the rest of our roommates—break the news, ask them questions—but we both need some space. We say we'll walk. Chace practically shouts it.

I stand robotically, my heart pounding. Chace is never one to let his emotions to get the better of him, so his reaction—overreaction—is alarming. But I suppose if it's going to happen, finding our friend dead is an understandable time to do so.

"Yes, you're free to go," Detective Lina says. "You have my number. Please use it if you need anything. I'll be in touch."

Nodding, I turn toward the door, and I'm almost knocked off my feet as Chace bolts out of the room.

"Err... Bye," I mutter and follow Chace. He's really not acting like himself. But how are you supposed to act when your friend has been murdered?

All eyes are on me as I walk down the corridor. The few police officers still here are silent, watching as I make my way out. The back door is cordoned off with yellow tape, so I head back to the main entrance. The few students and faculty who are in the building gape in the lobby as I pass under the tape. I keep my head down and walk as quickly as I can, shoving through the double doors, and I grind to a halt.

"Chace," I whisper.

He's leaning against the railing with his hands on his thighs and head bowed. I know he's heard me because he takes a deep breath.

"What happened in there?" I ask, tentatively reaching out and touching his upper arm. Even through his jacket, I feel his tension, muscles bunched tight and hard as rock.

Raising his head, he stares at me with a tortured look in his eyes. His face is so pale, it's like he hasn't seen the sun in years. "Sonny's heart was missing."

"What?"

"I thought something was wrong when we saw him, but I didn't know what. I don't know what the insides of a body really look like."

My mind is reeling. I shake my head and hold up my hand to stop him. "Wait. Chace, slow down. What are you talking about? How do you know this?"

"I heard the police talking outside the room. When I was leaving, two of the cops were speaking to someone on the forensics team. The bastard who murdered Sonny cut out his heart and left his body in our editing suite, and that detective is trying to tell us we're not in any danger?" Chace is livid.

I'm overcome. My vision blurs. I tighten my grip on the railing, and Chace pulls me against his chest. We lean on each other.

"Breathe, Lylah," he murmurs in my ear.

I do as I'm told and suck in a deep breath. My lungs sting with the cold as they expand.

"Are you sure that's true? Wouldn't the medical examiner need to see the body to know?"

And better yet, who would cut out a person's heart? How would they even begin?

7

Saturday
February 3

place one foot in front of the other, but I don't feel like I'm actually moving. Every step takes a lot of effort. My mind is spinning as I fight between rejecting what I saw and accepting that Sonny was murdered.

Where is his heart?

Chace is gripping my hand, squeezing so hard my knuckles crush against his. I don't tell him this though because, oddly, the pain grounds me.

We turn down the road, and our house comes into view. I almost break out into a sprint, but I don't know what it's going to be like inside. At least we don't have to tell them. The police have already been—Detective Lina sent them to break the news. That was about forty-five minutes ago. There are no police cars outside the house now, so they must have left already.

Charlotte, Sienna, and Isaac will be in shock—devastated—and they'll have a million questions that none of us know the answer to.

Before I unlock the door, Chace tugs on my hand. I turn to him. "I don't think we should tell them about Sonny's heart yet."

"What? Why wouldn't we?"

"The detective didn't mention it. That means the cops are keeping that detail from us for a reason. They do stuff like this. It's also…not news anyone wants to hear."

I nod, jabbing the heels of my hands into my eyes. My head is throbbing.

Chace continues, "I'm saying we should wait for them to tell us. Right now only the cops and killer know that information."

"And us," I whisper. "How are we supposed to keep this from our housemates? Our *friends*? Don't they deserve to know how he died?"

"It will only cause them more harm. Isn't it enough to know that he was stabbed to death?"

"Chace, you're not making sense."

He sighs. "If this detail gets out, we could jeopardize the investigation." I just stare at him.

"Lylah, you're looking at me like I have an ulterior motive. I don't. We both want the bastard who killed Sonny found, but if this information gets out before the cops want to release it, we could slow them down, we could put ourselves in dan—"

"All right," I say, interrupting him. "I get it, and I agree. But I don't feel good keeping secrets. So we need to talk with Detective Lina later and tell her what you overheard."

He nods. "That's all I'm asking."

I open the front door, and the house is eerily quiet. Looking over my shoulder, I make sure Chace is right behind me. He gives me a fleeting smile. We go into the living room together.

Sienna is in Isaac's arms, wiping her eyes with a tissue. Isaac stares at the wall in a daze, and Charlotte sits with her head in her hands.

Everyone looks at us as we walk in.

"I can't believe it," Charlotte says, her voice meek.

"Are you two okay?" Isaac asks. "You found him? What…"

Thankfully Isaac doesn't finish his question because I don't think I can answer what it was like. I've already had to go into details with the detective.

"I don't feel okay," I reply. My heart is still racing so hard I can hear my pulse. "When did the police leave?"

Isaac lets out a deep breath. "They left about five minutes ago. There wasn't much we could tell them, so they weren't here that long at all. One of them looked through Sonny's room."

"How is this happening?" Sienna mutters to herself, shaking her head. "It can't be right."

"It's possible that someone left Sonny for me and Lylah to find. Does anyone have any idea who could hold a grudge against all three of us?" Chace asks, perching on an arm of the couch.

"No, we already told the police," Charlotte says. "I mean, not everyone loved him, but I can't think of anyone who would want to do…*that* to him."

Cut him open.

"Okay. What about me and Chace?" I ask. "I don't think we have enemies, but if someone wanted us to find him, that's personal."

"I'm going to make tea," Sienna says. "Do you all want any?" Her body sways as she stands, and Isaac moves as fast as a cat to steady her. "I'm fine." Sienna steps away from his grip. "I'll make everyone drinks."

I follow Sienna out of the living room and down the hallway to the kitchen. Her posture is awful, shoulders slumped forward like they weigh too much.

"You okay?" I ask, leaning against the wooden counter.

She shakes her head while busying herself filling the kettle and getting five mugs from the cupboard.

We used to get six.

"When the police knocked on the door, I never expected them to say Sonny had been murdered," she says softly. "And knowing the killer left him where you and Chace would find him scares the hell out of me. They said it could be coincidental because the media building is positioned the best for disposal, but I think Chace is right. It seems deliberate."

I flinch at the word *disposal*. Sonny wasn't a piece of garbage. "It scares me too. I don't know why anyone would want to hurt Sonny… or me and Chace."

Sienna's charcoal eyes widen. "Are we all in danger?"

"Honestly, I don't know. I still can't get past seeing him like that."

"Oh, Lylah, I'm so sorry. Here I am going on about how hard this is, and I'm not the one who found him."

"It was awful. At first I couldn't stop looking at him. His chest…" I bite my tongue to stop the other details from slipping out. I'll never forget what I saw, but there is no reason Sienna needs to be haunted by that image too.

She turns to face me, leaning her back against the countertop. Her lip trembles. "Do you think he suffered?"

"I don't know." But from what I saw of him, it seems like he must have. I glance away and cross my arms over my stomach. "The police will have answers soon, I'm sure."

"Do you think so? I don't feel safe."

"I do think so. We have to believe that."

Sienna drops her voice. "What do you think happened, Lylah?"

I shrug. "Sonny was out, and he got into an altercation with someone he shouldn't have. That person snapped and...stabbed him. His body was taken to the nearest building and left in an open room."

And his heart was removed.

"An open room that just happened to be the one you and Chace booked?"

"Yes. If no one else booked the other rooms, they would be locked until the media assistant arrived. Since we booked it for so early they must have left that one open overnight," I speculate. "Let's not get ahead of ourselves. We need to trust that the police know what they're doing. Do you think we should reach out to Sonny's family and see how they're doing?"

"I don't know. Maybe in a day or so if they haven't called us? They might want to talk."

"They probably will. What I want to know is what do we do now?"

She tilts her head, frowning. "There is nothing we can do right now."

"Right. No, of course not," I reply.

"Do you need to be busy?"

Am I that transparent?

"I…I don't like waiting around. I need to *do* something."

"Well you have a lot of schoolwork to finish, don't you?"

I nod.

"So go do that if it will help."

We found our friend dead this morning. I'm hardly going to flick open textbooks and be able to concentrate, but I get what she means. "What helps you, Sienna?"

"Making tea and crying. It's okay to let it out, you know? You can cry or scream or do whatever you need to. But it's good to let out your feelings."

I sigh. Easier said than done. "I'll keep that in mind."

Keeping my emotions bottled up isn't good—I learned that the hard way—but I can't help it. I'm scared to really express my feelings in case I can't stop them. It was bad when my parents died. I felt like I lost all control.

Chace, Isaac, and Charlotte come into the kitchen.

"Spit it out, Isaac," Charlotte says. She looks at Sienna and me pointedly. "He thinks he has an idea who's responsible."

"Go on," Sienna urges.

Isaac clears his throat. "I think… I think it's Jake."

"Don't be ridiculous." The words fall from my mouth before my brain engages with the notion.

"Hear me out, Lylah. They cops said that Sonny was cut open, then moved to the editing suite. For a person to do that, he would have to be strong. *Really* strong. And Jake was. He'd have to have some sort of vendetta too, given how the crime played out. Jake is the only person who could have possibly wanted Sonny dead and also wanted you to find him."

Sienna puts her hands on her hips. "Really? That doesn't seem very likely. Why do you think Jake hated Sonny?"

Isaac sighs. "I know you say what happened with you and him wasn't a big deal, Lylah, but what if Jake saw it differently? He was good friends with Sonny. They kept in contact when he left school, but after a while, Sonny mentioned him less and less. What if Jake felt that you rejecting him cost him his friendship with Sonny?"

I want to deny it, mostly because the motives Jake would have make him seem pathetic and vindictive, but maybe that's all it takes for someone to lose it. Isaac is right about Jake's physical strength. And Jake was studying premed. He dreamed of becoming a surgeon. He could have known enough about anatomy to remove someone's heart.

The possibilities lodge in my throat, thickening until I feel like I might choke with guilt. Could I be the catalyst for all of this? If my rejection caused Jake to lose contact with his friend, and something snapped…

No, surely not. There has to be more of a reason to kill a person, right?

Charlotte takes a deep breath. "Think about it. Jake lost the girl he liked, then he lost his friends, then dropped out of university. It's been almost a year since the kiss, which maybe he marks as the start of his life going downhill. So what if that triggered…I don't know, something inside him?"

I can't hear anymore of this. They're not *trying* to blame me, but that's exactly what they're doing. It's not my fault that Sonny is dead.

Shaking my head, I head toward the hallway. "I'm going to my room. I need to lie down."

"Lylah, don't go," Chace says.

"I'll be fine. I just need a minute."

It's unlikely that I'll be able to nap after what I've seen or heard, but I don't want to be around people right now—not even my friends. I get halfway up the stairs when I hear Sienna break down into tears again, followed by the sounds of my housemates comforting her.

I go to my room and close the door.

Alone, I'm able to hear my own thoughts properly. But there are too many at one time, too many questions. Did Sonny have something serious going on in his life that he didn't tell us about? How personal was it? Why else would someone murder him in such a horrific way if it *wasn't* personal? The time and effort it would have taken to do that to Sonny… There had to be more to it. The killer surely would have to truly despise him to go to those lengths.

Already I can feel my anxiety bubbling, waiting to erupt. If I don't get ahold on it, I'll be in a place I swore I would never let myself get to again. Even with the help of a therapist, medication, and Riley, it was nearly impossible to pick myself up and rebuild my life. I'm not sure I'm strong enough to do that again.

Walking to my window so I can shut the blinds, I take a quick peek out first.

What the…?

There's a large gathering of people on the sidewalk outside our house and across from our house. I recognize a lot of them as our neighbors. It looks like they are holding a vigil. They're all standing with rose petals scattered around them. There must be thousands of petals. It's like someone had buckets and buckets of them.

When did this happen? The street was clear when we arrived home not that long ago. Did the news spread that fast? I watch Isaac and Chace walk outside. They stop at the end of the path by the gate and speak to someone. I don't recognize who.

Most of the crowd is gathered across the street, as if they are trying to lend their support but still give us some space. I scan the gathering of people and gasp. Standing next to a group of girls huddling together is a guy in a black hoodie. A guy who I swear I've seen before. He's staring at the house with his arms folded.

I grip the blind cord and yank them shut.

My heart is thudding, but I could be overreacting. It's winter. Lots of people are wearing hoodies and warm clothing. He could be with that group of girls, standing there out of boredom.

Or he could be the guy who took our photograph and left the creepy messages, covering his face so he can't be recognized—the culprit admiring the aftermath of his handiwork.

Do I call the police? They'd likely think I was overreacting, that I was seeing things. Almost everyone out there is wearing a sweatshirt or coat of some kind. It's probably nothing. Rubbing my forehead, I take a breath. I need to sleep to clear my mind.

8

Sunday
February 4

The next morning, I have to get out of the house. I've been given extra time to finish my media project, but throwing myself into work is a welcome distraction. I keep thinking about Sonny's body slumped on the floor, covered in blood. I need to think of anything else.

Chace has agreed to accompany me. Whether he needs a distraction too or he doesn't want to let me go alone, I don't know. Since the editing suites are still taped off, we head to the library. Even though the library is in another section of campus and nowhere near the editing suites, I still don't want to go alone. I may have used a little bribery, suggesting we stop by the dining hall to pick up some coffee and snacks.

"You holding up okay after last night?" he asks, glancing at me out of the corner of his eye as we walk.

I hid in my room for the rest of the day. Between anxiety, grief, and guilt, I couldn't bear the thought of facing my friends. I cried and tried to distract myself with social media. And when articles and rumors about what happened kept popping into my feeds, I shoved my phone under my pillow and binged movies on my laptop until I fell asleep—a heavy, dreamless sleep. I'm so grateful I never remember my dreams, if I even have any.

"Yeah, I'll be fine. It's all so upsetting. Isaac's take on the Jake thing on top of finding Sonny kind of rattled me."

"No one was saying it's your fault," Chace says pointedly. "But we called Detective Lina to tell her about Isaac's suspicions. She is going to look into it and contact Jake, even if it's just to eliminate him."

"Oh." I blink. I didn't know they'd called without me. "Okay. What did she say specifically?"

"She just said she'd look into it, so I guess she'll contact him and ask him to go to the station. I don't know, we'll see." Chace frowns, distracted by something in the distance.

There is a large mass of people gathered around the noticeboard outside the main dining hall. We fall in behind the crowd, Chace stepping closer to me.

"What's going on?" I push up on my tiptoes to try to see what has everyone's attention.

The people around us elbow one another, nodding in our direction and staring. It's like Chace and I are the center of some joke or gossip.

My heart plummets into my stomach.

Chace senses the shift too and wraps his arm around my waist, pulling me closer to him. I'm not complaining, but I wish it was because he had feelings for me, not because I'm sensing we need to stick together for safety.

Something is really wrong.

"What is everyone looking at?" I ask a girl I vaguely recognize from around campus.

She rolls her pale eyes. "There's something pinned up on the noticeboard with a knife. Something gross, like an body part or a piece of meat. There's blood *everywhere*. People are freaking, thinking it's a real heart—obviously it's not."

My knees go weak as the crowd parts and suddenly the board becomes visible. The large cork board is littered with random fliers, open party invitations, study groups, and takeout menus. Right in the centre though, is an organ. An organ from a body. A red and brown lump with bits dripping. It looks a bit like a chunk of beef. But it isn't. Blood has dripped down on to the fliers below it, leaving a red trail on the board and a puddle on the ground.

It's a heart. Sonny's heart. It must be.

"Chace," I whisper, tugging on his arm.

He guides me away from the crowd. "Don't get ahead of yourself, Lylah. I'm sure it's not real. I'm sure it's just a Valentine's Day prank."

It's not though. Knifing a heart to a bulletin board is *not* a prank.

"Be serious. We both know what that is," I say, pointing toward the *organ*. "The killer put it there on display like some trophy or threat, and—"

"Lylah, stop." Chace presses his forehead against mine. "Calm down before you hyperventilate. I'm going to call Detective Lina."

Before he can pull out his phone, two campus security officers come running. "The police are probably already on their way. Do we stay? I just want to go home."

"Detective Lina knows where we live if she wants us."

I shudder. "He was here again. On campus. Right near us."

"Don't think about that now," Chace tries to reassure me.

How can I not? The person who killed Sonny is still leaving threats. First the notes, now his…his *heart*. This can't just be about Sonny. The killer is threatening *us*.

Sinking into Chace's arms, I bury my head against his neck.

"It's going to be okay, Lylah. They'll find whoever is doing this," he murmurs.

"Clear the area," an authoritative voice shouts from behind Chace. "Back up! Now!"

The small crowd disburses, but they don't really go anywhere. They only move a safe distance away so they can still watch the action. Chace and I shuffle back with them.

"Let's go," he says. "We'll call Detective Lina later to let her know we were passing by and find out what's going on."

I nod in agreement, but my eyes don't leave the scene. I watch the police, who have arrived, and security officers examining the heart. It's quite clearly a heart. One is talking into a radio, no doubt calling for further help.

"Lylah?" Chace runs his thumb along my jaw to get my attention. "Come on. Let me get you home and take care of you."

His words are so soft and filled with promise that for a brief moment, there is so much I want to tell him about how I'm feeling, about my parents, about how I was after their death, about how I feel that anxiety creeping back now, but I keep my lips pressed together.

I can trust Chace, but I don't want to unload all of my crap on him. He's going through this too.

We walk along the path toward our house, the canopy of trees half sheltering us from a drizzle that dampens the ground. The rain has only just started, but I wonder if it poses a problem for forensics if Sonny's heart is still on the noticeboard.

God, there was so much blood.

My legs are freezing in my damp jeans by the time we get to our gate. On the doorstep is a bouquet of red roses.

Chace glances at me. "Maybe they're for Sienna from Nathan? Or a sympathy bouquet?" The words hold no weight. He doesn't believe them himself. Neither do I.

Pushing the gate open, Chace approaches the flowers like they are going to explode, and he crouches down.

"A dozen red roses," he mutters, turning them to see if there is a note.

"No...there are only eleven," I say, flicking my gaze over them again, taking a second count.

Chace frowns. "Why are there only eleven?"

My heart skips as I realize the answer. "Because the twelfth is in my bedroom," I whisper.

He lifts his eyebrow and straightens his back. "What?"

"The night before Sonny went missing, I found a rose in my bed. I assumed it was him pulling a prank. Remember last year? He left fake spiders in the beds of the girls in my hall?"

"You don't think it was Sonny?"

With my heart in my stomach, I shake my head slowly. "No, I don't think it was Sonny."

Chace lets out a long breath. "Whoever left these…whoever *killed Sonny* was in your room?"

My spine stiffens. It makes sense. "Yes, I think so."

Chace looks scared—like he did after overhearing those gruesome details from the police. He digs in his pocket. "I'm calling Detective Lina now. We should get inside in case we're being watched. But don't act suspicious. Bring the flowers inside?"

I let us into the house and carry the flowers into the living room while Chace dials the detective's phone. A red string holds the stems in place. I sit down on the sofa put the roses down, not wanting to handle them in case the police can lift fingerprints.

Chace hangs up the phone. "Detective Lina's coming over after she deals with the new crime scene, but she's sending a cop to sit outside our house until she gets here."

"She thinks the killer's coming for us? For me?" Why else would I have the final rose from the bouquet?

Chace sinks to his knees in front of me. "Nothing is going to happen to you, Lylah. The cops will find this guy, life will slide back to normal, and you can get back your plans for meeting Tom Hardy."

He always knows how to cheer me up. Giving him a sly grin, I take a calming breath. "I would enjoy that."

He rolls his eyes. "Of course you would. If you want to be a film editor though, you might not meet him."

"Ha. After working on this assignment, I think it's safe to say I don't want to do that professionally. I like being behind the camera. I will like it even *more* when I'm behind the camera shooting a shirtless Tom Hardy in a scene."

Chace tilts his head to the side. "So what does he have that I don't? Besides a shitload of money."

"Hmm... Yeah, just the money. Otherwise your qualities surpass his." My comment slips out before I can think about it. He doesn't look surprised or taken aback by what I've said, though I've never been quite so obvious before.

Chace smiles. "Glad to hear it."

●　　●　　●

Detective Lina took our statements and the flowers three hours ago. We've heard nothing since, not that I'd expect to. She'd asked us if Jake participated in pranks the previous year. He had. He never sent notes or flowers, but he'd egged buildings and had thrown water and flour on cars. She also let us know that cops were investigating the heart found on campus, but that it wasn't a human heart—it was a pig's heart.

There could be a lot of coincidences here. Valentine's Day pranks are rife, and someone could simply be trying to be funny. Or maybe someone's parents sent flowers, and the florist forgot to include a card. Or maybe they are meant for condolences, to honor Sonny.

It all seems unlikely though. I hate the idea of someone planning Sonny's death. If it was premeditated, which it seems to be since someone is sending notes and flowers, then the killer is even sicker than I originally thought. And maybe more dangerous.

Chace, Sienna, and Charlotte are at the store with two cops. I was going to go too, but I needed a few minutes alone. Well, as alone as I'm allowed to be. Isaac is in his room, talking to his family on the phone, and there are two cops outside—one patrolling the road at the front, and the other out the back. But I'm by myself in the living room, and that's when my phone rings. My brother's name flashes on the screen. *Crap, I haven't called to tell him. By now he's probably heard about Sonny on the news.*

"Hey, Riley," I say, accepting his call.

"What is wrong with you, Lylah? Your housemate was murdered and you don't call to let me know you are okay?" His deep voice sounds even deeper when he's angry.

"Riley, I'm sorry. I wasn't trying to scare you. Things have been... hectic. I've barely had time to process what's happened."

"What *did* happen?"

Like he doesn't know the details. Riley has a way of finding out everything about my life—even when it's not splashed across the news. When our parents died, he closed in tight. At first it was what I needed. I was free falling, and Riley held me together. But as I healed, and my sessions with my therapist started to pay off, having Riley as my shadow started to feel suffocating. He was all for me getting better, but he couldn't let go, let our relationship go back to the way it had been.

We'd gotten stuck in some unhealthy situations where he was constantly trying to save me. He made excuses for why I missed so much school, telling them I was unwell or had appointments, and completed assignments for me so I didn't fall behind. His life became all about making sure I was okay. He even lost a job because he took off so much time when I was at my worst, and that wasn't fair to him. College was the escape we both needed.

I was supposed to go home for a few days over Valentine's Day, but this year, I can't face it. Riley sounded so hurt when I told him a couple of weeks ago, but he said he ultimately understood that I'm where I need to be right now. I need to take care of myself.

"Lylah, what happened?" he repeats.

"Sonny was murdered. Stabbed. Chace and I found him in—"

"*You found him?!*" he roars. "Jesus, Lylah, are you okay? You should have called. I can be there in four hours. I'll leave now."

"No, Riley! I'm safe. I'm fine. You don't need to come."

"Like hell you don't need me! There's a killer on your campus!"

"I don't need you to come. Honestly, it's hard enough to keep myself together. It'll be worse if you're here."

He snorts. "Tell it like it is, sis."

"That's not how I meant it. But you know how you'll be, all overprotective and trying to fix the situation. I love you for it, Riley, I really do, but it's not what I need right now. I need space. Chace and my friends have been great. And there are resources, like therapy, if I need them."

"But they're not your family. They don't know you the way I do. We're all each other has, Lylah, so if you need someone to talk to, I'm it."

Rolling my eyes, I reply, "I've got this. I promise I'm a lot stronger than I was."

"You need to check in with me more. I've barely heard from you this semester."

"Sorry, I've been busy. I have a lot of work for my classes. I'll try to call more."

He blows out a long breath and changes the subject back to Sonny. "Where do I even start with these questions?"

I let out a dry laugh. "That's how I feel too. The cops are working tirelessly to find the killer."

Riley would be in his car immediately if I told him about the notes and flowers that came to the house we live in—the house *I* live in. The rose in *my* bed! So I don't tell him. His intentions are good, but he's assertive to the point of it being a flaw. I can't have him here pestering the cops and telling me what I should be doing every minute of every day.

Even the thought of it makes my heart sink.

"I don't feel right staying here when you're dealing with this."

"I'm not a kid, Riley. You don't have to play parent anymore. Just be supportive. Be my brother."

Though I can't see him, I know he's frowning. Riley was twenty-one and I was seventeen when our parents died. We've always been close, but I like that I've become independent.

"You call me the second you need me. I'll be there. Promise me, Lylah."

"I promise. Thank you for not going overboard."

"You're welcome," he replies sarcastically. "And Lylah?"

"Yeah?"

"Think about that therapy. Seriously, think about it. Don't let your anxiety take over."

He doesn't need to elaborate. When Mom and Dad died, I tried to get better alone. I felt so many emotions at once, and I started having panic attacks. After three months, I broke down and found a professional to see.

It was a dark time, but I managed to claw it together enough to start school as I'd planned. I'm not going to let Sonny's death take me off my path. I've worked too hard to get where I am now.

"I will. Love you," I say.

"Love you too."

I hang up, and my phone slides out of my hand. Some conversations with Riley are exhausting. I lean back on the couch and close my eyes.

Every time my parents come up in conversation, a stabbing pain shoots through my stomach. It's been nearly two years, and I'd hoped it would get easier, but I still miss them so much.

I breathe in deep through my nose and out through my mouth—an exercise my therapist taught me when I started to feel like I was going to fall apart. I can slowly feel myself start to relax when the doorbell rings.

Sighing, I get up. My housemates must've forgotten their keys or be carrying too many bags to unlock the door.

I glance through the window, but no one is there.

Another doorbell ditch?

My blood runs cold as I open the door.

An envelope is sitting on our mat. The world turns mute as the blood rushes to my ears. Bending down, I scoop up the envelope. It's addressed to Isaac. And it looks like exactly the one that came for Sonny.

No...

I turn it over and pull out the note. My hands are shaking as I read:

"Isaac!" rips from my throat.

"What?" he calls from his room down the hall. My voice is trapped in my throat as I look up and down the street. There are still a few folks leaving flowers, looking at the makeshift memorial in front of our house. Did one of them do this? Did one of them see who left the note? I feel so exposed. Vulnerable.

I draw back inside and shut the door, trembling.

Isaac's footsteps thud from his bedroom into the foyer. "Lylah, what?" His face falls and his eyes widen as he sees what's in my hand. "Is that another note?"

Nodding, I hand it to him.

"Jesus," he whispers. "Who was it addressed to?"

I look up at him, my vision blurring with tears. "You."

9

Monday
February 5

saac's eyes meet mine and we exchange a silent understanding. Sonny's murder wasn't an isolated incident, and we are not safe.

Isaac swallows hard and pulls his phone out of his jeans pocket.

My pulse pounds in my ears so hard I feel dizzy. Chace, Sienna, and Charlotte—they need to know what's going on. I need to text them.

"Come on, Lylah, we're going to the station to find Detective Lina," Isaac says. "We'll get the others to meet us there."

He's pulling on his coat by the front door, note in hand, waiting for me to get it together.

"I'm texting them now." I tap a quick message. "Isaac," I start, but I can't continue, my voice shaking.

"I know. Let's not panic and just go to the police, then we can do whatever they tell us to do. We'll be safe there."

Isaac flags the cops in the car outside and tells them what happened. The cops on patrol take us to the station.

Chace, Sienna, and Charlotte are waiting outside the station when we arrive, all of them looking nervous. The note is in Isaac's pocket, and I can't wait until the police have it and we never have to look at it again.

No one seems to know what to say to Isaac, because what do you say at a time like this?

Whoever is doing this knows our routine. The thought of someone so evil literally standing on our doorstep makes my skin crawl.

Inside, the officer at the reception desk calls Detective Lina to let her know we're here.

"Do you think Sonny's parents will want to see the notes?" I ask.

Chace shrugs. "I don't know. But I imagine they'll come by the house later now that they are in town."

I've been wracking my brain all night, trying to think of something to say to them. They've come to collect his things, collect *Sonny's body*, so they can bury him back in their hometown. There is nothing I can say to make any of that easier. Detective Lina and her partner, introduced to us as Alexander, meet us out front and usher us back to a conference room.

"Do you have it?" Detective Lina asks, pulling on a pair of disposable gloves from her pocket.

Isaac hands her the note he's pinching right at the corner. "This one is addressed to me. Lylah found it. First Sonny, and now me."

She takes the note and reads. Her forehead creases and her lips purse like she's sucked on something sour. "Where was it?"

"It was left on our doorstep, like before," I say.

"Jake is saying who he intends to *murder* next," Isaac adds.

"Tell us again why you think this is from Jake. Does this sound like something he would do?" Detective Alexander asks.

Sighing, Isaac continues. "He's strong enough to be able to, you know...*kill*. He has medical knowledge from his classes. He got rejected around Valentine's Day last year by Lylah. The rest of us have hardly gone out of our way to keep in contact. Jake is the only person I can think of who would make sense..."

Chace reaches out and gives my hand a squeeze. I know we are thinking the same thing: You would need to know what you're doing to cut out someone's heart. You would also need to be physically very strong. Jake fits both.

"Have you contacted him yet?" Chace asks.

Detective Lina gives Chace a thin-lipped smile. "Why don't you all take a seat in the waiting area. I'll get this into evidence and then will come and speak with you all, okay?"

That sounds an awful lot like her trying not to say they have nothing—no ideas, no leads. What if they've spoken to Jake and believe he's innocent? He has always been charming. I may not have had romantic feelings for him, but I thought he was a nice guy. I never thought he would give up his studies and leave school so suddenly, but he did. He wasn't the type to shy away from difficult or uncomfortable situations, but people can surprise you. He didn't come back after winter break, and he didn't give anyone an explanation.

I'm still thinking about Jake as we head into the waiting room. It's a basic room with three vinyl sofas arranged in a horseshoe shape, a vending machine for hot drinks, and a few dusty plastic plants. One wall is glass, so we can see the reception desk. I sit down with Chace and he finally lets go of my hand.

"Why is Jake doing this?" Charlotte mutters. "The notes, the flowers, Sonny, the heart knifed into the noticeboard."

"At first I thought it was Sonny's." The words spew from my mouth before my brain engages. But Isaac is being threatened next, and who knows which one of us it will be after him. My friends can't be kept in the dark anymore.

Chace's breath catches, and I feel him looking at me. I don't care.

"What?" Sienna rubs her face. "What do you mean?"

I have my friends' undivided attention. "The police didn't tell us this, probably because it could affect the investigation, but Chace overheard a conversation saying that Sonny's…his heart was… missing when we found him," I stammered. "But obviously the heart on the noticeboard was a pig's."

I expected an explosive reaction, but instead, I'm met with silence.

Chace's hand lightly brushes my back, telling me I've done the right thing by telling them. "Sorry we couldn't tell you earlier."

"Are you okay, Isaac?" Sienna asks. Her face is pale.

He shakes his head and looks away. When Isaac shuts down, it's usually best to give him space. Understandably, he needs some time to process, and we have to respect that.

Charlotte and Sienna begin talking in hushed voices, probably about Sonny's heart.

Chace digs his wallet out of his pocket. "Do you want a coffee?" he asks me softly.

"I think I saw Jake the night we found Sonny," I blurt. I keep my voice low so the conversation is just between us.

His eyebrow arches, and he sits forward, the drinks forgotten. "Where?"

"Outside, in the crowd. He was wearing a hoodie. He was staring at the house. Well, I think so. It was difficult to see since he was far away and it was dark."

"Jesus. You should tell Detective Lina."

"I know. I will when she comes back. Do you think it could be him?"

"Possibly. Seems a bit stupid to hang around though. Jake isn't stupid."

I hadn't thought of that. "Right. No, he wouldn't do that, would he?"

"It's probably coincidental. I think I saw about ten people in hoodies that night."

He's right. That guy only caught my eye because he seemed like he was watching our house. God, I hate second-guessing myself. I was sure at the time, but now I feel stupid.

"I'll get you a coffee," Chace says and squeezes my hand.

I watch him get up and walk over to the vending machine where the rest of our friends are settled. He brings me a hot Styrofoam cup.

Bowing my head, I prepare myself for yet more waiting.

•　　•　　•

"How long do you think we will be here?" I ask them after what feels like hours. I look at the clock on the wall—it's only been twenty minutes.

Isaac shrugs, Charlotte doesn't move, Sienna takes a breath, and Chace says, "I have no idea."

I stand and start pacing. After a few minutes, I expand my territory out to the lobby. I'm going out of my mind waiting and drinking coffee. The caffeine was probably a bad idea. I spot Detective Lina walking out of another room and call out to her. She holds up her hand. "Sorry to keep you, Lylah. I'll be with you in five." She disappears behind another door.

I need to know what's going on. Is she questioning someone? Is it a suspect in this case? Is she working on another case?

As I turn around to join the others, someone catches my eye standing at the reception desk. "Zak?"

Jake's older brother, Zak, gives me a fleeting smile. "Hi, Lylah."

I don't really know what to say. Why is he here? His brother could have murdered my friend, not that he would have had anything to do with that. Zak visited Jake at school every two or three months until he dropped out, so I kind of got to know him. We all hung out together in a group.

He runs his hand over his short black hair. "I don't know what to say to you," he admits.

"Is Jake a suspect?"

"We're not sure."

"How so?" I ask, not following what he means.

"We haven't seen him in weeks," Zak tells me. "The last anyone in the family heard from him, he texted to say he needed space to figure out life and was going to do some backpacking or something. He hasn't contacted our parents for a few days. When the police called asking about him, my mom freaked out thinking they were calling to say he was dead. But it's almost as awful to think he could be a suspect. I can't believe it, Lylah."

"That's Lylah? And stop talking like he's guilty, Zak!" snaps a girl who's come up behind him. She has the same black hair and deep brown eyes as Jake and Zak, so I assume she's their sister. Jake told us that he lived with his dad, brother, and sister but I've only ever met Zak before. She looks quite a lot like Jake.

Glowering, he turns to her. "Shut up, Sarah. I'm not saying I believe he did this." Zak turns back to me. "My brother couldn't have done this. Even if he didn't get along with Sonny, that's not motive for murder."

Ignoring Sarah, I say, "I didn't want to think so, but we need to find him so we can settle it either way."

"This is ridiculous, of course *she* would think that!" Sarah shoots daggers at me from her brown eyes and stalks off toward a man who can only be their father.

"What does she mean by that?"

Zak sighs. "Jake told us about the kiss."

My face reddens, and I don't know why I feel embarrassed. "It wasn't a big deal. He seemed totally fine when—"

"You don't have to explain, Lylah. You didn't like him that way."

"No, I didn't."

Silence falls over us. I've always liked Zak, but right now he feels like the enemy. He will, understandably, want to protect his brother, believe the best of him. Me? I'm not so sure about Jake.

"I should go. Can we meet up later?" he asks suddenly.

I open my mouth, ready to give him an excuse, but he sees straight through me.

"Lylah, please. Bring your friends too. I want to help. Jake isn't responsible for this, and maybe we can work that out together if you hear me out."

"You want to convince us your brother isn't a sick murderer?" Chace's voice booms behind me, and I jump. His eyes flame with hatred.

"That's not going to happen," I say, backing Chace up. "When the cops find Jake, if he's innocent, I'll apologize. But until then, he's the only person we can think of who could hold a grudge."

Zak's posture changes. He straightens his back and puffs out his chest. "A killer is on the loose, and you're playing guessing games."

"Your brother *is* the killer," Chace says. "Lylah, come back in here with us. This conversation is going nowhere, and we probably shouldn't be talking to the suspect's family."

"You don't know he did anything wrong!" Zak challenges, his voice thick with worry.

"He's not the one who was carved up and left in our goddamn editing suite, that's how I know!"

Chace is unnecessarily mean, but emotions are high. Sonny had a horrible death, and we found his body.

"Let's go, Chace," I say, reaching out and placing my hands on his chest. He doesn't move when I apply pressure. I'm trying to get him to go back in the waiting room, but he's too strong for me to force.

I widen my eyes at him, pleading. "Chace, please."

This time he listens. His hand circles my wrist, and he steps back into the waiting room, taking me with him. Although he's walking away from Zak, his attention is still fully on him.

"What was that about?" Isaac asks once Chace and I are seated again.

Chace finally snaps out of his stare-off with Zak and shrugs.

Sienna closes the door, scowling at Jake's family, who are now talking to Detective Lina. I guess she won't be with us in a minute after all.

"Zak doesn't think Jake had anything to do with this... But he's been kind of MIA since before Sonny's murder."

"The very fact that Jake hasn't been in touch makes him look guilty as hell," Isaac says. "Why can't they get in touch with him?"

I shrug. "Zak didn't say. He went off to find himself or something. Maybe they're worried that something bad has happened to Jake too. They want to believe the best in Jake, obviously. No one wants a killer in their family," I reply.

"Well they have one, and the cops better find Jake soon," Chace says, narrowing his eyes at Jake's family.

I get that Chace needs answers and is looking for someone to blame, but he seems so definitive. How can he be so sure? Or is he just desperate for answers and an end to this? I look over as Detective Lina shows Jake's dad into a room. Two other officers take Sarah and Zak into separate rooms.

"They're being interviewed," I mutter. "If they discover where Jake is hiding this could all be over soon."

If.

10

Monday
February 5

Detective Lina decided that the five of us should have around-the-clock protection, so I have a cop—Officer Grey—with me on the way to the library. There is a car parked outside our house and, until Sonny's killer is found, we will all have officers acting as our shadows.

This should make me feel more comfortable, but it's attention I really don't want. Sonny's murder and the rest of us being stalked is all anyone can talk about on campus. People who used to say hi to me now either stare or look the other way, whispering to their friends. It's like they think they'll become a target if they interact with me. I don't know. Maybe they would. But I hate being avoided like I have some contagious disease. I thought about escaping—packing a bag and heading home to see Riley—but that wouldn't solve anything. As much as I love my brother, he couldn't comfort me like my mom would've. Besides, I can't take time off without it having a negative impact on my grades.

In my pocket, my phone vibrates with a text message making me jump. My hand flies to my racing heart. So much for the police detail making me feel less skittish.

I pull out the phone. Riley. Of course, it's Riley. How are you?

Sighing, I tap a reply. I'm fine. Promise. Going to study.

You sure? I can come if you need me.

I'm good. Honest. Try not to worry about me.

You're my baby sister and the only family I have left.

He doesn't elaborate, but he doesn't need to. When we lost Mom and Dad, we lost everything. Everything except each other. There is no one else. No grandparents, no aunts or uncles, no one. We are a family of two.

I send him three heart emojis and slip my phone back in my pocket. Riley shouldn't have to pick up my pieces time and time again because I'm not strong enough to hold it together. He's had to do enough of that already.

"Lylah?" Officer Grey prompts since I've stopped outside the library.

"Sorry. Are you going to come in too?"

He gives me a curt nod. Dressed in black suit trousers, a cream shirt, and a heavy jacket, he doesn't look much like a police officer. But it's painfully clear he's not a student. Still, I'm grateful he's not in uniform.

"Of course," I say. Nothing is going to happen to me in the library with so many people around, but his instructions are clear: don't let Lylah out of sight.

I push open the door and keep my head down. At least it's warm in here. He follows me along the short corridor and into the main part of the library. Although I don't make eye contact with anyone, I can feel people around watching me.

Grey leans in. "Are you okay?" he whispers.

The walls close in until I feel like I'm standing in a cell. Everyone around me seems so much bigger, like they're giants.

There's no air in here. I need to get out.

"Can we leave?" I ask Grey. Of course we can, I don't actually need his permission. *Move your legs, Lylah.*

"Yeah, come on," Grey says.

Somehow I manage to make myself move. Grey accompanies me back outside, this time walking next to me, rather than a step behind. His blue eyes are alert and concerned.

"Lylah, are you okay?"

I breathe deeply once the fresh air hits me. "I'm fine now. Sorry, that was really embarrassing."

"What happened?"

"They were all watching me."

He nods. "People will do that. Ignore it."

"Easier said than done."

He replies with a sympathetic smile. "This won't be forever."

No, but how long will it take for the police to find the killer?

I decide I'd be more comfortable working at home, so we start walking back. Soon, I spot Zak by a café on the corner. He's alone, unless his dad and sister are inside. His arms are folded, and he looks deep in thought, eyebrows furrowed together.

Against my better judgement, I start toward him with my bodyguard trailing behind. We haven't been told to stay away from

Jake's family, but given the circumstances, it's probably best we do. Still, I can't quite bring myself to stop. If anyone in Jake's family is willing to do what's necessary to find Jake, it's Zak.

He sees me and walks toward me with long strides. "Lylah, hey." His eyes flick over my shoulders, probably looking for one of my friends.

"I'm alone," I say. "Well, aside from Officer Grey, that is."

"Right, you have…protection." Clearing his throat, he looks at the ground, ashamed.

"We don't blame you, Zak. I know this is awful for you too."

He raises his eyes. "I think Chace blames me."

I shake my head and take a step closer. "No, he's angry, scared, and confused, but he knows this isn't your fault."

"Thank you."

"Have you heard from Jake yet?"

"No. His phone has been turned off for the last four days. I tried this morning and my dad is constantly calling and texting. He won't answer anyone."

"Four days. So his phone was on after Sonny died?"

Zak wets his bottom lip with his tongue. "Yes."

At this point, I don't even know if that means anything. It's still not proof that Jake killed Sonny and sent those notes. We need something solid so the cops can make headway.

"How is your dad?" I ask.

"He's devastated. We haven't had contact with Jake, and now he's a suspect in a horrible murder investigation."

I want to ask if his family still thinks Jake is innocent, but they probably do. I wouldn't give up on someone I love.

"What are your theories?"

"He's been hurt. That's pretty much all we got." Zak's nostrils flare as he takes a sharp breath.

"Pretty much? What aren't you telling me, Zak?"

"Nothing."

"If you know something, you need to tell me. Or tell the police."

"Lylah, I know you want answers, but I don't have them."

"I think you're lying. Your dad and sister seem sure that Jake is innocent. Why aren't *you* sure, Zak? What do you know? Was something going on that we don't know about?"

Officer Grey steps closer to me, visually warning that he will step in if he feels like he needs to.

Zak rubs his temples. "Stop pushing, Lylah. I had one moment of doubt because the police are pushing it, but that's it."

I still don't believe him.

"Sonny is dead, Zak. If there is anything you need to tell the police, you *have* to do it. Isaac has been threatened. Other people lives are at risk here. Including mine."

"Lylah," Officer Grey warns.

Zak ignores him completely. "I'm sorry for that, Lylah, I really am. But I can't help you. I've always liked you and your friends, so if there was anything I could do to help, I would. I'm already trying to contact my brother, and I'm cooperating with the police. Whatever you think I'm hiding, you need to get it out of your head. There's nothing I know that the police don't. I've been completely honest."

"Okay," I concede. "I'm sorry for pushing. This is all impossibly stressful. Jake was our friend. I don't *want* it to be him."

"But you still think it is. Are you sure there's no one else that might have done this? Jake hasn't been to this school in months, so why would he do this?" He bows his head.

I hate talking about his brother like this, but Zak needs to face the reality that his brother could be a murderer.

"You must think I'm an idiot for still believing he wouldn't do this," he tells me softly.

"No. Of course I don't."

"I can't give up on him, Lylah."

We're at an impasse, so I change the subject. "Where are you staying?"

"Knights Hotel. It's nearby."

"Is it nice?"

He snorts. "Not really. But it's cheap, and we don't know how long we'll be in town." He eyes Officer Grey. "Does that guy follow you everywhere?"

Rolling my eyes, I cross my arms. "Everywhere but the bathroom."

Zak laughs. "Is it driving you crazy?"

"Yeah."

"I'm glad you have protection." He smiles, holding my gaze a fraction too long.

Biting my lip, I shift on my feet. "Um, thanks. That's…er…flattering."

Holding up his hands, he says, "Whoa, I wasn't coming on to you! I meant I'm glad all of you are safe."

Oh my God, is my face actually on fire? It feels like it is.

"Oh, I know you weren't."

I'm such an idiot! How self-centered I am to assume he only meant me?

"What are you doing with her?" Behind Zak, Sarah stands with two coffees in her hands, trying to strike me down with a glare.

Sighing, Zak turns to his sister. "We were talking."

"Well, don't. You know what *it* and *its friends* think of Jake."

It. Nice one.

"Drop it, Sarah," Zak growls.

She shoves a coffee at him, and it almost spills as he takes it. "I can't believe you're siding with her!"

"I'm not siding with anyone! Lylah's done nothing wrong."

"She's accused our *brother* of murder, and now our whole family is being treated like suspects."

I can't help but lash out. "How do we know you're not?" I shouted.

Officer Grey steps almost completely in front of me. "We need to leave."

"Lylah!" Zak snaps.

I ignore him. I'm sick of Sarah and the snotty attitude she's giving me. This might not be her fault, but it's not mine either.

"You can go to hell, bitch," she spits. "You have no idea what you're talking about. You strut around here, throwing people away when you're bored of them, and then have the audacity to incriminate one of them in murder case."

"Sarah, stop. This isn't doing any good," Zak growls, playing referee.

"Enough!" Officer Grey snaps. "We're leaving, Lylah." He turns to Zak and Sarah. "I suggest you two do the same."

A few students stop to openly and unapologetically gawk at our exchange. Sarah is getting more and more agitated, her shoulders tilting back and eyes narrowing.

She's giving the crowd a good show. And I suppose I am too.

"Whatever, this is pointless. I'll speak to you later, Zak," I say.

He gives me an apologetic smile.

"You won't speak to him later. Stay away, Lylah. I mean it!"

Officer Grey puts his hand across my stomach. "Let's go. Now, Lylah."

"Ignore her," Zak calls. "I'm sorry," he says more quietly to me.

"It's fine," I reply. Officer Grey steps forward, making me move back. "All right, I get it. We're going home now," I tell him and turn on my heel. He's right behind me, keeping close.

I can't blame Sarah for being angry, but we're all getting gossiped about, so you'd think she would keep a low profile.

"Yeah, run along. Jake didn't need friends like you, and neither does Zak. Stay away from us, or you'll be sorry," she shouts after me.

I turn back to her and narrow my eyes. "That sounds a lot like a threat, Sarah."

"Enough!" Zak snaps. He takes her elbow and guides her in the other direction.

"Lylah," Officer Grey says again. "You're not doing yourself any favors here."

I watch them go. They're clearly having a hushed argument by the way she's waving her free hand around and scowling at him. Zak doesn't look at her or back at me. He walks like he's on a mission.

Officer Grey stares after them, tense.

What is he thinking? Does he think she could know more than what she's told the cops?

Would she conceal Jake's whereabouts and let him get away with murder?

11

Monday
February 5

My attempt at doing something normal was a bust. I slam the front door, chuck my bag on the floor by the side table, and look around for my housemates. No one spends a lot of time in his or her room, so if no one is in the living room or kitchen, it's likely I'm home alone.

Before Sonny died, I loved coming home to an empty house and getting a bit of time to myself. Now, I have a knot of stress in my stomach at the thought of being on my own, despite having Officer Grey outside to keep watch.

"Hey?" Chace says from the living room.

"It's me," I reply, my shoulders lowering with relief. He's sitting on the sofa watching an early episode of *Game of Thrones*.

"You weren't at the library long," he states.

I shake my head, then flop down on the sofa beside him. I feel like a failure. All I wanted was to get back to a routine, but I ended up freaking out. When Mom and Dad died, Riley and I got a lot of unwanted attention. People were only trying show their concern and help, but for me, it made losing my parents feel even worse.

Frowning, he shifts on the sofa until he's facing me, muting the volume on the television. "What happened?"

"You know when you walk into a room and everyone turns to look at you?"

"Ah. People were talking about you, about Sonny…all of us."

My palms itch. "I don't like being the center of attention like that. I'd rather be ignored."

"That's not going to happen with all that's going on, Lylah. You're going to have to learn to ignore them."

"Yeah, that's pretty much what Officer Grey said."

That's also what Riley told me after I had my second panic attack when my parents died. But right now, ignoring stares from strangers is like asking a fish to breathe in the desert.

"You've never cared what people said about you before," Chace reminds me.

"This is different. And what do people usually say about me?"

Chace laughs. The sound is deep and gravelly. It does things to my insides that make me forget about everything else.

"No one is saying anything bad. I promise."

"That you've heard," I say with a frown. "Where is everyone else?"

"Sienna and Isaac went to the gym before class, and Charlotte was going to meet a friend to get some notes for class."

"They all have someone with them?"

His head tilts to the side. "Yeah…"

"Just checking."

He pauses and gazes into my eyes. "Are you okay, Lylah?"

Chace sounds like my brother.

"I worry about them," I say.

"They're safe," he assures me. "Did something else happen?"

"I ran into Zak, who was really nice, and Sarah, who wasn't so nice. She told me to stay away *or else*."

"Like brother like sister," he scoffs. "She's as intense as Jake."

"You would compare her to a killer?"

He shrugs and opens his mouth, but is silenced quickly by sirens screaming down the road. Chace and I leap to our feet and dash toward the front door and out onto the front step.

The vehicles pull to a stop outside a house two doors down from ours where a few people are gathered on the sidewalk.

He looks at me. "Well, at least the crowd isn't gathering outside where we live."

"Yeah, but what's going on?" I instantly think the worst.

Gatherings of people used to mean parties. Now they mean death.

Detective Alexander is the officer who was home with Chace. He is on his phone and walking toward us. He touches Chace's arm and gestures for us to go back inside the house and stay there. Officer Grey runs toward the commotion.

This isn't good.

I duck back into our foyer with my hand covering my thumping heart. "What's going on?" I demand of Detective Alexander. Chace shuts the door and folds his arms.

Hanging up the phone, the detective says, "There's been an incident."

"What kind of incident?" I ask.

"Do either of you know a Nora Wilson?"

"Yeah. Well, kind of," I reply.

He frowns. "Kind of?"

"She's also a student at the university. I know her enough to say hi or exchange small talk. We've gone out in a group with other friends, but we're not close. I don't think any of us really *know* her."

"I don't think I've ever spoken to her," Chace says in agreement.

"Is she okay?" I ask.

He clears his throat. "She's been murdered."

Overwhelmed with emotion, I lean against Chace. "That's terrible…"

"Do you think Sonny knew her?" the detective asks.

"Potentially, but she's not really the type of girl that Sonny would go for," I say through the lump in my throat.

"Why's that?"

"I think she's very into her studies. I always see her in the library. Like Charlotte, Nora doesn't go to parties much. I wouldn't think she'd have been on Sonny's radar."

"That's helpful," the detective replies, nodding.

Chace speaks up. "What happened to her?"

What he's really asking is *Was this the same person who killed Sonny? Was it Jake?*

Detective Alexander clears his throat. "She was stabbed, but I don't know any more than that."

"Does she have her heart?" The words are out of my mouth before

I remember that is restricted information we are not supposed to know.

The detective's eyes widen, either shocked that I know this detail or at my bluntness. *Yeah, I don't want to be asking these questions either, but here we are.*

"I'll take that silence as a no, she doesn't have her heart anymore," I reply. "Nora must have been killed by Jake too."

Chace shakes his head. "But that doesn't make any sense."

Detective Alexander tries to calm us. "We're not jumping to any conclusions."

"What's going on?" Isaac shouts, coming in the back door.

"We're in the foyer," I call back.

He and Sienna join us, their security detail trailing behind them. Isaac drops his bag with a thud. "What happened out there? No one would tell us anything, and part of the road is blocked off."

"Has Jake been found?" Sienna asks.

"No, it sounds like Jake has killed someone else. Nora," I say.

The detectives all glance knowingly at one another.

"What? I thought he wanted me next," Isaac says.

I shrug. "We all thought that, but…"

Sienna's perfectly shaped eyebrows leap. "Nora? Nora wasn't exactly our friend, though she was a bit obsessed with you, Lylah. She really wanted you to like her. But we never spent much time with her. Why would Jake hurt her?"

Alexander listens to our conversation intently, no doubt making mental notes.

I shrug. "Maybe we got it wrong. Maybe Jake has a longer hit list than we originally thought."

"Just putting this out there," Isaac says. "What if it's not actually Jake? I mean, did he even know Nora?"

Chace scoffs. "I think Jake's proved that we never really knew him, so he could have known her."

"That's true," I say in agreement with Chace. For all we know, Jake could have had a relationship with Nora. "I wonder what she could have done to make him so angry."

I wonder if that is why Nora always tried to hang out with me—because she saw me with Jake. Maybe the two of them had a thing, he cut her loose, and she couldn't accept it? So she tried to get him back by being friends with me? Nora lived in a different dorm than us last year, so Jake could have slept with her, and we would never have known.

"Yeah, but Jake was hung up on you, so it doesn't make sense for him to have been with her," Sienna says. "Especially since we never saw them together, and she didn't mention him whenever she was around you."

"Great, let's keep bringing up my relationship with Jake." I feel bad enough already. To think that I was a catalyst for so much hate makes me ill.

Alexander clears his throat. "Let's not get ahead of ourselves. Detective Lina will be here in a minute, and we'll have some questions for everyone."

I really don't know how much help we'll be. I didn't know Nora well enough to know about her personal life. The times we hung out together were rare and included other people, and our conversations didn't delve that deep. And Jake didn't exactly put himself out there with many people outside of our group or his class. So I can't see the connection. But someone needs to figure it out before someone else ends up dead.

•   •   •

Two hours later, I'm exhausted. Detective Lina had us all go down to the station, where she got us thinking of possible links between Nora, me, my friends, and Jake. Now my head is pounding. There is absolutely no tie that any of us can think of.

We've been over every detail, from first meetings to a week-by-week rundown of our time in college. It was especially challenging since the first year was a total blur.

However, I'm confident I can remember every nanosecond of my time with Chace.

I'm pathetic.

I haven't seen my housemates for ages, as they are being questioned separately.

I'm in the waiting room, watching the clock tick by. It's only been fifteen minutes since I was released from the interview room, but the fact that they're all still being questioned makes me nervous. Why did mine go so quick?

Chace and I were called in first—probably because we found Sonny—so I expected him out at the same time as me.

Across the hall, the door to an interview room clicks open, and I leap to my feet.

It's Chace. He looks tired. His usually light eyes are dark with stress. He rolls his shoulder and closes the door. "You okay?" he asks, dipping his head.

"Yeah. That was intense. She seemed to repeat questions a lot or ask them in a different way, like she thought I was lying."

He comes closer. "She doesn't think that, Lylah. The police have to make sure they're thorough."

"Could you think of anything?"

"Nope. I think Detective Alexander hates me though."

"Why is that? What did you do?"

"Nothing...but thanks for your heartwarming confidence," he says with a hint of sarcasm. "I wasn't able to tell him anything he didn't already know. He's frustrated. Kids are being killed, and they have no leads on Jake. Detective Alexander has a nineteen-year-old daughter, so he's extra concerned."

"Maybe the killings are more random than we thought. That's something we all need to fear."

It's heart-stopping knowing Jake is out there. I think I would rather not know the suspected killer, that way I wouldn't see Jake's face everywhere.

He's out there, free, and it's only a matter of time before he strikes again.

The note said Isaac is the next target, but he diverted from his plan.

I'm not sure what that says about the killer's mental state, but I know it petrifies me.

12

Tuesday
February 6

Since Nora died, we've heard nothing from the killer. There have been no notes, no flowers, and no graffiti. Nothing. Jake is either doing a wicked job at hide-and-seek or he's laying low to plan his next move.

I've barely slept. I'm starting to feel the fatigue that plagued me for months after my parents died. My body aches and my eyes sting from lack of sleep. When I do drift off, I have nightmares, only this time it's not my parents' death I see in my dreams—it's Sonny's and Nora's.

Since Jake has seemingly vanished from contact, the cops want us to provoke him into making a move so they can catch him. They're not sure if Nora's death threw him off course and made him go into hiding, but they're determined to catch him before he can kill again.

Detective Alexander seems to approve of his partner's plan to draw out the killer, but I'm scared. What if that there is another murder?

But if we refuse to help, it could mean that the killer gets away.

So I'm in my room getting ready. I'm not willing to sit by and do nothing if there is a chance I can help. I owe it to Sonny and Nora to try. In an hour, we're heading to a club that the cops have already scoped out. Officers went there before it opened to speak to the manager and staff and get their teams ready for tonight.

I pull the brush through my long hair and stare at my reflection in the mirror. When I left home and came to college, I was determined to be a different person. I wasn't going to stress over the little things to the point of making myself ill. I was going to think positively and not always see the worst-case scenario.

For a year and four months, I've managed to do that pretty well. Until now. I look like the scared, anxiety-crippled girl I was desperate to leave behind. Looking away from the mirror, I put down the brush.

It's amazing how quickly you can revert back to old habits. My stomach churns with disgust that I've allowed myself to go to this place again—even with the circumstances.

Vibrations on my wooden bedside table make my heart leap. It's a text message. I peer over, already knowing who it'll be.

Riley. Rolling my eyes, I unlock the phone and open the message.
What's going on, Lylah?

I can't tell him what I'm about to do. He'll blow up my phone trying to get in touch with me and show up wherever I am. I already feel like I'm weakening, so having Riley here will only make that worse. I'm crap at being strong around him.

I tap out a reply: Not much. Still no word from Jake. Cops

outside the house and everywhere we go. Stop worrying so much. I'm fine. Love you.

That's not good enough. Then, Have you thought more about coming home for a while?

I let out a frustrated sigh. I'm okay. No need.

I bite my lip in anticipation of his reply. He's been trying to convince me to come home more frequently for a while, but there are too many memories that I'm trying to escape. And I can't fall into bad habits.

"Are you almost ready?" Sienna asks, letting herself into my room and sitting on my bed. "Are you nervous?" she continues.

Putting my phone down, I tell her, "I'm in this one hundred percent. Honestly. But it's a bad idea, isn't it?"

She laughs. "We're absolutely insane for doing it. Despite Sonny's shortcomings, I believe he would do the same for us though."

"He definitely would," I agree. We may not have gotten along the whole time, but if anyone dared mess with us, he would have gotten in their face, I'm sure of that.

Our little household is like a family: we argue and get frustrated with one another, but we always have everyone's backs. So we're going to help Sonny get the justice he deserves by trying to force the killer out of hiding.

"How do I look?" Sienna asks, doing a twirl in the middle of my bedroom. She's wearing a short navy-blue dress that looks painted on. If anyone has the figure for it, it's her. She has her black hair pinned in a messy yet glamorous bun.

"You look amazing."

She grins. "So do you. Chace will love the dress."

I glare at her. Sienna is forever telling me to go for it with Chace, but I'm far too scared to make the first move. It would be unbelievably awkward if he turned me down, though from how he's acted recently, I don't think he would.

Chace is a big part of my new life and helping me become the person I want to be, so potentially jeopardizing our friendship by kissing him feels far too risky.

I sigh. "Let's get tonight over with first."

Her shoulders slump. "Do you think *he* will turn up?"

"It's worth a try, I guess. If the police think the killer is still watching us, then hopefully he'll follow us to the club where the police can nab him."

Except I have this nagging feeling it won't go as planned. Jake was always intelligent, probably more intelligent than the rest of us combined. Will he be able to see through the ambush?

Sienna shakes her head. "I *really* hate him. I still can't get my mind around how someone could do that to another person. I mean, cutting them open and removing their heart? God, it makes me feel sick just thinking about it. And I've been trying really hard not to think about it."

This is the first time since I told them about the heart thing that it has come up. No one wants to discuss it. "Yeah, I'm at a loss here too. I know people are capable of evil, but I never thought we'd know one of them."

"Let's focus on doing everything we can to draw the killer out of hiding," she says. "For Sonny."

I nod. "For Sonny. And Nora."

We go downstairs and find Charlotte, Isaac, and Chace in the living room. Their faces are solemn, obviously as nervous as me and Sienna.

"Shall we get this over with?" I ask, turning out of the room and grabbing my coat by the door. The detectives stand in the hallway looking serious.

Charlotte has decided to stay home, and the closer we get to leaving, the more I'd love to stay with her. I'm torn between wanting to find justice and us all being safe until that happens.

We all gather for our last instructions.

"Remember, there will be eyes on you the whole time. There is no need to worry, but please try to stick together as much as possible. No one goes anywhere alone," Detective Lina says.

Gritting my teeth, I fold my arms and try to feel brave.

"And if we need to go to the bathroom?" Sienna asks, almost sarcastically. "Who will stop Jake from stabbing us to death in there?"

Isaac tilts his head. "Don't you girls always go in packs anyway?" His intonation is exactly how Sonny would have said it, which makes Sienna and I smile.

Detective Alexander didn't know Sonny, so he doesn't pick up on the humor. "We have people everywhere. You're safe. We'll start outside the club, and after the Valentine's lights are switched on outside, we'll make our way into the club in the hope that Jake will follow."

Tonight, just over a week before Valentine's Day, is almost as busy as December when the campus Christmas tree lights are turned on. As if a big Valentine's Day event is even necessary.

"The cars are outside," Detective Lina says. "Let's nab a killer."

I reluctantly follow her with my lip between my teeth. I'm ready for this all to be over.

Sienna and I get in the first unmarked police car, and the boys ride in the car behind. From outside, it should look like we took a car service, though Officer Grey is our driver.

Silence lays heavy over us. Supposedly, if we act like our lives have returned to normal, that we aren't broken up by what has happened, it should enrage him.

That part I'm not too thrilled about.

"Do you think Jake would try something stupid? Like stabbing someone random in the club?" I ask as we approach the strip.

Officer Grey looks at me in the mirror. "It's unlikely."

I'm not sure if I'm encouraged by that or not. Unlikely isn't a definite.

He parks, and we get out. We're to walk the strip and go in ahead of the guys. I wish I could squeeze Chace's hand for encouragement.

The club is heaving. Since Limbo closed down next door, the other five clubs have been busier. University students need to let off steam somewhere. I don't mind large crowds, but I hate it when I can barely move. Limbo was Jake's favorite club, but this place was always his second choice.

Detective Lina hopes that our decision to come here will send a message to him—we know who you are and we're not hiding.

Being strong seemed impossible the day we found Sonny. I wanted to curl up and wait for it to be over. But now that the dust has settled, I've gained a bit of clarity. I know laying low isn't an option.

As scary as it is to think someone is coming after you, I won't let Jake rule my life. I won't stop living because he wants me to.

The boys arrive. "You two want to find a table?" Isaac asks. "Chace and I will get drinks."

Sienna nods. "Stay together."

Like we're going to walk off alone.

I stick to Sienna's side as I glance around the room. But I'm not looking for a table—I'm looking for Jake.

"There's one!" Sienna grabs my hand and tugs me along. I walk, but I'm not paying any attention to where we're going. The club is quite dark and people are dancing, and every flash of light that hits someone's face makes me think I see one of Jake's traits.

We stop at the table and Sienna sits. "Lylah?" she calls, waving her hand in front of my face.

I look down. "What?"

"Are you going to sit?"

"Yes," I drop onto a chair next to her. *Act normal, Lylah.*

"You shouldn't be looking for him."

"How can I not?"

She tilts her head and a lock of hair slips from her bun. "If he's watching, he'll know you're searching. We're supposed to be on a normal night out."

I avert my eyes, feeling foolish. She right, of course. But I'm not as good at acting as Sienna. Hell, even Isaac and Chace are way more relaxed than me. I'm on edge, my back is rigid, and pulse is racing.

Jake could be inside this building.

"I just need a drink to relax."

She smiles. "Yeah."

The boys come back and I down half of my vodka soda.

Chace leans in closer. "I don't think we should get drunk tonight."

"I remember the word 'normal' being thrown around a lot, and this is what I would do on a normal night out," I remind him.

He laughs and puts his hand on the small of my back. "Come and dance with me?"

As if I'm going to say no to that.

Looking up at him through my lashes, I nod.

We leave the table where Sienna and Isaac are arguing about which one of them could run five miles the fastest.

He turns me around on the dance floor and pulls me close. I don't know if he's more aware of what goes on inside my head now that I've told him some of how I feel, but he does seem to know when I need him.

"When this is over, we're all going away," he says.

Grinning up at him, I indulge in the thought. "Where?"

"Er… Magaluf."

"You mean Shag-aluf? Really?" Magaluf is where everyone goes on spring break for casual sex.

Laughing, he tilts his head back. "I knew you'd say that."

"I'll let you take me to Vegas," I offer.

He raises his eyebrow, giving me a suspicious look. "You want to get off-our-face drunk and be married by Elvis?"

Yes.

"Please, I'd make you work harder for it than that," I say.

He laughs and presses his forehead against mine. My brain short-circuits. He's close. Like, real close. Holy crap, I can feel his breath and smell his aftershave. It's Chace overload and my heart is trying to break out of my chest.

I slide my head onto his shoulder, closing my eyes to savor the moment. When I open them, I freeze. I see him.

Shit. Jake. I'm sure it's Jake. My fingers dig into Chace's neck.

"Lylah?" Chace asks. Frowning, he follows my line of sight. "What? What is it?"

"Jake. I think I've just seen him."

Chace's reaction is immediate. He pulls out of our embrace and grabs my hand. With his free hand, he starts messing around with his phone, probably sending a message to Lina.

"Are you sure?" he asks, forcing us through the sea of students on the dance floor.

"It's dark—but it looked like him."

"That's good enough for me," he replies, still tapping on his phone. We head back to the bar where Sienna is getting a new drink.

One of the many undercover police officers reaches the bar just as we do. He leans in. "Are you sure?" he asks.

I shake my head. "I only got a quick glimpse."

"Stay here," he says and heads in the direction where I think I saw Jake.

"He's here?" Sienna asks.

"We think so," Chace replies. "Where's Isaac?"

Sienna's eyes dart around the room. "He went to dance with some girl I don't recognize," she says.

"We're getting you out of here now," Detective Lina shouts over the music.

"We don't know where Isaac is," I reply. I'm not leaving without him. No chance. He got the last note. What if he's next?

Her mouth falls open a fraction. "Okay, so much for sticking together," she says, shaking her head. "We'll get you in a car, and I'll find Isaac."

"I don't want to get in the car without Isaac," I press. My pulse is pounding so hard it makes my head swim. He's missing. When Sonny went missing he turned up dead.

"Lylah," Detective Lina snaps, "I'm trying to protect you. Please get in the car."

I grit my teeth. "Have you caught Jake?"

"We're working on it."

Whatever. She wants me to trust her decisions, but so far they've led to nothing.

"Jake sent Isaac a note. I'm not going anywhere until—"

Chace cuts me off by grabbing my hand and tugging. I scowl at him, but he ignores the look. "Get in the car, Lylah."

"What? No. Why are you taking her side?"

He rolls his eyes. "There is no *side*. It's safer."

"Are you coming too?"

His eye twitches. Like I suspected. He's planning to stay and look for Isaac. Damn hypocrite. "Just go with the detective."

"Come on, Lylah," Sienna says. "I don't want to stay here, and I don't want to be alone."

God, this sucks. It feels like I have to retreat because I'm a girl, while only the men can be brave. What a load of bullshit.

Sienna takes my other hand, and Chace lets go. He watches me, and I can tell from his slight frown that he feels bad, but he won't back down. I appreciate that he cares, more than he'll ever know, but

I'm mega-annoyed that he thinks he can ship me off. Who does he think he is?

I turn on my heel and stomp toward the exit without glancing back at him.

"What's up, Lylah?" Sienna asks as we're escorted back to the car. "Is there something going on with you and Chace?"

One of the undercover cops opens the door for me. I want to get in without acknowledging him, but I was brought up to be polite, so I give him a fleeting smile. It's the best I can manage.

He slams the door shut, but it doesn't snap me out of my current mood.

"Nothing is going on. Chace is an ass."

"He's an ass for wanting you to be safe?"

Yeah, it doesn't sound rational. "Yes."

"Okay…" She clears her throat. "He was right to tell you to go."

My gaze slides over to her.

"I know it's not what you want to hear, Lylah, but we tell each other how it is. The guy likes you, I don't care what you say."

I have been inadvertently hurt by him dozens of times when he's gone out with other girls, so nothing is certain until Chace spills his feelings.

"Whatever," I mutter. I'm not in the mood to have yet another conversation about my feelings for Chace. Sienna has always said that we're too close, that he's too caring for him to think of me as just a friend. But we both know she's only trying to distract us. Her knuckles are white around the handle of her handbag she's clutching it so tight.

Someone knocks on the window, and we both jump in our seats, my heart skipping a full beat.

"Isaac!" Sienna says.

I breathe slowly, sagging against the fabric. He's okay.

He gives us a nod and follows Chace to the car in front.

"Thank God he's okay," I whisper, my shoulders relaxing. The remaining officers and detectives file to the cars as we prepare to leave.

The officer with us starts the engine, and we pull onto the road.

I lay back against the seat. "Well, that was a waste of time."

The officer looks back in the rearview mirror. "We're trying to trace the man you saw."

He nods to the window, and when I glance out, the club is emptying. Hundreds of students shiver on the street in the freezing cold.

"If Jake is there, he'll be found," the officer says.

Right, like Jake would file out of the club with everyone else. He's probably long gone. But we can hope for the best.

13

Wednesday
February 7

I n the morning, I wake without a hangover. *Winning.* Every time
we've been out, I've always had a headache the next day. It's kind
of nice not to want to hack off my own head.

I pull back my covers, and instantly, I regret it, as freezing air
rushes over my body.

Is the heat not on?

Dashing to my closet, I grab my bathrobe and wrap it around my
body. I head to the thermostat on the wall by the stairs to turn up
the heat, but it's off. It's the middle of winter. Why on earth would
anyone turn the heat off?

At the top of the stairs, I freeze. There's a white box right inside
the front door. It's about shoe box size, but square.

My heart thuds, and I clench my fists. I must be the only person
up. Someone else would have seen this for sure if they were awake,

but I don't want to open it on my own. My pulse races. What am I about to find in that little white box?

I step backward without taking my eyes off the package and knock on Chace's door. "Are you up?"

No answer.

"Chace?" I call a little louder, and knock again.

This time he hears and mumbles through the door, annoyed, "What?"

"There's something downstairs. I don't want to look at it alone."

He doesn't reply, but I hear movement as he gets out of bed and thunders across the floor. The door flies open. "Someone's in the house?"

"No. Some*thing*, not some*one*. There," I say, pointing at the box. I'm scared about what's in the package and, more importantly, how it was left inside for us. But I can't help but notice and appreciate Chace's naked chest.

"What the…" he starts. "Lylah, stay here." He moves down the stairs, rubbing his arms in the cold.

"No, I'm coming with you." As long as I have company, I can be brave.

Rolling his eyes, he says, "How did I know you'd say that?"

I follow him down, one step behind.

We reach the bottom, and I twist the thermostat there too. The boiler finally kicks in, making clunking noises as it fires up to heat both zones of the house.

Chace stops and looks at me. "That was on high when I went to bed last night, and I was the last one up."

"I so don't want to hear that."

"How is he breaking in? Was one of the doors left unlocked? We have security outside, so I don't understand how this happened."

"We need to be more careful." I shudder. "He could have done anything while he was in here." Gasping, I grip Chace's arm. "We don't know he hasn't. Sienna! Isaac! Charlotte!" I shout.

"Jesus, Lylah, talk about overreacting."

"I'm not overreacting. He could have hurt them!"

"What's with the noise, guys?" Isaac asks, stumbling out of his room.

Charlotte is out next. "What? What's going on?"

"There's a box," I say, looking up the stairs for Sienna.

She surfaces seconds later, and I let out a sigh of relief. Her sleek black hair is still pulled up in a topknot from last night. "This had better be good, Lylah." Folding her arms, she walks down the stairs. "Jeez, it's cold."

"Jake was here during the night. He must have turned off the thermostat when he left this." Chace steps aside so they can get a good look.

"Oh my God, don't open it. We should we call Detective Lina!" Sienna exclaims.

"I can't wait that long. Someone call her, but I'm opening it," Chace replies. He crouches down and reaches out slowly like he expects the box to explode.

I hold my breath as he lifts the lid with the tip of his index finger. Flipping it open, he peers in, and then jumps to his feet. "Fuck!"

Oh God. No way. No, that can't be…

But it is.

Turning away, I press my fist against my mouth and wretch. *Don't throw up.* Even though it's in a plastic bag, the smell is overpowering. It stings my nose and attacks the back of my throat.

Charlotte sprints into the living room screaming and Sienna makes a dash for the bathroom as Isaac swears and pounds at the screen on his phone, I assume calling the police.

Is that…Sonny's heart? Or Nora's? Or a pig's heart like the one on the noticeboard? And if it was from a pig, where are Sonny's and Nora's hearts?

"How could he do this? We've done nothing to him. How could he?" I rant, breathing heavily to try to make my lungs work properly. It doesn't help. The harder I breathe, the sicker I feel.

"Lylah," Chace calls, trying to snap me out of my panic. He ushers me into the kitchen and holds on to my upper arms. "Are you okay?"

I shake my head and whisper, "No. Why is he doing this?"

"I wish I knew," he replies, pulling me against his chest.

Closing my eyes, I sink into his embrace, wrapping my arms around his back.

"Detective Lina's on her way, and cops outside are checking it out now," Isaac says, stomping into the kitchen. "Are you all right, Lylah?"

Chace doesn't let go, but I feel him shake his head.

I always try to put on a strong front. But Jake has stripped me of every ounce of strength I had. I need to get it together. Except I have to let myself be scared. That's what my therapist would say.

I can hear the cops talking in the hallway, but thankfully, their voices are muffled, so I can't make out what they're saying.

"Where are Sienna and Charlotte?" I ask.

"Sienna's still puking up her guts, and Charlotte's crying in the living room. She didn't want company," Isaac replies.

Charlotte has always been a very private person, but I am surprised she wants to be alone. I don't want to be alone ever again.

Then in a hushed voice, Isaac says, "He really cut out his heart? He didn't just cut his chest but… I mean, how do you even…"

Chace shakes his head. "I don't know, man."

"His *heart*, Chace," I whisper.

"I know." His waving voice gives away his disgust and fear.

Jake is cutting out their hearts and leaving pigs' hearts for us to find. I don't know why he's not using the real thing. I don't understand what he's doing with the real hearts or why he even feels the need to use something else.

To be honest, I don't want to understand.

My words start tumbling out. "I can't imagine what his family will go through when they're told his heart turned up in a box! Well, his, Nora's, or another pig's. How can anyone be so callous? I should have just kissed him."

Chace holds me so he can look into my eyes.

"This isn't your fault, Lylah," Chace says.

"He's right. Jake is sick in the head. The dude needs to be placed in a psychiatric facility."

"I think I need to sit down." I pull out of Chace's grip. Neither of them stops me as I leave the room. Charlotte wanted space, so rather than going all the way into the living room, I sit on the bottom step.

Chace follows me, moving so quietly I almost don't hear him. He looks concerned, like he has no idea how to handle me right now.

Riley would know. He's pulled me back from the brink and fixed me so many times. But I don't want to be dependent on my big brother. I won't call him to pick up my pieces. I'm supposed to be a fully functioning adult, and he deserves a normal life where he doesn't have to cancel dates because his emotional wreck of a sister is having a meltdown. He said he met a nice girl a few weeks ago. My brother seems happy. I don't want to diminish that with my drama.

It's fine. I can handle this myself. *Just breathe, Lylah*, I tell myself. *Deep breaths, in and out.*

"Lylah." Chace kneels in front of me. His deep, green eyes watch me with caution. "I need you to believe that all of this isn't your fault."

"Look, I know Jake is obviously ill, but I can't help thinking that if I'd paid a little more attention, this wouldn't have happened."

"If that is the case, then we're all guilty. No one could have known what he was capable of."

Logically, I know what he's saying makes sense. But isn't there something that we could have done? Something that would have prevented Sonny's and Nora's deaths? If we'd known—noticed—that Jake was suffering, we could have gotten him help, and we all would be walking a different path.

The doorbell rings, saving us from a conversation that would inevitably go in circles. Chace rises to his feet and goes to the door. Through the glass, I can see people in uniforms.

Detective Lina is the first one in, followed by Detective Alexander and three cops.

"Where is it?" Lina asks, her face ashen.

Chace nods to the floor.

The house is soon flooded with more cops and a forensics team. We move out of the way and watch from the kitchen. Our house looks like a circus scene—people everywhere and flashing lights from someone taking photos of the evidence.

Detective Lina spends a while with us, going through our statements. I've done this enough now that the process is familiar. But by the afternoon, I'm still thinking about the heart. I can't stop thinking about the heart. It looked like a lump of beef in a box. But we're not sure yet if it's Sonny's, Nora's, or another pig's.

The police are trying to keep the heart thing under wraps. The pig's heart on the noticeboard was passed off as a prank, which the general public believes, because they don't know that Sonny and Nora lost theirs. Chace was right. The police are keeping that fact a secret to prevent panic and potentially identify the killer.

When the police saw the contents of the box, it was the first time they looked a little lost. Detectives Lina and Alexander spoke in hushed voices with their shoulders slumped, looking less in control than they had been the last time I saw them. The only person with any control here is Jake. He's proved that time and time again. Now he's making human remains deliveries in the dead of night. There is a cop stationed outside, yet he still managed to get in. What could be next?

Detective Lina tells us the latest plan. Like last night, she wants to create a scenario to lure out the killer—then trap him. Later tonight, we are supposed to go to the Valentine's firework display on campus, but I see that being as successful as trying to catch Jake at the club. Still, we have to try. Waiting for him to make a move will be too late for his next victim.

●　　●　　●

Charlotte flat-out refuses to come with us again, and I can't really blame her.

Sienna, Chace, Isaac, and I are channeling all of our anger, grief, and hate into finding the killer at the fireworks show, so we're going. We've all posted on our different social media pages that we'll be there, hoping to make ourselves targets.

Detective Lina goes over the rules again before we leave. They're obvious things like *don't chase Jake if we see him*. As if that's going to happen. I'm not running after a murderer! There will be a lot of cops around, double the amount they had at the club. One of them can take on Jake.

I hope it works.

* * *

That night, I pull on my coat and we head out the door. This time, we're walking alone, and undercover cops will trail us.

"It's hard to act normal," Isaac says.

"That's because you're a freak, bro," Chace replies, trying to lighten the mood.

Isaac punches Chace on the arm. "Shut up, dickhead. You know what I mean."

Sienna rolls her eyes and gives me a grin. The banter *is* normal, like it used to be. I've missed the casual conversations and lighthearted bashing of one another.

"You're both idiots," I say.

But the closer we get to where the fireworks display is being held, the more nervous I become. "Do you think we have a good chance of catching him?" I ask as we arrive, making our way through the masses of people. It looks like the entire student body has turned up. Music plays in the background somewhere, but it's barely audible over the sound of hundreds of voices.

Chace wraps his arm around my back, his fingers curling around my hip. "We have to believe so. Don't leave my side, okay?"

Yeah, I have no problem with that.

Over the PA system, the university's president makes a short speech before the display. He's met with a deafening cheer, drowning out his words. I'm huddled in front of Chace with Sienna and Isaac beside us. We've moved into the crowd a little, but we're close enough to the outskirts to make a run for it if we need to. I've lost track of the detectives, but they've promised to stay close.

I ball my hands into fists. *Please let this work.*

Above us, the sky lights up red with the first firework explosion of the night.

Valentine's Day, well more like Valentine's *month*, is under full swing now.

Campus is absolutely packed. People are standing on the grass in the hundreds, all staring up at the night sky.

The next fireworks go off with a bang that echoes through the night.

I half watch the display and half look around to see if I can spot the undercover cops and Jake. It's impossible to see much though. It's dark, obviously. Most of the streetlights are out until the fireworks are over, and there are so many people.

As it's winter, there is a sea of hoodies, probably mostly men who don't want to wear a coat for fear of being labeled a wimp. Any one of them could be Jake. I don't really know the cops' plan. Are they wandering around looking at the face of every person here? I can't see what more they can do unless he tries to attack us, which doesn't fill me with much confidence.

The fireworks finally finish with a round of applause, then the streetlights slowly blink on, and everyone heads to the clubs to party. The display only lasted fifteen minutes, but it felt a lot longer.

I'm bumped from all sides. Sienna and Isaac are close, but they're separated with the mad rush of everyone who wants to be first at the bar. Chace is right behind me, watching for any signs of Jake.

I scan the outskirts of the crowd. The last time I glimpsed Jake, he was watching me from the doorway of the club. If he's here, he'll likely be situated to make a quick escape.

As the crowd thins, the streetlights suddenly die, cloaking the area in darkness.

People cheer loudly, the way they do if someone drops a glass in the dining hall. Instantly, I'm on edge. My heart races as my palms start to sweat.

"Chace!" I turn to reach for him, but he's disappeared. I call to Sienna and Isaac, but they were farther away. I can't see a thing. I blink to try to get my night vision. "Chace!"

Everyone starts to pull their phones from their pockets for light. I spin back. "Chace!" I shout. *Where is he?* People are being obnoxiously noisy, cheering and chanting now that the lights were off.

My body goes cold. *This must be Jake's doing. He's coming for us.*

All I can hear now is my heavy breathing.

"Chace!"

Dark shadows move around me, and I catch glimpses of faces as I stumble, frantically calling for my friends. I'm terrified that the next face I see will be Jake's. I'd close my eyes if that weren't more dangerous.

Why aren't the lights coming back on?

My heart is beating so hard it hurts. I press a hand against my chest, willing my heart to slow down, and fumble for the flashlight feature on my phone with the other. I hold it up, lighting a short distance in front of me.

Chace isn't anywhere. I can't see him at all, and I didn't hear him reply.

Someone smacks into my back, wrapping an arm around my waist. I freeze. Whoever it is, he's strong and holds me so tight my ribs scream in protest. "Shh," he hisses into my ear, and chills run down my spine.

It's not Chace or Isaac. Could it be a cop? They would have said by now.

I don't turn my head because I'm petrified of seeing whoever is behind me, of being able to identify my attacker. He starts to back up, forcing me to go with him. That's when I struggle. A scream rips form my throat. But a large, gloved palm presses down hard over my mouth.

It's Jake. It must be.

"Jake!" I yell into his hand, but I can hardly hear it.

"Shh," he whispers in my ear again, so close I feel his hot breath against my neck. I squirm, but he has me in an iron grip.

Where are the cops, and why haven't the lights come back on yet?

He drags me off the grass and down an alleyway between buildings.

I lift my feet off the ground, twisting my body in a bid to get him to let go.

No one else is here. No one knows where I am or what's happened. I can only rely on myself now. He could kidnap me, *kill me*—I need to fight.

His hand drops from my mouth and seals around my waist with the other.

"Help!" I shout as my voice cracks. "Get off—"

He chuckles and starts to smother me with his hand again, this time harder, so I'm unable to make a sound. Then his mouth clamps down on my neck. I feel teeth press into my skin above my jacket collar. I swear he's going to pierce the skin.

I stop moving. Fear makes a statue of my body. Tears roll down my cheeks. Then, suddenly, I am released. His hands slam into my back. I stumble forward with a scream.

Gasping, I reach out to break my fall, but it's too late. I hit the pavement with a scream. My palms sting. In the darkness, I can faintly see raw patches where the skin has broken.

Lights begin to flicker on in front of the buildings. Groaning, I look behind me, but he's gone.

"Lylah!"

My head whips around, and I sag in relief. Chace runs toward me.

I push myself to my feet. "I-I'm okay," I say as he reaches me.

"What happened? You're shaking."

I'm shaking?

Chace pulls me into his embrace. "What happened?" he demands. I can tell he's upset, but trying to seem calm.

It takes me a moment to be able to speak. "He grabbed me. He dragged me back here, and then he shoved me and took off."

"Lylah! Chace! There you are," Detective Lina says breathlessly. She's followed by the three cops who were supposed to be watching us. They have flashlights.

Stepping out of Chace's arms, I relay the information again. Two of the three cops run off in the direction I point, but Jake—or whoever it was—is probably long gone.

My cheeks feel like they're on fire. I know I have to tell her the rest of what happened, though it feels like a violation. "He bit me," I mutter, looking down.

"Bit you?" Detective Lina repeats, her voice a little higher than usual.

Hooking my finger over the neckline in my coat, I pull it down. She leans in to get a decent look.

"I don't think we'll get any evidence from this. There are no indents and it's fading quickly. We can swab for DNA though."

Evidence? Like comparing the bite mark to dental records? I almost wish he'd bitten me harder so there would be something to work with.

I give my permission to swab the mark. I'll do anything.

Chace hasn't said a word.

"Did he say anything? Did you get a proper look at him?" the detective continues.

"He said *shh* a couple of times and laughed. I didn't see him at all. He held me from behind. I think it was Jake."

"Are you sure it was him?" she asks.

"Yeah...I mean, I don't think I've ever heard him *shh* before, but it could have been his voice. At least I think so. Everything happened so fast, and I was scared. I was struggling to get free."

Detective Lina nods. "It's understandable. I'm glad you are okay. Isaac and Sienna are already in a car on their way back to the house. Let's get you all home."

"Wait," I say, bending down. There's an envelope on the ground near where I fell. The detective takes the envelope from me and opens it. I crane my neck to read it over her shoulder.

My spine ripples with fear. Spinning around, I head toward the car, trying to even my breathing with one of my exercises. I feel so exposed.

"What did it say?" Chace asks, catching up to me and grabbing my hand.

This night needs to end.

Hell, this whole nightmare needs to end.

I tell him flatly, then say, "He proved that to be true."

"I'm sorry, Lylah, I should have held on to you better so we wouldn't have gotten separated. I tried to find you, to call for you, but it was dark, and everyone was so damn loud," he says through gritted teeth, his forehead creased with guilt.

"There's no reason for you to apologize. I lost you too."

Clearing his throat, Chace rubs his jaw nervously. *Why is he so uncomfortable?*

"Your neck…"

"What about it?"

"Are you okay? Does it hurt?"

"I'm fine. It didn't really hurt. I think I was in shock. I've never felt so vulnerable. He could have dragged me away and killed me." I shudder.

When we reach the car that brought us here, Chace opens the back door and we slide in the back seat. Detective Lina and her partner get in the front.

"He didn't kill me," I repeat. But my nerves are frayed. Is he planning something bigger?

No one says anything. I'm sure Detective Lina has some theories, but she doesn't share them—so I push.

"Tonight was about letting me know that he can do what he wants, wasn't it? He didn't kill me because he doesn't want to—yet. But why did he come for me? If I'm not next on his hit list, why not go after someone else? I don't get it."

"Lylah, I wish I had the answers you're looking for," Detective Lina says. "But I agree that tonight was about fear. He probably hadn't planned to harm anyone."

"We may never understand," Chace says. He reaches across the middle seat and tentatively puts his hand on my thigh. "But the important thing is that you are all right. You're safe."

I cover his hand with my own and lean my head back. In this moment, I believe him.

14

Thursday
February 8

It's almost one in the morning, and I'm lying in bed beside Chace.

He hasn't left my side since I was grabbed. I think he feels guilty, as if it was his fault.

He's been asleep for an hour, and I can't take my eyes off his face. He's the only thing holding me together right now. I don't want to think too much about what happened or what Jake's note could mean. So I focus on Chace's features: the way his dark lashes create a shadow on his cheeks in the dim moonlight, how his lips pout slightly as he sleeps.

My hand itches to reach out and touch his hair. It looks so soft. I thought I was going to faint when he insisted on staying the night with me. I think he's worried that Jake will come for me.

I am too.

When we headed to bed, Chace wasted no time stripping down to his boxers. Thankfully, his back was to me, because I was openly gawking. I excused myself and went to the bathroom to change into my pajamas. The nice silk ones, obviously.

His muscular arm is over my stomach and has been for about ten minutes. It's maddeningly intimate—and the only reason I'm not obsessing about Jake.

Instead I'm lying here, wide awake, obsessing about Chace.

I need help.

He shifts onto his side, and he's suddenly *very* close. I hold my breath.

Oh my God, wake up and kiss me!

Biting my lip, I close my eyes tightly. This is torture. Pure, beautiful torture.

"Lylah?" he whispers my name.

I must look like totally insane with my eyes squeezed shut, chewing on my lip. When I open my eyes, Chace is gazing at me.

"You good?" he asks, his voice deep from sleep.

"Fine. Just having a hard time falling asleep." I can still feel Jake's breath on my shoulder right before his teeth bit into my skin. They did swab it for evidence, but now we have to wait for the results.

"You're overthinking." It isn't a question. He knows I am. It's a relief he thinks it's about Jake though.

He tugs me into his arms and holds me tight against his chest. His very, very naked chest. "Sleep, Lylah," he murmurs against my forehead.

His toned chest is hard under my palm. I'm not getting rest anytime soon. I can feel Chace's heart thumping fast and loud. Mine feels the same way.

After a while, his body relaxes. He must have drifted off. His breathing lulls me, and I succumb shortly after.

• • •

Last night, being held by Chace was exactly what I needed, but this morning, it's like it never happened. I'm in the kitchen with Detective Lina, and Chace is still sleeping in my bed. It's early, and I'm freaking out about going to the library today.

"Do you think I should leave town? If I'm the one who hurt him, maybe he'll stop channeling his hate to everyone in my life."

With a sympathetic smile, Detective Lina rests her arms on the table. "You may be the focus of his rage and obsession, but you're not the only one he is targeting."

"But do you think he would leave my friends alone and try to find me instead?"

"I think he's more likely to get angry and lash out, maybe start spree killing. If I thought you leaving would help the case, I would have suggested it by now. You said you prefer to keep busy, so go to class as normal, but at no point will you be alone."

With a nod, I get up. I focus on something I can control—my rumbling stomach.

Once I've eaten and dressed, I head out with two cops in tow. Jake grabbing me yesterday has left me on edge, jumping at shadows. He's unlikely to try anything while I have protection with me.

I hope.

It's still as cold as the South Pole, but the sunshine makes it more bearable. Campus is up ahead; I can see the brick library from here.

"Lylah?"

Tensing at the sound of my name, I turn my head to the side. I'm poised to run, adrenaline coursing through my veins. But it's not Jake.

"Zak." My shoulders relax. "How are you?" I ask, stepping closer to him.

He raises his eyebrow.

"Dad and Sarah are waiting for me, but can we meet later?"

His question catches me off guard. I didn't expect him to want to meet up. Does he know what happened last night?

I hesitate, then say, "Sure. When and where?"

"The Bar? We'll be able to talk, but it's not so quiet that we'll be overheard. Say…at nine?"

"You know I'll have a cop with me, right?" If he wants to talk without anyone around he's going to have to find someone else because I can't do that.

"Of course. I wouldn't want you walking around with no protection, Lylah."

"Okay. Well, then, I'll see you there."

Zak nods and without another word, walks away. He doesn't look back.

I carry on to the library and spend an hour making notes. Well, I sit at a table for an hour. Ten minutes is dedicated to studying, and the rest of the time, I try to ignore people's stares while wondering what Zak wants to talk about and glancing from door to door in case Jake came in, making sure the cops shadowing me are alert and also watching the door.

But Jake wouldn't come here. Too out in the open.

Eventually, I shove my things back in my bag and throw it over my shoulder. The undercover cops are right there with me, rising to their feet and following me like a dogs.

We walk home in silence. These cops aren't that talkative, but that could be because they're concentrating on the task at hand. I would find it distracting if someone was constantly talking to me while I was working, so I don't try to engage in small talk.

We get home in minutes because I'm walking so fast.

One cop follows me inside, while the other joins the detail in a car outside our house.

Chace and Sienna are the only ones home. I find Chace in the living room. He's sitting on the sofa starting at the TV. The TV is off.

"Chace?"

He looks up and smiles. "You're back."

"Looks like it." I sit down next to him. "You're watching a blank screen. Anything you want to talk about?"

Chuckling, he shakes his head. "Did you get much done?"

"Nope. We're still the talk of the campus. I'm considering handing out Polaroids so people don't have to stare. But I did run into Zak. I'm meeting him at The Bar tonight."

Chace's face falls. "You're going out with Zak?"

"No, not like that. He asked me to meet him at The Bar. I think he's having a real tough time."

"Why did he ask you and not someone else?"

I frown at his question. "Because I'm the only one who doesn't treat him like his brother's actions are his fault. You're hardly under-standing, any of you. And I imagine his dad and sister are still really emotional about Jake."

The last time I spoke to Zak may have ended in a public argument, but none of my anger or frustration was aimed at him. His sister is the one who had gotten to me.

"So they should be. He's ruined people's lives—he's *taken* people's lives."

"Chace, stop. That has nothing to do with Zak, and he is in pain too. Why are you being like this?"

"Like what?"

"Argumentative."

"I'm not. Go out with whomever you like, Lylah. I don't care!" He stomps off, his footsteps thudding away from me.

What just happened?

Chace doesn't usually say one thing and mean another, but the way he said that was not at all convincing.

I bite my lip. *Oh my God! He's jealous!* Suddenly I don't really mind that he's stormed off.

Is it wrong to find that adorable?

"Why're you smiling like a fool?" Sienna asks, walking into the room and looking back in the direction where Chace ran off.

"No reason. I need to take a shower before I go out later!" I practically skip upstairs like I'm tipsy already.

●　　●　　●

When I get to The Bar, Zak is already there, sitting at a table along the wall. After last night, I don't really want to be out, but I do want to talk to Zak. He has a right to know what's going on. And a right to know that I don't blame him for what his brother has done.

Detective Alexander is with me tonight, and I won't be straying far from his side.

Zak smiles when he sees me.

I sit down. "Hey."

"How are you, Lylah?"

"That's a loaded question."

He winces. "Sorry."

"Has anyone been by to talk to you about…recent events?" I ask him, wondering if he already knows what happened to me.

Shaking his head, he scoots forward on his seat. "What's he done?"

"You believe it's Jake now?" I ask, my voice unable to hide my surprise.

Zak's eyes drop. "I don't want to, but…I have doubts about him. Things don't add up. The profile for the killer—being strong and having medical knowledge or training—it all points toward my brother."

I give him a sympathetic smile. That can't be easy for him.

I recount what happened, and Zak's mouth falls open. He slumps. His eyes briefly dart to the cop behind me, like he's unsure if he should talk in front of him. Detective Alexander's not going anywhere, so he's going to have to learn to relax around him.

He doesn't move and doesn't talk as I ramble on and on about what happened, going over parts more than once, for a solid twenty minutes.

Clearing his throat when I stop talking, he asks, "Were you hurt? God, I have so many questions. I don't really know where to start."

"Yeah, that's how I feel most of the time. It's like Jake hates us all. I know he left college, but I didn't think he had that kind of animosity."

"My dad and I have been going through each moment we spent

with Jake since he moved back home," Zak started. "I can't help thinking we've missed something big. A clue to his grand plan or hint to where he could be. I don't know. I'm driving myself up the wall trying to remember our conversations. Maybe if I'd read between the lines… But nothing sticks out."

"There might not have been any clues, Zak. These aren't exactly the sort of plans you share."

"No, I know. I'm just trying to do something useful, you know?"

"We feel pretty useless. Do you still plan to stay in town until he's found?"

Zak nods and sits back in his seat. "I can't go home yet. Besides, the cops have turned our house upside down and none of us are ready to deal with that."

"Do you and Sarah both live with your dad still?"

Chuckling, he shakes his head. "No, I'm the only loser here."

My eyes widen. "I wasn't insinuating that you're a loser."

"I'm kidding. I was renting a place, but the landlord wanted to sell, so I'm back home until I find another apartment."

"What was Jake's plan after he dropped out?" I ask, moving the subject back to the information I wanted to find out. "He only told us that college wasn't for him, and he was going home to consider his options."

"I don't think he had a plan. It was obvious that he regretted leaving. All he ever wanted to do was practice medicine, so I wasn't buying his change-of-heart bullshit. But he wouldn't admit that something else changed his mind."

"That something being me?"

"I don't know. We assumed he wasn't doing as well as he'd hoped and maybe needed some time off. He was going to live at home and get a job for a while. Jake didn't have money. Hell, he had a student loan. That's what I don't get. How is he affording to live? Where is he staying? How does he know how to kill the streetlights on campus? How does someone who went to school to learn to save lives start taking them instead?"

"No idea." I shake my head solemnly.

We sit with our own thoughts for a few minutes before I break the silence.

"We should get a drink. After last night, I could really use one."

"Vodka soda, right?"

I grin. "Ah, you remembered."

"Hard to forget when you almost threw up on my feet after a night of drinking them."

Cringing, I watch Zak get up and go to the bar. It must have been the last time Zak visited before Jake dropped out. I had one too many—rather, six too many—and threw up on the walk home. It was horrific, and I was so embarrassed. I've never allowed myself to get that drunk again.

I turn to look at Detective Alexander. He's nearby at the bar, sitting on a stool, drinking a Coke. His gaze is mostly on me, but he's also watching the crowd. His job must suck. I'd be bored stiff sitting there for an hour doing nothing.

Zak returns a few minutes later. It's ten, so most of the students have moved on to the clubs. I definitely prefer The Bar when it's quieter.

"Thanks." I take my drink and sip. "A double?"

"My brother pulled you down an alley. I figured I owed you a double."

"You owe me nothing, but thank you. Are you still working for that motorcycle shop?"

"Yeah, still selling cool bikes to uncool men embracing their midlife crises."

"Ah, in a few years time, I'll send my brother your way. He's definitely headed for an early midlife crisis." It wouldn't surprise me actually; Riley's had to be a proper grown-up far too early in his life. At the tender age of twenty-one, he inherited a teenager.

I take another sip. God, I needed this drink.

Zak laughs. "Definitely send him my way. You should come too. I'll take you for a ride on the back of my bike."

"I'm pretty sure I'd be awful on the back of a bike. Seriously, if you were to lean I'd probably go the other way."

"Yeah, that's not good."

"But I would love to see the lake by your home. It looks gorgeous in the photos Jake used to show me."

"That'd be great. I probably wouldn't tell Sarah though."

"Does she still think Jake is innocent?"

"The evidence has been stacking up, so as much as we hate to admit it, we all believe you. Jake has done a great job of concealing his true feelings. He was reapplying for college and planned to go north to finish his degree. I found the brochures at our holiday home when I had to let the police in to search it. I thought he'd lost everything, but he was rebuilding."

I frown. "He was?"

Zak nods. "Yeah. Maybe he thought he could pick up his life

after… I don't know. Getting inside his head is after recent events is, frankly, impossible."

Jake was supposed to have lost everything. That was the reason he wanted us dead. The anniversary of my rejection the trigger. Someone who's lost it all and only wants revenge doesn't plan their future. At least I don't think they would. Now, nothing makes sense.

But Zak is probably right. Jake was likely using starting over as a cover.

I spend another thirty minutes with Zak before heading home.

• • •

The house is super quiet when I let myself in. Detective Alexander left me at the door after making sure I got inside safely. It's now up to the cops outside on patrol to protect us.

"Where is everyone?" I ask Charlotte as I plop down on the sofa. She's curled up watching TV.

"Gone out."

My eyes widen. "Are they all together?"

Charlotte shakes her head. "Nope. Sienna's with other friends, Isaac's with some girl at a bar, and Chace met up with…some guys? I can't remember who. Detective Lina was not amused that we've all gone in different directions tonight and they've had to send out extra cops to accompany everyone."

I'm not surprised that Chace has gone out, and I'm not bothered that he's out with friends—particularly since he seemed jealous of the time I was spending with Zak.

"Well, she wants us to carry on like normal," I said. As if that's possible. We can all keep getting out of bed and leaving the house, but nothing is normal.

"That's exactly what Chace said. How was your night?" she asks.

"It was fine."

"Really? Was it not weird being out with Zak?"

I shrug and sink back into the cushions. "Why would it be? He wants Jake caught too. Imagine what it would be like to have a killer in your family. I feel bad for him."

"So that's the reason you went out tonight?"

"Not the only reason. Zak is cool. We all used to get along before Jake turned psycho."

"I wish I could still see Zak in the same light, but I can't. I used to think he was okay. He always made sure to ask how I was and how school was going when he visited. It was awkward being around him and his family at the police station. I don't know what to say."

"He's still the same person. You can talk about anything with him, except accusing him of doing something wrong. He's no more guilty in this than any of us."

"Yeah, I'll probably just avoid him until this is over and he goes back home."

Laughing, I nod. "That'll work too. What have you been doing then?"

"TV. I don't have a social life, remember?"

"That's because you spend your evenings in front of the TV!"

Charlotte is about to reply when there's a loud knock on the front door. We both startle.

"Girls, it's Detective Alexander. We need to come in."

We?

I get up, and Charlotte lunges for my hand. "He said we! Who's with him?"

"We won't know if we sit here!"

I peer through the window, then open the door.

"Zak!"

Zak is leaning on the detective. His head is bleeding. I gasp. "Oh my God, what happened?"

"It was *Jake*," Zak rasps.

15

Thursday
February 8

Detective Alexander supports Zak, who is slumped against him. I usher them into the kitchen. Charlotte holds back, watching from a distance.

"I was jumped around the corner. I managed to get him off me, but smacked my head against a wall in the fight." Zak collapses onto one of the dining chairs. "Alexander saw me stumbling past your place. I'm *not* going to the hospital."

Oh my God.

"I think you need to, Zak," the detective says. Zak growls low in his throat and shakes his head. Detective Alexander turns to me. "Do you have a first aid kit?"

I dash to the cupboard in a fluster. "Yeah, the landlord provided one. Shouldn't we be taking him to the emergency room though?"

Detective Alexander scoffs. "We can't force him." He reaches into his pocket and dials a number.

"I'm right here!" Zak grumbles. "I don't need to go to the hospital. I'm fine."

"You're bleeding!" I say. A small stream of blood trickles down the side of his head.

"Barely. Honestly, I'm just shaken up and embarrassed."

"There's nothing to be embarrassed about," I say. "You were jumped!"

"Are you sure it was Jake?" Charlotte asks.

I wince inwardly. Of course it was, but that must be really hard on Zak.

Taking a deep breath, Zak shrugs. "Well, I didn't get a good look but the way he ran reminded me of Jake. He has a distinctive run. It must have been him."

I smile. "I remember." Jake picks his legs up high when he runs, making it look a bit comical. At first, I thought he was just drunk, but he ran the same way playing soccer with Chace and Sonny too. "Did you get a note before this happened?"

Zak looks up, his eyes haunted. "No," he breathes. "Does that mean it *wasn't* the killer?"

"Maybe," I say as I rummage in the cupboard for the first aid kit. I find it underneath some deflated blow-up party decorations and hand it to the detective.

"I've called in the incident," Alexander says, putting his phone away.

I sit down across from Zak and lean over the table, where Alexander is treating him. "Zak, are you okay?"

"He's my *brother*," he mutters. Zak sucks in a ragged breath, unable to finish his sentence.

"If this is Jake, he's not thinking clearly at the moment, Zak," Detective Alexander says.

No one wants to believe that Jake would attempt to hurt, let alone murder, his own brother, but I'm not buying that it was a random mugging. Whatever is going on with Jake, he's obviously not stable. The guy has serious issues.

Maybe hurting Zak wasn't part of the plan though. Maybe he crossed paths with him while Jake was watching us, and he panicked. Zak would easily recognize him.

"Do you want me to call your dad?" I ask.

"No! He can't know about Jake attacking me."

"*Potentially* attacking you," Detective Alexander clarifies. "Let's not get ahead of ourselves."

My eyes flick between them. "Zak, he's going to know something happened. You have a cut on your head."

"I'll make something up. My brother has already broken his heart. If my dad knew he was capable of hurting family too… Please don't tell him."

I hold up my hands. "Okay." He's obviously going to find out, from the police probably, but I'll honor Zak's wishes and not tell him myself.

Detective Alexander tends to Zak's head, which has stopped bleeding and thankfully doesn't look as bad as I initially thought.

"Why do you think he tried to attack you?" Charlotte asks. "I mean, it doesn't make sense. He doesn't usually attack impulsively like that. This wasn't planned so it doesn't fit with the other attacks."

"Or it might." I look at Charlotte and then back to Zak. "Think about it, Zak and I hung out tonight. That could have angered him."

Charlotte takes a breath. "Right. He's jealous."

Guilt lays heavy in my stomach. "Damn it, Zak. I'm so sorry." My heart sinks to the floor. "I think I made you a target."

Zak takes a minute, like he's trying to process a really complicated equation or figure out Facebook after a big update.

"It's not your fault, Lylah. This is on him." Zak lowers his head, too ashamed or too emotional to look at us. I know a lot of men don't like to show how much certain things affect them, and I'm guessing Zak is one of them.

"We will find him," Detective Alexander says. "If it was Jake, he made a choice, and he will shoulder the responsibility of those actions. There are consequences."

Detective Alexander is a man of few words. Unless he's speaking to you or interrogating you in a professional capacity, it is strange to hear him being so…human. It's nice.

"I'm going to need a formal statement from you, Zak," he continues.

Zak frowns. He could refuse in an effort to protect his brother, but what would that achieve? It's not like Jake isn't already in serious trouble.

"You know you have to," I say quietly. Brother or not, Jake has to face what he has done.

Zak bows his head lower. "I don't want to go to the station in case anyone sees."

"You could do the statement here," I offer. "That's okay, right, Detective Alexander?"

He nods.

"Lylah, let's leave them to it," Charlotte says.

I follow Charlotte into the living room so the detective can take Zak's statement in private. Closing the living room door, I lean my back against it.

"He tried to kill his own *brother*. Well, maybe tried to kill," I say. The words don't sound right as they leave my mouth. You're supposed to protect your family. I would be devastated if I were Zak.

"Jake has completely lost it. What's he going to do to us, Lylah? I kept thinking that if I saw him, I could to talk him, reason with him. I mean, we weren't that close, but we were friends. I thought. There is no chance of talking with him anymore, though, is there? We're all going to die."

I'm silent. It's a harrowing thought.

Charlotte drops onto the sofa like her legs can't take hold her weight anymore.

I move over to her, sit next to her, and give her a side squeeze. "Charlotte, it won't come to that. They'll catch him. We'll be more vigilant."

She wipes a tear from her eye. "You sound pretty sure. I'm not sure of anything."

I'm hoping. It's the best I can do. It's not like I have a lot of experience with murderers.

"We can get through this if we stick together. Jake wants us separated because that makes it easier to get to us. Let's not allow him to do that."

Charlotte looks me in the eyes. "Do you think all of this is because of you?"

Me? I swallow the lump in my throat and open my mouth to respond, but what is there to say?

"No!" she cries, realizing she's upset me. "I didn't mean it like that. I'm not blaming you. The police are right. This is all Jake's fault. I just meant that being turned down doesn't seem like a legit reason to go all Freddy Kruger."

"Who knows what's going through his mind," I said. "Detective Lina said that sometimes people just…snap. Like a small interaction can feel big to another person. A lot of stalkers meet their victims through a chance encounter that the victim barely even remembers. Something must have been different in Jake's mind for a while, but now it's blown up."

She scoffs. "I wish his head would blow up."

"I don't think spontaneous combustion is going to solve anything here."

Laughing, she shakes her head and pulls her legs up on to the sofa, wrapping her arms around them. "Well, you made me laugh at least. But I don't think I'll feel better until Jake is caught. I never wanted to find myself in a position where I was living in fear again."

"When did you live in fear?" I ask gently. Charlotte has shared very little about her childhood and family. I don't even know if she has siblings.

She shrugs.

"Sorry, you don't have to talk about it."

"It's…my mom took off when I was a baby, and my dad was a violent alcoholic. My home life wasn't pleasant. I never knew what I was coming home to. Leaving for college was the best day of my life. I haven't seen or spoken to him since."

"Not at all?"

"Nope. He's probably forgotten he has a daughter. I don't care."

I can't imagine getting to that point. She must have gone through hell. "I'm sorry, Charlotte. You deserve a better life than that. I hope you're happy here." Frowning, I add, "Besides the situation right now."

"Thanks, Lylah."

Thankfully we've all managed to keep our families away. It's too dangerous for them to be here, for everyone. Their presence could be seen as an obstacle between us and Jake, and it could cause him to react. Detective Lina explained that it was better to have the police deal with this. They know what they're doing. I know for a fact that my brother would get too involved.

Someone knocks on the living room door, but they don't wait for a response. Detective Alexander smiles as he pushes it open. "Everything okay in here?"

"Yeah," I reply. "Where's Zak?"

"An officer is taking him back to his hotel."

"Has there been any other sign of Jake?"

"Not that I've heard. We're working all our leads. If you need me, I'll be outside."

"Thanks, Detective Alexander," Charlotte and I say in unison.

I turn to her. "Jinx."

That makes her smile again, which feels like an accomplishment.

Once he's left, Charlotte heads down the hall for a bath. I make a pot of coffee and get comfortable. Chace, Sienna, and Isaac are still out, but it's only five minutes to midnight. I don't expect them anytime soon. I curl up on the sofa and switch on the TV. While I'm waiting for a movie to load, I text Zak. We had exchanged numbers on a night out a few months back, but I've yet to need it until now.

Are you okay?

It takes him a few minutes to reply. Yeah, I'm fine. Sry to turn up on your doorstep like that.

Glad you're all right, I responded. If you want to talk, you know where I am.

There are about a hundred questions I'd like to ask, but I don't want to push him. I can't begin to imagine what's he's going through. *This is all such a big mess.*

Thanks. His message doesn't give me anything to work with, so I don't reply. He probably wants to be alone anyway.

As the opening credits start to play, my phone rings.

Chace. He doesn't usually call when he's out for the night. "Hi," I say.

"Lylah, what the hell is going on? I just heard about Zak from the cop that's with me. He got a message from Detective Alexander. Is he okay? Are you okay?"

"Yeah, he was alone, and he got jumped. Detective Alexander found him walking past our house and cleaned him up, and then another officer took him home."

"You weren't with him?"

"No, we went separate ways, and it happened on his way back to his hotel."

Chace is quiet, and I hear a car door slam shut.

"Where are you?" I ask.

"On my way home. Where's everyone else?"

"Charlotte's here, but Isaac and Sienna are both still out. Should we try getting ahold of them?"

"If Jake's been hanging around the neighborhood, fuck knows where he is now. We should all be together."

I text Sienna and Isaac to clue them in, then try to focus on my movie while I wait for them to come home. I chew on my lip until it's raw. A fat lump starts to rise where I've bit down too hard on it. My hands won't stay still. I wring them as my mind works in overdrive trying to think of a way to stop Jake. So much for the distraction.

An hour into my movie, Chace gets home. My shoulders relax with the relief of knowing he's safe. He joins me on the sofa.

"Are you okay?" he asks, staring into my eyes like he's a human lie detector.

"Chace, I'm fine. I promise."

He leans back against the soda. "Good. You're watching horror?"

"Yes." I glance at him out of the corner of my eye. Does he think that's in bad taste? Is it in bad taste?

Throwing his arm over the back of the sofa, he replies, "All right."

I smile to myself. *All right.*

A few minutes later, Charlotte emerges in her pajamas, and not too long after, Sienna arrives in a whirlwind, flinging open the door. "What the hell, guys!" she shouts, raising her arms. "He hurt Zak!"

"Where's Isaac?" Chace asks.

She freezes as she kicks off a stiletto. "He's not here? We split up after some friends asked me to go to another bar. He texted me a while ago. He was already on his way home."

It's as if I'm on a roller coaster, slowly climbing into the sky, and when we reach the top of the track, suddenly, I'm falling.

16

Friday
February 9

t's 4:30 a.m. My emotions are flitting between fear and anger—
switching every five seconds. It's not unlike Isaac to stay out all
night, and it's not like he always tells us where he is. But under these
circumstances, he would call. I *know* he would call. Especially if he
got delayed. He told Sienna he was heading home.

Surely, he would know that we'd worry.

But that's the scary part. What if he *can't* call?

Jake could have him right now.

Or he could simply be asleep in some girl's bed. Like Sonny, Isaac
is also a big fan of all-night shagging sessions with anyone who is
up for it.

Please let that be the case. My brain argues with itself. *Come on,
Lylah. That's not the case. The last note was addressed to Isaac. What if
the killer made his move?*

Detective Lina covers a yawn with the back of her hand. She is still trying to get a trace on Isaac's phone after rushing here the moment Officer Grey called her to report Isaac missing. But so far, she finds nothing.

His phone battery could have died. Or someone could have taken out the battery.

The back and forth in my head is driving me insane. I just want to hear from him. But it won't happen. Isaac is gone. I can feel it.

Charlotte and Sienna are half asleep on one sofa, and Chace and I are wide awake on another. No one wants to go to bed because we're scared of what news we might learn if we wake up. So we wait. And wait.

We wait either for Isaac to walk through the door or to find his body somewhere.

I've drunk my body weight in coffee since we started calling him at midnight. I'm awake and alert, but I also have to pee every five minutes.

Riley called around ten to check in again. I had to lie to him so he wouldn't come. Another missing person would make him react for sure.

"Try Isaac's phone again," I tell Chace. If anyone has a chance at him answering while he's with a girl, it's Chace.

He gives me brief smile and taps his phone. He's only calling to keep me happy. He doesn't think Isaac will answer any more than I do. I can't shake the feeling inside that I know Isaac is gone. Have I given up on finding him?

It's a horrible thought, which leaves a nasty taste in my mouth. How can I give up on my friend? But what's the use in pretending?

Out of everyone here, Isaac is probably Chace's closest friend. Chace wouldn't really give up on him without proof, would he? Maybe it's not about giving up, but accepting reality. We've lost Sonny and Nora. Jake is more than capable of killing Isaac too.

I stare at Chace's phone with baited breath. *Come on, Isaac. Pick up.*

Chace lets it go through to voicemail before hanging up. "He's been back later than this before," he says, putting on a positive front.

"That's true. Some days we're getting ready for class when he strolls in," I reply.

But never when a deranged murdered who's threatening us is on the loose.

I keep my mouth shut, not wanting to voice the words and make everyone even more scared for Isaac's safety. Riley always told me to be confident, voice my beliefs, even if I'm worried they may not be received well. Apparently, it's better to get it all out than keep feelings inside that eat away at you. At the moment, I think Riley is full of shit.

The front door creaks open, and we all leap up at the same time. Detective Lina appears from inside the kitchen, rushes to the door, and her shoulders sag with disappointment.

I sit back down and put my head in my hands. It's not Isaac.

Out in the hallway, the detective has a muffled conversation with two officers. Frowning, I strain to overhear what they are saying. Something's happened.

She comes into the room, and no one dares to speak.

"One of the officers found this outside," she finally says, holding up an envelope. The note has already been removed. It's facing her, so we can't see it.

"What does it say?" I ask.

"Editing suite."

I close my eyes and curl into a ball on the sofa. *Isaac is dead*.

"We have officers on their way," she says. "As soon as we have more information, I'll let you know. But for now, I need you stay here. This is the safest place for you."

She doesn't know that. Jake could still be outside.

"Are you leaving?" Charlotte asks.

"I am. You have two officers in the house and four outside. No one leaves or comes inside."

Chace rubs his forehead with the tips of his fingers. "Can I come with you?"

"No," she says flatly.

"He's my *friend*, Detective."

"I'm sorry." Her voice is firm. She isn't going to back down. Detective Lina turns around and gives instructions to the cops with her. We're no longer part of this.

Chace glares at her back and ushers me and Sienna into the kitchen, leaving Charlotte with Detective Lina and the two cops. "Out, go," he says, navigating us to the back door.

"What?" Sienna whispers. "We can't go out alone. She *just* said no leaving."

"I have to slip out if I want to get to the editing suite," he replies. "I have to see for myself. You two need to cover for me if Detective Lina or the cops realize I'm gone."

I don't hesitate. "What? No, I'm not letting you go alone. If you're going, so am I."

"Lylah, what could be waiting for us…" he starts.

Bile stings my throat. I remember vividly what Jake is capable of. "I know, but we're in this together."

Chace raises his hands and opens his mouth to protest, but I beat him to it. "Come on," I mouth, waving at him to follow me.

"Guys, this is a terrible idea," Sienna whispers.

"I agree. Lylah should stay with you," Chace argues.

"Not happening. Now come on."

Chace sighs sharply, knowing I'm not going to change my mind and that we don't have a lot of time. "Cover for us," Chace says to Sienna as we slip out of the back door. We're sheltered from the road by the high wall and gate, but the cops will see us if we're not super careful. We need to time this perfectly.

"What if he's out here?" I ask, glancing around in the dark. "He's into sports, likes to run, and if we're alone, we're sitting ducks."

Chace tugs me against the back garden wall, opposite the gate where the cop car is parked. "You're safe with me, Lylah."

Chace is strong. I'm sure he could take on Jake and win, but I don't want it to come to that.

"Should we take a weapon with us?" We definitely should have taken coats because it's freezing, but that would have raised a few questions.

He stills and raises an eyebrow. "You get the guns, and I'll grab the crossbow."

"Not funny, idiot!" I snap, whacking his stomach with the back of my hand. I shiver.

Chuckling quietly, he nods to the wall. "I'll help you up. We need to go before they realize we've left." Chace kneels down, threads his fingers together with his palms facing up, and waits for my foot.

I place the sole of my shoe in his hands. Pushing off, I reach high and grab the top of the wall. It's damp from the light rain and ice cold. I dig my fingertips into the brick so I don't slip.

This is ridiculous. We're breaking out of our own house.

I swing my legs awkwardly over the wall and look down at Chace. He smirks at me with hands on his hips. "Smooth, Lylah."

"Just hurry up!" I jump down to the other side and wipe my hands on my jeans. Thankfully, no one is around, and the cop car is out of view. Behind our house is a pedestrian-only zone. The road ends by our back gate.

Chace jumps up, grabs the top of the wall, and swings himself over. His fluid movements put me to shame.

I frown. "No one likes a show-off, Chace."

He grabs my hand, and we take off toward campus, breaking into a run. My heart is pounding wildly. Adrenaline blasts through my veins, urging me on.

I won't turn back, even fearing what we're about to find. Isaac is our friend. I ache to be there when he's found. He deserves to have people who love him there, not a room full of strangers.

Chace sets the pace, which given the fact he's a runner, is incredibly fast. I manage to keep up, though I'm not sure how.

Whatever has happened to Isaac, I need to see with my own eyes. I want nothing more than for the note to have been a ruse. I'm happy for it to be a joke if it means Isaac is okay.

We round the corner, and Chace stops dead. I almost body slam him. Ahead is a cop car, stopped, lights flashing. It looks like it was abandoned outside the media lab. Its engine was still running. They stopped in a hurry.

"We have to go in there now, before others arrive," I say.

Chace nods, and we take off at lightning speed again. My thighs burn in protest and my shins feel like they're splintering. I'm not used to this kind of physical activity. The freezing air bites into my cheeks and burns my lungs.

We pause by the front door, and Chace cranes his neck around the corner to get a better look. In the distance, I hear sirens, many different tones. They blend into one another, but I can tell there are multiple. More cops and the paramedics are likely on their way. Maybe the fire department for extra backup.

Chace nods. "We're clear."

If there were time, I would tease him about that comment. It's like we're in an action movie. Though now I've discovered I prefer watching one to living one.

Careful to keep our footsteps light so we're not heard, Chace slips through first, and I twist my body to the side and sneak in after him.

We know this building like the backs of our hands, so we take each turn without thinking. Up ahead is the editing suite. We will finally know Isaac's fate. Will he look just like Sonny?

"I'm scared," I whisper as Chace pushes the door with one hand.

The cops are close; I can hear them around the corner in the next hallway. Their muffled voices are probably trying to make sense of whatever Chace and I are about to see.

"I am too, Lylah, but we have to do this. I can't abandon Isaac."

I clench my fists until I can feel my nails cutting into my palms. We walk slowly. I feel like I'm wading through water.

"Which room?" I whisper.

"It's… I'd imagine it's the same one Sonny was in."

Oh God.

The hallway looks so much longer than it normally does. It's almost as if it stretches with every step I take. I feel like I'm back in the hospital, waiting to see my parents.

Then I can only hear my breathing. It's fast and loud. But Chace doesn't tease me. He doesn't say anything.

The suite is just steps away. I lick my dry lips. The door is open. My legs give way again, and I hit the tile hard.

Isaac lies on top of the table. His chest is bloody, and his arms hang over the edge, his face pointed up toward the sky.

His eyes are wide open.

Chest cut open.

Heart missing.

17

Saturday
February 10

Nineteen hours. That's how long it has been since we last saw Isaac alive. Detective Lina was furious that we bolted to the media lab despite her orders to stay at the house, but I don't care. Her life isn't the one being threatened, and she isn't exactly doing a stellar job of protecting my friends.

Chace has barely said a word since we found Isaac. They were close friends. He's lost both guys in our house. I don't know what I'd do without Sienna and Charlotte.

Chace is lying in my bed staring up at the ceiling. I've tried talking to him all day, but he's only replied with curt yes or no answers, or he hasn't responded at all.

I'm completely lost with how to help Chace. I can't process seeing Isaac like that, let alone know how to help him. Grieving for Isaac is impossible when I am consumed by fear.

This must be how Riley felt after our parents died.

I lay down on my side next to Chace. He doesn't react. "Are you hungry? You haven't eaten all day."

He shakes his head.

Of course he's not.

"I don't really know what to do here," I admit. "What can I do to help you?"

Releasing a breath, he closes his eyes. "Nothing."

"If I make you something will you eat it?"

"Lylah, if you make me a meal, I'm going to frame it."

I laugh, despite being the butt of his joke. I'm an awful cook. But it's really nice to hear him say something other than grunted one-word answers.

"Very funny. I meant a sandwich. Or I could order in?"

His eyes meet mine with such intensity that I'm transfixed. It's like I'm frozen until he looks away and breaks the spell. "Thanks for not kicking me out of your room," he says softly. "I really need the company."

"I'm not going anywhere…and apparently neither are you," I reply with a grin.

He meets my eyes again, but this time, he doesn't look away. It feels like the air is getting thicker.

"You're going to need to be more careful," he responds.

"What? Like when using the stove?"

His lips twitch. "No, in general. When you go out."

"We all do."

Chace falls silent. I'm missing something.

"What's going on? I'm not following."

"Nothing makes sense right now, so why do I have to?"

"Because it's frying my brain! Not knowing how to be supportive is stressing me out. Do you want more protection? Do you want food?" My voice gets an octave higher, which makes his mouth part in a heart-stopping smile.

"Order something so you don't have to cook, and I'll try to eat. I want *you* to have more protection, Lylah. I want *you* to have the entire fucking army surrounding you." He frowns, his eyes still glued to mine. "I don't know what I'd do if anything happened to you. I can't lose anyone else."

"Oh," I reply like an utter moron.

Oh? That's really all I could say?

Chace breaks eye contact and sits up. "Have the detectives called recently?"

Why is he changing the subject? Hysteria bubbles under my skin. He was basically declaring his undying love, right? Now he wants to talk about the two detectives who we're not fond of at the moment and who aren't really our fans right now either.

Calm down. He's concerned about you as a friend. Like a sister.

"Lylah?" Chace waves his hand in front of my face. I swat it away, my heart jumping at his interruption.

"What?"

"Pizza?"

"Yeah. Sure."

I grab my phone, half reeling from our conversation and half wondering if the detectives do have any news. They wouldn't be allowed to withhold any developments just because they're angry with us though, only if releasing that information would impair the investigation.

I'm pretty sure of that. Maybe.

When the pizza is delivered, Chace and I eat in my room. Sienna and Charlotte were both downstairs and not hungry. No one is feeling very chatty. We all miss Isaac and can't help but wonder who is next.

The only time I've left my room today is to use the bathroom and answer the door for the pizza. Classes were canceled. The entire campus was shut down. The administration said it was in respect for Isaac, but I think it's because this shit is now serial and everyone is afraid. If I was brave, I would check social media for updates, but I have no doubt it's a media circus: people posting their condolences for Isaac and his family, appreciation to Isaac for getting them a day off, thousands of theories. I'd rather not read those.

The cops were able to keep their suspects under wraps after Sonny's and Nora's deaths, but not anymore. Sienna told me this morning that the entire student body seems to be hunting for Jake. Maybe they'll have better luck than the cops.

At ten, Chace falls asleep in my room. It's the second night we've shared a bed. I change into my nice pajamas and slip between the covers next to him.

I could get used to this.

●　　●　　●

When I wake in the morning, Chace is already up. His hair is damp from his shower. He gives me a smile from the end of my bed where he sits.

I push myself up on my elbows.

"Morning," he says.

"How long have you been up?"

"About thirty minutes."

He looks better this morning. There's color back in his cheeks, and his eyes don't look as defeated.

"You should have woken me when you got up, Chace."

"No, I needed to sort myself out, and you looked peaceful. I'm so sorry about yesterday." He runs his hand over his face and sighs. "Finding Isaac like that…"

I sit up and reach for his hand. "Don't apologize. You lost your best friend."

Sienna and I have been close since we met, and I would be beyond devastated if she died.

"I want to be here for you, Sienna, and Charlotte too."

"Chace, just because you're the only man in the house now doesn't mean that you're responsible for looking out for us. You need to take time for yourself too."

Clearing his throat, he stands. "I'm making coffee. I'll see you downstairs."

I watch him walk out of my room with his shoulders bunched tight, wishing there was something I could do to help him. He must be feeling so much pressure when all he should be concentrating on is mourning his friends.

We all should.

Throwing off the covers, I get out of bed. It's a little chilly, but it's worse since I'm not wearing my fuzzy jammies.

Once I'm showered and dressed, I check my phone.

Riley. He's not pleased. I promised I would give you space as long as you're OK. YOU'RE NOT, LYLAH! ISAAC IS DEAD!!! I'll be there today. NO EXCUSES.

Well, that's just great. He's clearly angry with me for not telling him the news myself.

Chucking my phone on my bed, I head downstairs. There's no point in replying to Riley's message. I won't be able to convince him to stay home again.

I grab the banister and take the stairs slowly. This is all getting so out of hand...not that it was ever in hand. My breath catches. On the beige welcome mat is a cream envelope. Chace obviously hasn't seen it. Charlotte and Sienna would have shrieked if they'd found the note. It almost blends straight into the mat.

"Chace," I call, stepping toward the envelope like it could explode. My teeth find my bottom lip, and I look around as if Jake is going to appear beside me. I call again, this time louder and more frightened.

Chace hurries into the hall with Charlotte and Sienna close behind. They notice the envelope immediately, and Sienna mutters something under her breath.

I release my lip. "Do you think it was left just now?" Chace left my room about fifteen minutes before I came down here so there wasn't much time. Besides, it's morning. It's light out. Surely Jake wouldn't risk coming here when he could be seen so easily?

Sienna shakes her head. "I was asleep."

"I didn't notice it last night," Charlotte says. "But you would have to be looking in that exact spot to see it on the mat."

Chace bends down to pick it up. "It's not addressed to anyone."

"What? That's weird." I reach out and put my hand on his back. His muscles are locked tight. "Should we wait for the police?"

"No," he replies, opening the envelope.

It's not a new threat, but it still gives me chills.

"He's recycling his psycho notes. He should get some new material," Chace spits. The anger and hatred in his voice makes him sound like a different person.

I can't find any amusement in his remark, so I snatch the note out of his hand and cut him a look. "It's not funny. We know how dangerous he is."

"I'm calling the detective," Sienna says. Charlotte follows her into the living room.

Chace bends his head to look more directly into my eyes. "Hey, sorry for the sarcasm. Are you okay?"

"I'm fine, I guess. Riley is coming today."

Chace grips the letter in his fist, crumpling it. "Your brother, really? I'm glad I've managed to convince my parents to stay home every time they call…so far. I don't want them here in case Jake turns to them, and they think they'll bump me up his list if I have them around me constantly. He already likes doing the implausible. Imagine what he'd get out of killing a man with his parents near."

I wish Riley would agree to that. If something happened to Riley because he came to protect me, it would kill me. But there is no way I'll ever convince him to keep his distance; he would rather anger Jake by being an obstacle between me and him.

"Yeah. Riley's not happy that I didn't tell him about Isaac. He wants the case solved now, and he wants to make sure the cops are doing what they're supposed to. Like they're just sitting around twiddling their thumbs!" I don't tell Chace that Riley doesn't think I'm safe here, because I don't want him to feel even more pressure.

"The last time I spoke to him on the phone, he wanted me to move home. I explained that it wouldn't matter where I am. In fact, leaving all the police protection here would make it even easier for him to get to me."

Chace raises his eyebrow. "I take it he didn't like that."

"Nope. His text said he's arriving today. I hope he doesn't hang around long. He's going to be a nightmare, demanding answers and telling people how to do their job. Plus I don't want him here in case he becomes a target. I mean, look what happened to Zak when we met for a drink. If Jake can attack his own brother, there's nothing stopping him attacking mine."

"Well, there might be one thing."

"What's that?"

"Jake's probably not going to feel romantically threatened by your brother."

I turn my nose up at the disgusting thought. "Ew. There is that, I suppose. Hopefully Detective Lina will be able to convince him to leave the investigation in their hands. He sounds like he wants to go all Sherlock on the case."

"She's probably got the best chance. Not sure I'm ready to have your brother puff his chest and glare at me twenty-four-seven though. I usually have more time to prepare."

I slap his arm. "He doesn't hate you."

"Lylah, he spent the entire day calling me Chacey and threatening to castrate me if I got within two feet of you."

"He's protective."

Chace's eyebrows shoot up in the cutest way. "Protective."

I lift my shoulder in a lazy shrug. "Uh huh." I know he's overbearing, but I'm the only family he has. "You would be too in his position, especially since we're getting more notes like the one you're currently holding."

"Yeah, I guess." He looks down at the note in his hand, releasing it slightly until he's holding it at the edge with only the tips of his fingers. "We should probably get this to the cops stationed outside."

"Mind if I wait in here?"

"Course not." With a smile meant to comfort me, Chace goes to the front door to start this process all over again.

18

Saturday
February 10

Riley's car pulls up outside the house just as the detectives are leaving. Forensics will examine the note, but no one is expecting much. Now that we've gotten several of these, we've learned Jake is far too good to leave a fingerprint or any DNA.

Not even the postmortems have turned up anything. The autopsy on Sonny's body showed that he died of multiple stab wounds. They were able to tell the general height of the killer and that he's right-handed, which Jake is, but that also describes most males on campus. Hell, even Chace fits the bill.

We're all pawns in his game, and it feels like we're only ever going to see the killer when he wants us to. The thought sends my anxiety into overdrive.

"What the hell, Lylah!" Riley pulls me into his arms as he rushes inside.

I know I'm supposed to be a proper grown-up now since I'm living on my own, but as soon as Riley is around, I feel so much younger again. It's not necessarily a bad thing. He's always been protective, a safety net I can always fall back on. But I get that I shouldn't rely on my sibling like I would a parent.

"I'm sorry. I didn't want to worry you." As soon as the words leave my mouth, I know they're not going to be received well.

Riley grips my upper arms and holds me out so he can glare. "Don't be ridiculous, Lylah, you're my baby sister. We need to talk."

Great.

"Sure. My housemates are in their rooms, so we can talk in the living room."

They're in hiding. Chace knows Riley isn't his biggest fan, but he doesn't know it's because of how I feel about him. And Sienna and Charlotte wanted to give me some space to explain what's going on.

My housemates are lucky they've managed to keep their family at a distance through all of this. Chace's family is apparently talking closely to the cops, but haven't swooped in because they believe that would be worse for Chace. They're petrified of doing the wrong thing. I don't really know what's going on with Charlotte's family, but since she said they weren't on good terms, I'm not surprised we haven't seen or heard from them. And Sienna's parents are in Korea visiting family. I get the impression she hasn't been totally honest with them about our situation.

Sonny's parents have also come in town, but they haven't been by the house. I suppose it's something they will do when they're ready. I can't go in both Sonny or Isaac's rooms either.

Riley and I sit on the sofa, and I wait for the lecture to start. Riley has the same shade of blond hair and the same dark-brown eyes as me. We've always looked similar, just like our mom. She would be glad he's here with me now.

"I should have come when I first heard about Sonny."

"No, I needed some space to process. To be with my friends. We've been supporting each other, Riley. I need you to know that."

"But the murders are all over the news now. Since Isaac, people are saying there's a serial killer on the loose. I didn't even know another girl—one of your neighbors!—had been killed because my little sister didn't feel the need to tell me."

"Come on, Riley," I say. "I'm sorry, okay? It's just hard to talk about…"

"You don't want me here, and I can't figure out why."

I sigh. "I'm scared that I'll rely on you as much as I did when Mom and Dad died. Things have been going really well here. I like being independent. I've been doing well in my classes, and my anxiety has been in check thanks to therapy. I haven't needed to see my therapist in a little over four months because I've been successfully using the tools she gave me. You know how big that is for me. I haven't wanted to jeopardize that."

He nods. "I know. And all of that makes me so proud of you, Lylah. But someone threatening you, murdering your friends? That's a good time to lean on your family."

When he puts it that way, I suppose he's right.

"It'll be two years soon," he says as if it's news to me.

"I know. I think about Mom and Dad all the time." I grip my necklace between my thumb and index finger.

He tilts his head, eyes narrowed. "What I mean is, we need to pull together at this time of year even more. I'm going to stay here until Jake is caught. Or you can come home with me."

"No, I don't want that. Either option. I can deal with this alone. I don't want you to get dragged into this too."

Shaking his head, he stretches out his legs in front of him. "Not happening."

My chest burns. "Riley, please—"

"Would you leave me if the situation was reversed?"

Damn it. "That isn't the point." It so is—I wouldn't leave him, but I don't want him here where he could be hurt.

He stands. "I'll make us some coffee so you can tell me *everything*, and after that, I'm going down to the police station to see what the fuck is going on."

Closing my eyes, I flop back against the sofa as he walks out of the room. Having him here makes me feel like a helpless teen again.

Riley returns with two coffees and sets them down on the coffee table. "How have you been dealing with this on your own? I want the truth, Lylah. Don't tell me what you think I want to hear."

I sit up and grab my coffee. I hesitate but don't sugarcoat my response. "It hasn't been easy, and a few times I could feel myself slipping back into my old ways. But I haven't, and I'm determined not to. Chace's support helps."

Riley rolls his eyes.

"Don't be like that. He's one of the good guys, I promise."

"I'll be the judge of that."

Of course he will.

I continue. "When we found Sonny, we were devastated, but we thought that was it, a single incident. Then there was another note, another threat. Everything snowballed so fast it made me dizzy. No one has a handle on it, and I'm scared."

"Damn, Lylah. I hate that you've been going through all this, especially at this time of year."

"None of it makes any sense. Jake seems to be the most likely suspect, and the detectives think so too. He tried to kiss me last Valentine's Day. Four months after I rejected him, he left college, and now, eight months after that, he's killing."

"What about the girl?"

"Nora. We think she and Jake knew each other, but no one knows how. Either that or he's trying to throw everyone off by hitting other targets too."

I shrug and take a sip of coffee.

"And the police have no idea where he is?"

"Not a single clue where he could be or where he has been… besides the crime scenes." Saying the words out loud makes me feel defeated. When will this ever end?

Riley thinks for a moment. "How is he doing this alone? Carrying a dead body can't be easy."

He doesn't know about Jake cutting out their hearts yet. And no one knows where Sonny's and Nora's and Isaac's are.

"Jake used to work out a lot, almost obsessively. He had weights in his room, he ran, he went to the gym twice a day. The guy was strong. I don't know if he had help. His friends and family are all accounted for. His dad and brother are staying in a hotel nearby, assisting the police as they can."

"And you're sure it's not better for you to come home?" He looks skeptical. "I know you were all friends, but doesn't it make you worry that these people were friends with Jake too?"

"Detective Lina, the officer in charge of the investigation, doesn't seem to think there is reason to leave. She said it could cause the killer to go on a spree. I don't want to be the reason for that, Riley. Here, we can be a support network for each other."

He nods. "I'll stay instead then, Lylah."

"You can stay in a hotel."

Chuckling, he lifts his eyebrow. "Charming. You won't even let your brother stay at your place."

"It's not only my place. I have roommates, and we want to keep things as normal as we possibly can. Detective Lina can arrange protection for you."

"I don't think so," he scoffs, frowning like I've offended him. "What do the notes say?"

"Mostly things like 'you'll be mine.'"

We sit in silence for a moment as he considers it, then asks, "What are you holding back?"

I sigh. Riley does know me well. "We tried to trap him twice. Once in a club, I thought I saw him but I must have been mistaken because when the cops cleared the area, he was nowhere to be seen."

"And the other time?"

"At the fireworks display on campus. The streetlights went out, and"—I brace myself for Riley's reaction—"he grabbed me. Don't shout. He didn't hurt me, but he left a note making it very clear that he can get to me—to us—whenever he wants."

"He damn well can't," Riley spits through clenched teeth.

He can. But there's no point in stressing that to Riley. It'll only infuriate him.

"Despite my less than warm reception, I am glad you're here," I admit.

"See? I know when you need me and when you're lying," he replies, nudging my arm. "So… What's happening with Chace?"

I roll my eyes. "Don't start."

He holds up his hands in surrender. "I'm not starting anything. I want to *really* get to know the reason why you rarely come home anymore."

I look away. Guilt drenches my body. It never really occurred to me that Riley could need me too. I've always been so caught up in how to not be a burden on him that I've never really thought about what he might want.

"Riley, I'm sorry. You gave up so much to take care of me. I want you to live your life. You lost, what? Two years? I should be asking you about *your* new girlfriend."

"Drink your coffee, Lylah. We stick together. I haven't lost anything, and I wouldn't change a thing about taking on your dramatic ass after they died."

"Wow, thanks." I grin. "You realize you've avoided the question about this new girl of yours though, right?"

"Lylah?" Chace calls. Before I can reply, he walks into the room. "Riley."

My brother's jaw tightens. "Chace."

"What's up?" I ask Chace.

He scratches the back of his neck. "I'm going out for coffee and wanted to know if you wanted to come. I didn't realize Riley was here already."

"You're going *out* for coffee?" I ask. "I can make one here."

"I'm not letting Jake scare me into staying in. Cabin fever is setting in, and I need to leave this house for a while."

I feel it too. Sitting around the house for days on end is getting difficult. I sit up straighter with the thought of getting out of the house that's missing two tenants and away from a brother who's probably got a thousand more questions.

"Go if you want to, Lylah," Riley says with a sigh. He frowns at Chace over my shoulder.

"I do want to get out for a while, but you just arrived. Do you want to come?"

"I'm glad we got to catch up. Now that I've seen you, I want to go to the station and find out what the hell is going on with this colossal mess of an investigation. Someone needs to be doing more."

Oh God. "Don't do anything to embarrass me, Riley. Please."

He grins. It's the same smile he would give me when we were kids—right before he did something stupid that would get us into trouble.

I shake my head. "Just don't tell me what happens unless you get any real information."

"Look after her," Riley demands from Chace. He holds his gaze for a few moments.

"Always," Chace replies, causing my heart to flip in my chest.

But I can't help but notice there's something off about Riley and Chace's interaction. It's more than just the tension between them. Riley is protective, but I don't know why Chace is being standoffish.

Riley stares after Chace as he leaves the room.

My brother can usually read people well. What the hell is Riley doing? Why is he treating Chace like he's a bad guy? Why all the glaring and pointed looks?

No way. Could Riley suspect Chace is somehow involved?

19

sit at the small bistro table in the coffee shop and fiddle with my necklace. Two cops sit at a table next to ours. My nerves are shot. Chace is still at the counter, waiting for our order. Chace, my crush, and the guy my brother seems to think could be a murderer.

There is no way Chace has anything to do with these deaths. Absolutely none. He doesn't have it in him, and even if he did, he wouldn't have had the time—he's been with me.

I shake the thought from my head, annoyed at my brother for planting such a horrible seed.

Chace looks over and gives a wave. He's been standing there for more than five minutes. How long does it take to make a cappuccino and a latte?

Coming here was Chace's idea, so we have to stay, but I hate the way we're being watched and gossiped about. Across from us is a group of four women, probably in their early twenties. They lean in, and the brunette opposite me moves her mouth at a hundred miles an hour, speaking in a hushed voice. Her eyes lift to us, but they're back down the next second.

This attempt to keep some normality in our lives is not working. I angle my body away from her so she can only see my profile.

"Like, I would be so upset if any of *my* friends died. I would do something! If there's a killer after them, why are they in public?"

The voice comes from behind me from a different table, so I can't see who's speaking. But I hate them. Hate that they can't see how much we are hurting. Hate being the center of rumors. Sinking lower in my seat, I silently curse Chace's idea for getting out of the house.

We should lay low.

Chace *finally* gets our drinks and comes over. His head is high, green eyes focused on mine, unwavering, like he's willing me to stay calm.

I'm not calm. My heart is racing, my palms are sweaty, and I just want everyone to let us drink our coffee in peace.

"People are talking," I mutter as he sits down across from me.

His left shoulder lifts in a lazy shrug that screams *Who cares?* I wish I didn't care.

"Let 'em, Lylah. Their opinions don't matter. And we deserve a moment to step away from all of our sadness and stress." He places my latte in front of me and kicks up his leg, resting his ankle on his knee. He seems relaxed. I wish I were.

I take a sip of my drink and force my back straight. I don't have to give anyone the satisfaction of knowing how much they're bothering me.

It's a lot, by the way.

Chace smirks, his eyes glowing with humor. "Much better. Now tell your face you're not listening to them."

I mouth *piss off* and take another sip.

"Are you going out with Sienna and Charlotte tonight?" he asks.

Raising my eyebrow, I put down my mug. "No. Absolutely not. Nope."

"Lylah, come on—"

I'm finding it really hard to be here, so how would I survive a more crowded setting with a hundred people talking about us? "It doesn't feel right," I reply.

"The night will be whatever you make it. Sienna thinks you need to do something that doesn't involve obsessing over Jake, and I agree. It's unhealthy. Isaac would tell you to go. He would tell you get out there and show this fucker he won't break us. Besides, Sienna has managed to convince Charlotte to go out, so you can't flake on them."

But he's killed three people. I'd say we're all pretty broken. Though Chace has a good point. I'm just not sure it's good enough to convince me to change my mind. Charlotte, Sienna, and I would often go out together for a drink, and we always had fun. If I could ignore everyone around me, a night with my girlfriends is probably what I need.

"I'll think about it."

"Thinking is the problem, Lylah. All we've done since we found Sonny is think. Go out and have fun for Sonny and Isaac. Please!"

"*You're* not going out."

He laughs. A full belly laugh I haven't heard for a long time. Butterflies swarm my stomach. I love that.

"And the award for most childish comeback goes to…"

"Very funny, Chace. I'm merely pointing out that you're not following your own advice."

"Charlotte and Sienna haven't invited me out though, have they?" he says with a hint of sarcasm. They only want to go out because they need a distraction. We're being threatened—and in our own home—so it doesn't exactly make any of us feel secure there. "I would usually go out with Sonny and Isaac."

I dip my head, my face heating in shame. If I touched my cheeks, I'd probably get a third-degree burn. Here I am moaning about being scared to go out with the girls, when the guys Chace used to go out with are both dead.

Before I can apologize, he says, "Don't tell me you're sorry. And stop looking like that. You've done nothing wrong. Lylah? Hey, up here."

He reaches over the table and cups my chin. I meet his intense gaze.

"Stop stressing over everything."

Wincing, I reply, "I shouldn't have said that. I didn't think."

Dropping his hand, he sighs and changes the subject. "What's your brother up to? Is he staying with us?"

I shake my head. "Definitely not. He'll be staying in a hotel. I like having him close, but I can't have him in the house. He can be a bit overbearing. He's probably yelling at the detectives right now."

Chace grins. "I wish we could see that."

I don't. My brother's embarrassing when he gets going. I understand he's only looking out for me, but every time he defends me, I end up feeling like an incompetent child. "Can we drink up and leave?"

Raising his eyebrows, he asks, "Why? Do you have a hot date?"

I give him a smile. My heart is flying. Rolling my eyes, I reply, "Yes."

For a second, it's as if we're the only two people in the world.

"Let's go."

I stand, draining the rest of my latte.

Chace laughs. "You don't need to have every last drop."

Putting the mug on the table, I frown. "Do you even know me?"

Chace helps me put on my coat. He didn't bring one. Idiot. It's freezing outside.

He waits for me to lead the way, but he stays close as we pass tables of people who conveniently stop their conversation as we pass.

Not obvious at all.

I splay my fingers on the door, shoving it open. Outside, I take a deep breath and close my eyes.

"That wasn't too bad after all, huh?" Chace says.

When I open my eyes, he's smirking again.

"Sometimes I really dislike you."

"I don't believe you, Lylah."

Yeah, I couldn't convince myself of that either. Not even the times I cried myself to sleep because I saw him out with another girl. There have been many, *many* times since we met that I wanted to hate him. But I've never managed it.

Chace and I walk across campus, our two officers still following us. I'm grateful for them, but I hate that we need around-the-clock protection.

It's only 1:00 p.m. but it's getting dark thanks to gray rain clouds. It's also damp and cold. There aren't many people around. Campus is always quiet on Saturdays.

The few people milling around are watching me and Chace while pretending to look everywhere but at us. Everyone seems to have a theory on why Jake would want to harm me and my friends. The most popular one is that I cheated on Jake with Chace. They don't have a clue what the truth is, but that doesn't stop them running their mouths.

"That was a massive fail, Chace, admit it." I force my gaze to hold his.

"You love going out for coffee with me whether we have an audience or not. You know that."

"Have I ever denied it?" The words leave my mouth before my brain full engages. I wince. *That didn't come across as desperate at all. Well done, Lylah!*

The rest of my housemates are aware of my feelings for Chace, Sonny and Isaac used to give me knowing looks, and Sienna and Charlotte and I have talked about my crush many times, but I don't know if Chace is aware. I'm probably not the best at concealing my emotions, so maybe he knows.

That's not very encouraging since he's never mentioned it.

Recently, though, even before this mess, we've gotten closer. And he was definitely jealous when I went for a drink with Zak.

"No, you've never denied it," he whispers, looking into my eyes like I'm hiding the answer to life.

We've stopped walking. When did that happen?

I swallow what feels like a mouthful of sand as Chace's gaze stays glued to mine.

Is he going to kiss me? Oh God, please say he is!

"You okay, Lylah?" he asks. I think he was trying to tease me, but his voice is breathy, and his chest is rising and falling too fast.

I nod. "You okay, Chace?"

Damn, I was going for calm, but my voice comes out like Minnie Mouse.

His mouth curves in the most beautiful smile. "I know I shouldn't even be thinking about this right now, not with everything going on, but I can't help it."

I'm lost, and I really, really want to know what he's thinking about. I wait for him to finish his thought.

"You, Lylah. I don't even know when I started thinking of you as more than a friend. But I want more. This is crap timing with all these goddamn awful things going on, but I don't want to wait. I want something good to make living in this nightmare bearable."

"Oh."

Yep. After seventeen months of wanting to be with him, he tells me he has feelings for me, and my reply is oh. *Is there anyone out there more awkward than me?*

His dark-blond eyebrows raise, and he tilts his head to the side. "Oh?"

"No, I didn't mean that." I hold up my hands. "That came out wrong. I was stunned. But my mind is working now. At least I think it is. What I wanted to say, and what I should have said instead of being a monumental—"

I'm silenced by his lips.

He steps closer, holding me against his chest with his strong arms.

I imagined what it would be like to kiss Chace a million times, but my fantasies were nothing compared to this.

Warmth spreads through my body as his lips brush mine with the most maddening pressure. My fingers push into the muscle of his lower back. He pulls me tighter, and I'm sure I'm going to faint.

Chace's fingertips slide down to my hips, driving me insane.

I run my hands up his chest, feeling every indent of muscle, and then circle my hands around his neck. I feel his smile against my lips.

All too soon, Chace pulls away. I bite my lip, but it isn't because I'm anxious. *Wow, and I thought I liked his smile before.* He plays it cool, but he looks as giddy as I feel. I know I'm grinning like an idiot, and I don't care.

After a moment, Chace says, "Well, we should get home. You've got a girls' night to get ready for."

Suddenly, I don't want to go.

So I don't come across as a lovesick fool, I nod. "Yeah, let's go." *Also, we're just feeding the cheating on Jake theory by being out together.*

When we get home, Chace heads straight to his room, and I go to mine. We held hands on the way back, but neither of us said a word, so I don't really know what's going to happen with us. Usually I would obsess over that, but I think we both made it clear how we feel.

There's plenty of time to discuss the details.

I spend the rest of the afternoon in my room, then take my time getting ready in the evening, curling my hair, picking out a killer black dress and heels, and applying a subtle amount of makeup.

I'm ready before Sienna, but Charlotte is already waiting in the living room. Her almost white hair is ironed straight with the front pinned back. She's wearing a knee-length navy dress with a modest neckline. She's never been one for revealing too much skin.

Sienna comes down, her heels clicking on the wooden stairs. Her dress is royal blue and just barely covers her butt, the neckline plunging to show off her cleavage.

"Ready?" I ask. This feels wrong, but I put a smile on my face.

Even Sienna, the party queen, seems less than enthusiastic. Yeah, it's Saturday. But we all need a few hours when we're not stressing about a killer. I spend most of my time worrying who Jake will come for next—if he'll come for me. A few glasses of wine with my girls will be a good distraction. And it's a massive middle finger to Jake from Isaac and Sonny.

I don't see Chace before we leave because he's in his room, but I'll find him when I get back. The wine will give me the confidence to strut into his room and kiss him until we're both light-headed. The thought makes me smile.

We leave the house with our three chaperones in tow and head into town. There are cops back home with Chace too.

"Something is definitely going on with Lylah," Sienna says in a dramatic voice, disregarding the fact that I'm right there.

"I agree," Charlotte replies. "I can only assume it has something to do with a certain green-eyed hunk back home."

"Do you want me to leave while you talk about me?" I ask.

"Are you two together yet?" Sienna asks. Her eyes examine me for any hint of a lie.

"Maybe?" I can feel myself blushing.

She claps her hands together. "Finally! But what do you mean by maybe?"

"We both admitted how we feel about each other, and then we kissed. I think he got what I meant through my rambling."

Thankfully, we arrive at our favorite bar before I have to answer any more questions. I push through the door first to guarantee that, the girls and our undercover police escorts right behind me. We've only had protection for a few days, but I'm forcing myself to pretend this is normal. Like Chace said, we have to carry on. Jake can't win.

"There's a table," I say, pointing to one of the tall tables with stools. "I'll get the first round. Rosé?"

"Perfect," Sienna replies, linking arms with Charlotte and leading her to the table.

I head to the bar, knowing one of the officers will be close. "Three glasses of rosé, please," I say to the bartender.

He stills and blinks a few times before responding. He must recognize me. "Sure. Large glass or small?"

Swallowing, I clear my throat. "Large. Definitely large."

The bartender gets our drinks, and I pay. He avoids eye contact throughout the whole transaction, looking uncomfortable as he hands the drinks over. I mutter a thanks and head back to my friends.

It doesn't matter what the bartender thinks of me. Besides, he might not be passing judgement. Maybe he doesn't know what to say. There's not much you *can* say in situations like this—even I don't know what to say.

Back at the table, Sienna holds up her glass. "To Isaac and Sonny."

Charlotte raises her wine and says, "We miss you guys."

"We love you," I add quietly, and we all take a sip.

Out of nowhere, a guy wearing a tracksuit hustles over and slaps an envelope in the middle of our table. "This is for you."

I practically leap off my stool, pushing myself away from the table where the envelope sits.

No.

Not again.

Please.

Before our police protection can respond, Sienna digs her acrylic nails into the guy's arm. "Who gave you this?" she demands.

He wrenches himself out of her grasp. "Don't touch me, bitch. Some dude in a black hoodie gave me thirty bucks to deliver it. Back off."

I can't stop staring at the envelope. I'm petrified to find out what's inside.

The officers take over. One pulls the guy to the side, while the other two close in on us.

"We're leaving," one of them says, picking up the envelope with a gloved hand.

It's thicker than the preceding notes.

What could it be?

The three of us follow the cops outside, one ushering the deliverer by the arm.

Outside the bar is eerily quiet. At least the area is well lit.

"I need to see what's in there," I say. "Please, just one look."

He raises his eyebrow and then sighs, conceding. "One quick look." Tipping the contents into the palm of his other gloved hand, he looks up at me.

"Oh, God," I whisper as my lungs deflate.

There are small Polaroid pictures of me, Sienna, and Charlotte out on campus, in the coffee shop, at the library, and near our house. All candid. We had no idea someone was taking our photo. There is one, just one, of me and Chace in the editing suite. We are sitting close together, our heads almost touching. It was a completely innocent moment, but it could definitely be construed the wrong way.

"What is wrong with Jake?" Sienna rages, glaring at the photos.

"That's enough. I'm taking this man in for questioning and giving the envelope to evidence. My colleagues will take you home," the officer who grabbed the delivery guy says. He handcuffs the man who delivered the note as he protests his innocence. He's probably just a pawn in Jake's game.

The officer stuffs the photos back in the envelope and hands them over for processing.

"Thank you," I say. I know he probably shouldn't have shown us yet, but I appreciate that he did. This is our life, and we'd likely be shown it at some point anyway.

The other officers escort us to the sidewalk toward home. "Come on, ladies. We'll take your statements at your house."

I nod robotically and do as I'm told, but my legs feel like they're made of concrete as I walk toward home in a daze.

20

There's a ringing in my ears that won't go away. I can't believe how much bolder Jake is getting.

He's been following us around, taking more pictures. "How have we not seen him?" I ask, collapsing on to the couch in our living room sometime after midnight.

Sienna shrugs. "Maybe he's changed his appearance. He was bulking up at lot before he left from all that time in the gym. He could be double the size by now. It also isn't hard to dye your hair."

"Maybe he's just really good at being a creep," Charlotte adds.

Char is right. Jake's certainly proved that he's intelligent and can get around undetected.

Neither cop joins us in the living room. Instead they both go into the kitchen to speak with the officer who's been here with Chace.

Chace. *Oh God, he doesn't know yet.*

I turn and shout for him. He's going to be livid knowing we've been followed again, I didn't get to look at the photos for long, so I'm not sure exactly when they were all taken, but they definitely weren't all taken on the same day. We had on different clothes, and they were taken in multiple locations.

My body shudders, a bolt of ice shooting through my spine. How long has Jake been following us? I wish we knew what he wanted.

"Chace?" I call again and get up to find him. There's no way he didn't hear me. All three officers come out of the kitchen, standing in the hallway with matching frowns.

Oh no. "Chace!"

I sprint up the stairs, taking the steps two at a time. "Chace!" A herd of footsteps thud behind me as the rest of the house follows suit. I run to his door and shove it open without a second's hesitation.

His room is empty.

My heart starts to race. I step to my room and open the door. Empty.

"Chace!" *No, this cannot be happening. Not him.* "Where is he? Where did he go?" I demand from the officer who was supposed to be watching out for him.

"He's not in the bathroom either," Charlotte says.

I can't breathe. Why can't I breathe?

"Whoa, Lylah. Don't panic," Sienna says. Her hands circle my upper arms and I stumble forward.

"Jake has him, doesn't he? He's going to make sure I find him and—"

"Hey!" Charlotte snaps. "Stop that. We don't know anything yet. He could have gone for a run."

"Without security?" I turn to the officer who's failed at his job, and try to block my imagination from all the terrible things that could have happened. "Where is Chace? Where were you? You were supposed to be with him!"

Except the officer's not listening to me because he's on his phone.

He holds up his hand. "He's okay," he tells me, then goes back to his conversation. "Stay where you are. I'm coming." Hanging up, the officer grinds his teeth. "Chace is fine. He skipped out. I'm going to meet him now."

My shoulders slump in relief, and I close my eyes. "Thank God he's safe."

"Come on. Detective Lina will be here soon," the officer who opened the envelope says. "Why don't I put on the kettle and make us all some tea while we wait."

He's the nicest officer to accompany us so far, but they change so often I can never remember their names.

With my heart still pounding from the shock, I follow closely behind Sienna. Her presence keeps me from launching into a full-blown anxiety attack.

I sit and put my head between my knees, my mind in overdrive.

"Are you okay, Lylah?" Charlotte asks. Her voice is soft, like she's talking to a toddler.

"I'll be okay," I reply, straightening. "But why would Chace leave the house alone? He knows better with Sonny and Isaac dead."

Sienna shakes her head and folds her arms. "You'll be able to ask him soon. Right after I've punched him in the stomach for being such a massive idiot!"

Despite the lack of humor in this situation, I laugh. "Take a number and get in line, Sienna."

"Are they in the living room?" Detective Lina asks, bursting into the house and calling from the front hallway.

Where is Chace?

"Thank you," she says to one of the officers standing out there. I hear three steps, and then she's at the living room door. "Girls," Detective Lina says. "Chace is safe, with an officer, and is being escorted home." She takes the photos from the envelope. "We need to talk about these."

"Jake's been following us for a while. Some of these aren't recent," I say. "The last time Chace and I were in the editing suite before this week was a month ago, in early January, not long after we got back from the holiday break."

She splays the photos out on the coffee table. "When would you say the others were taken?"

I take each one in. Chewing my lip, I try to think back to when I was wearing the outfits in the photos. It's not easy considering I can't even remember what I had for breakfast.

Sienna leans forward, blocking my view. "It's hard to say. Most of those outfits are in the wash now. I haven't done laundry in two weeks, so I'd say between one and two weeks."

Wow. Sienna has two dressers jam-packed full of clothes, so it doesn't surprise me that she can avoid laundry that long. Who would have thought one of the perks would be providing the police with an accurate timeline?

Detective Lina nods. "Okay. Thank you. Do you think any of these photos were as recent as Sonny's murder?"

"Um, possibly. I can't say for sure," I reply. The others nod in agreement.

"Do you think Jake has been following us while we've had protection too?" Charlotte asks. If that is the case, I won't feel safe. Ever. These undercover officers are supposed to be watching for Jake. They're trained for that kind of thing…but they still haven't caught him.

The officer arrives with a tray of tea, and Detective Lina is quiet while we get settled. The officer pours himself a drink and, instead of leaving the room, sits down. I don't want to talk in front of him because I don't want him to think I'm questioning how he's doing his job. But in all fairness, I *am* questioning how he's doing his job.

"So are you any closer to finding him?" I ask. *Does he have a hit list? Does he want all of us dead? Who is he punishing? What did we do to him that was so bad? We don't deserve this.*

Detective Lina tries to reassure us, but I'm only half listening. The second I hear a key in the lock of the front door, I'm on my feet. He's home.

Chace enters the room, smiling sheepishly. He holds up his hands. "It was stupid, I'm sorry."

"What the hell were you thinking sneaking out?" I snap. "We were worried sick!"

"I'm sorry, Lylah. I thought I'd be back long before you got home." His face falls. "Why are you home anyway? What happened?"

Detective Lina launches into a lecture. "Chace, we have provided protection for a reason, so—"

"You really don't need to say it. What I did was stupid and it won't happen again. I swear."

She nods, satisfied that Chace is done being an idiot.

For as much as I care for him, I'm still not convinced.

"The girls were given these," the detective says, gesturing to the coffee table.

A quiet expletive that I don't quite catch leaves Chace's lips.

"You got these while you were out?" he asks us, and we nod. "Jake was there. Jesus. Why is there only one with me and none of Sonny or Isaac?"

Maybe because they were already dead?

I shrug. "Some guy was paid to hand the envelope to us. Jake must have been close though. How else would he know where we were?"

"We'd only been at the bar long enough to order one round of drinks too," Sienna says. "It makes me sick to know he was following us tonight."

Detective Lina interjects, "Please try not to let it get to you too much. I know that's a tough ask. We have every available officer on the streets trying to track the perpetrator down. He couldn't have gotten far."

She didn't mention Jake by name. I know the police have to look at different options and that having only one suspect when there is no definitive evidence is dumb, but Jake is the only person it can be.

I glance at Chace with hope. This could be over tonight. We'll get to be normal again.

Or a new, different normal anyway. Without Sonny and Isaac.

He smiles, seemingly to reassure me. But his eyes still show skepticism, which doesn't ease my worry.

"He's been tracking us and leaving us notes this whole time, and you've still found nothing," Chace snaps. "Sorry, but that's the truth. You've got no idea where he is, meanwhile my friends are *dying*."

Why can't a whole team of police officers and detectives find one man?

"Chace, I understand your frustrations, but I can assure you we are doing everything we can. We're following every lead, and we will continue to do so until the killer is found."

"Right. How many of us will be dead before you do that?" Chace storms out of the room before anyone can reply.

Chace was a lot closer to Sonny and Isaac than Sienna, Charlotte, and I were. They spent a lot of time together—hanging out, playing football, going for drinks, playing video games.

Sienna puts her hand on my shoulder. "He'll be fine, Lylah."

"I think I should try talking to him." I've never seen Chace like this before. Worry churns away in my stomach.

Chace often makes me feel nervous; he's the only person who has ever given me butterflies. Right now though, they are fluttering so hard I feel sick.

I excuse myself, head up the stairs, then knock on Chace's door. He doesn't immediately answer, but the bathroom door is open, so he must be in his room. I don't realize I'm holding my breath until my lungs start to burn. How long has it been? Thirty seconds? Forty? Is he okay? Does he want to be left alone?

"Is it you, Lylah?" Chace calls from inside.

I suck in a massive breath in relief.

"Yeah, it's me."

I wait.

One. Two. Three.

He opens the door.

"I'm sorry. Despite the good morning, it's been a shitty night."

"Yeah. I get that."

Chace steps aside so I can come in and closes the door behind me. I've been in his room hundreds of times before—we've even hung out together on his bed—but being here now feels different.

Chace grins and tugs my hand, pulling me back to the bed, and we lie down. He wraps his arm around my shoulders and rests the side of his head against mine.

"I'm going to have to tell Riley about what happened at the bar when I see him tomorrow," I whisper. "He's going to freak out. Are we going to be okay, Chace?"

He sighs. "That's a pretty broad question. But yes to all of it."

"Why did you go out on your own tonight?"

He sighs. "No lectures. I had to get out. The house was too quiet, and I felt the loss of Sonny and Isaac. Like, *really* felt it for the first time since they died. As dumb as it was, I had to get some air and be alone. I don't think I'm going to be good company, so if you want to leave to chill with Sienna and Charlotte, I'll understand."

I shake my head gently and nudge my hand over his. Chace threads his fingers through mine. "We can be bad company together. I don't want to be anywhere else."

Chace takes a shallow breath and whispers, "Thank you."

21

Monday
February 12

I wake up feeling fuzzy. Blinking to focus my vision, it takes me a few seconds to orient myself. I fell asleep in Chace's room last night again. Sitting up, I look next to me at the empty bed.

Where did he go?

And why does my head hurt so badly? It's probably stress.

I check my phone. It's almost 11:00 a.m. I pad out of Chace's room and into the bathroom. I run the cold water and drink straight from the faucet. It tastes so good. Now I just need some painkillers to keep my head from splitting in two.

I go downstairs in search of them. Chace is in the kitchen, sitting at the table with an envelope in front of him.

What now?

He doesn't look up, but he must have heard me. Chace reaches out and hands me the note. Jake has used letters cut from magazines again, but I barely even see the note. What I'm fixated on is the lock of long, blond hair.

"Oh my God. Is that real hair? Wait… Is that *my* hair?"

Please, please don't let it be my hair.

Chace's head doesn't move but his eyes meet mine, distressed.

"How did Jake get this?" I lean in to examine the lock up close, as if I'll be able to tell who it belongs to for sure.

It's the same color as my hair, but that doesn't mean it's definitely mine. Blond is hardly a rare hair color.

"I've called Detective Lina. She'll be here soon."

"Why didn't she tell whoever's outside to come in? Did something happen to him?"

Chace tilts his head and frowns. "I don't know," he says. Now I wish I hadn't said anything. "Something's wrong." Chace makes a move to take a step and my heart drops.

"Don't go out there!" I exclaim, sidestepping in front of him and gripping his upper arms. "Chace, wait for the detective. Please. This is her job."

"We can't do *nothing*."

"Yes, we can!"

"Lylah, Officer Benjamin Woodard is outside. He's one who sits outside our house most evenings making sure we're okay. His wife recently gave birth to their first child. If you were her, wouldn't you want someone to check on him?"

Guilt crashes over me like a tsunami. He knew so much about this officer, and I didn't even know his name. "I'm sorry," I say. "You're right, but be careful."

I follow him to the door. "Stay here," he orders.

He unlocks the bolt, but I can sense his hesitation. It's like he's scared of what he'll find.

I'm scared too.

But our fear is nothing compared to what this officer's wife will feel if he's not okay out there.

The sky is dark thanks to a dull, overcast sky, but there is no mistaking what we find when we open the door. The officer's car door is wide open. From this angle, we can't see inside.

"No," Chace whispers. He steps out into the frosty morning air and looks up and down the street. It's deserted.

"Chace," I say, my voice breaking with fear.

His breathing is as heavy as mine, sending short, small puffs swirling up in the cold air. "I have to look."

I want to cling to him until the detective arrives, but Chace will do what he wants no matter what I say. "Don't touch anything."

He shakes his head. "It wouldn't be the first dead body I've found, Lylah." His retort is sarcastic, but it makes my heart ache in the worst way. This is all wrong. We shouldn't be used to dealing with dead bodies. I pray we aren't dealing with one now.

Chace can only take three steps before Detective Lina's car comes careening up the street, lights flashing and siren blaring. She parks in front of the open vehicle and gets out. There is another officer with her, Detective Hayes, if I remember correctly. I probably am not remembering correctly.

My memory is horrendous. Chace knows about these people and their families, and I can't remember anyone's names besides Detective Lina and Detective Alexander and Officer Grey. I feel awful because these people are literally risking their lives to protect me and my housemates.

Detective Lina waves us off, telling us to stay where we are.

I'm not arguing with that, so I keep my feet planted in the doorway.

Chace stops where he is, halfway down the path. It's so cold that my skin pebbles.

The two cops take tentative steps toward the open car door.

Oh no.

My heart falls. From Detective Lina's body language and somber expression, I know Officer Benjamin is in that car. And he's dead.

Turning around and striding toward me, Chace takes me into his arms, burying his face in my neck.

I cling on to him and will myself to stay strong when I want to scream and cry. A police officer was killed on duty protecting me and my friends. The guilt is overpowering.

"Inside, now," Detective Lina barks.

That's all the confirmation we need. We follow instructions, but I want to ask a million questions.

Is he there? Is he alive? Of course he isn't alive. Was he stabbed like the others? Does he have his heart?

Jake is relentless. There used to be a moment of calm before the next storm, but now, one thing happens straight after another.

The closer to Valentine's Day we get, the more he seems to be killing, and the more notes he's sending.

"He killed a *cop*," I mutter as Chace calls for Charlotte and Sienna. What chance do we have if he's murdering the very people who have been assigned to protect us?

"Why are you shouting, Chace?" Sienna snaps from the top of the stairs. Her dark hair is matted, and she rubs her eyes.

"Officer Benjamin is dead."

Straight to the point.

Her eyes widen. "What? The cop outside?"

Charlotte opens her door down the hallway. "Wait, what were you saying? Jake killed a police officer?"

Sienna slowly lowers herself to sit on the top step. "He's going to get us."

I glare at her, really damn annoyed that she's giving up. Sure, maybe the odds are stacked heavily against us, but that doesn't mean we're completely helpless. "Don't say that!" I shout, my eyes brimming with tears. I need some hope to cling to.

I head into the living room to call Riley. I need my big brother. I don't care if that makes me less independent. I need the support of my family.

"Lylah, are you okay?" Riley asks, answering my call on the second ring.

I explain what happened with a few quick sobs. "I'm freaking out," I tell him.

"When was this?" my brother roars.

"We just found out. My head is spinning."

Riley spits out a string of swears. "How shit are the cops at their job? There is one killer and dozens of them. I'm on my way to you. Don't move."

"Riley, I—" I just want to talk and for him to listen for a minute before he rushes over, but he hangs up the phone.

I guess he's had enough of my talking. And I can't help but be grateful he's coming to take care of me. We all need someone, right? I shouldn't feel like a failure for wanting to lean on family during times like these.

I'm sure that's what my friends would tell me, what my therapist would have told me. Being strong doesn't mean I don't need other people. And I think I'm finally starting to understand that.

● ● ●

Riley arrives about ten minutes after we hang up. Sienna lets him in after the police have cleared him. I wrap my arms around my big brother. He hugs me back.

"No one is ever going to hurt you while I'm around, Lylah. I promised Mom and Dad to always look out for you. I won't break that promise."

I know Riley probably couldn't stop Jake if he wanted to kidnap or kill me, but I do feel safer with him around.

"I can't believe that officer is dead! And that he cut some of my hair." I fiddle with the back of my head, where earlier I finally noticed a piece of hair that was shorter than all the rest. "I didn't notice he cut my hair."

"How would you notice that, Ly?"

"Well… Okay, I don't know. It give me the creeps that he's been so close."

Riley grinds his teeth, his hands balling into fists.

I need to change topics before he starts ranting. "Want a cup of tea?"

He laughs without humor. "Sure, kiddo."

Riley follows me into the kitchen where Sienna, Charlotte, and Chace sit around the table staring at a note.

"I thought you gave that to the detectives," I say.

"We did," Chace responds.

"Another one came in with the mail a little while ago. We just found it," Sienna says. "We're waiting for the police to finish outside and come back in to show them."

I lean over to read it.

Jake must be getting desperate. He's never sent so many notes all at once before. The last two haven't been addressed like the earlier ones, but I know this letter is for me. I can feel it. I mean, my hair was with the last one. He's using hair instead of ink to address the person he's threatening.

I take an involuntary step back. I'm the center of Jake's sick vendetta. I must be. It's the only thing that makes sense. I would be out of my mind to comply, but if I don't, one of my friends will be killed. Jake doesn't make empty threats. He's proved that already.

My brother and my friends will tell me not to go. If they were in my position, would they take their own advice though?

Riley gives me a stern glare. I've never seen him look so much like Dad. "The guy is tripping if he thinks anyone is meeting him."

"Agreed," Chace says. "The detectives should be in shortly."

Sienna stands. "I'll get some coffee going."

Riley and I sit at the table. I read the note again and again. My heart palpitates, and I press my fists to my chest. *Calm down. Please calm down.*

"Lylah?" Riley's hand squeezes my shoulder. "You're okay."

Two notes in one day—both with no name. Does he just assume we all know it's me he wants? I take a breath. And another, trying to keep them steady and slow so I don't hyperventilate.

Sienna brings over the hot drinks, but no one makes a move for them.

If I don't meet him, Charlotte, Sienna, or Chace will be next. Riley could be a target now too. I can't lose anyone else. Especially not my brother.

Would Jake save me for last? Or will he kill me on the spot if I meet him?

I've never really thought about my own mortality, even after my parents died, but I'd be okay dying to save someone I love. My friends mean a lot to me. Each person around this table has helped me through so much, whether they know it or not. How can I gamble with their lives?

Chace's green eyes keep catching mine. He shifts uneasily in his seat, and I would give anything to know what he's thinking.

The silence that rubs against my skin like shards of glass.

My phone vibrates in my back pocket.

My heart pounds. It's Jake. I know before I've even taken my phone out of my pocket. It has to be.

My heart thuds. What would they all think if they knew the killer was contacting me directly? What if they thought I was somehow *part* of all this?

Careful not to alarm or alert the others, I subtly slide the phone from my pocket and check the screen under the table. My breath catches in my throat.

On Valentine's Day, you will be mine.

22

Tuesday
February 13

I wake up in Chace's arms, so it's officially the best morning ever. He's wrapped around me like koala clinging to a tree, so I'm roasting hot. But it's nice. I haven't been able to shake my chill since I received Jake's text. So far I haven't told a soul. Chace knows something is off, but Riley, surprisingly, hasn't said anything or noticed I've been acting weird.

Gently, I move Chace's arm, and he rolls onto his back. I hold my breath. He sighs, still sound asleep. I don't want to wake him. He was unsettled last night, tossing and turning. I couldn't sleep either. Jake's text message has been on my mind all night.

Making the wrong decision will be fatal. Meeting a murderer in a secluded place is insanity, but ignoring a murder's threats could be worse.

I can't win.

Maybe if I tell Detective Lina, we can set up the meeting to look like I am alone, and the police can catch him.

Except there are so many risks and no guarantees.

I take one last look at Chace and slink out of bed and his room. Since it's 5:30 a.m., no one else is up. That suits me, because I need a coffee and some time to think.

I brew a fresh pot and sit down at the table with my phone and mug. My hand shakes as I open the text I received a few minutes after the first one yesterday.

Can't wait until Valentine's Day. Meet me at Limbo tonight. 10 PM. Alone.

Limbo is an old club everyone on campus used to go to, which closed down late last year. The building is still empty, but there's a lease sign outside, so I don't think it will be empty for much longer.

If I meet Jake tonight, I should formulate my own plan. I'm no criminal mastermind, but I'm not stupid either. I could think of something to outsmart him. He's getting more and more desperate, and he's out there, alone, with no support, and his mind isn't clear. Obviously. So I probably could do this. I could *maybe* do this.

But I'm not like him. How could I win playing him at his own game?

I have to tell Detective Lina. The police orchestrate these kind of traps all the time. They'll know what to do. If I go alone, I'm only putting more people in danger and risking Jake escaping.

This has to stop, and I'm the only person who can stop it.

"Lylah?"

Chace's voice makes me leap out of my skin. He stands in the kitchen doorway, his bare chest on show. It's very distracting. *Eyes up, Lylah!*

He frowns, ignoring my ogling of him. "What're you doing up so early?" He rubs his eyes.

"Couldn't sleep."

"Really? You're going to pretend you're not okay because of a bad night's sleep? Let me in, Lylah. Please." The concern lacing his voice compels me to spill my secret. I hate how hurt he sounds. We should be deliriously happy to be starting a new relationship. Chace means everything to me, and I don't want secrets between us. I'm anxious enough about all that's happening, I can't start lying to the people I care about.

I take a deep breath. "Yesterday, I received a text," I tell him. "From Jake."

His eyes widen further than I've ever seen them. "What the hell, Lylah?! Why didn't you tell me sooner? What does it say?"

I know he's mad I didn't immediately tell him, but I stand by my decision. I needed a little time before dragging anyone else into it.

I drop my phone into his open palm. "I wasn't sure what to do. I didn't want to stress you out even more after yesterday."

His forehead creases as he frowns. "You realize there is no way I'm letting you meet him, don't you?"

I roll my eyes, more at myself than him. I'm not about to let him tell me what I can and can't do, but right now, I kind of like his protective instinct.

"It's all I thought about all night," I say.

He tilts his head, places my phone on the table, and without breaking eye contact, sits down. Although he's concerned, his posture is rigid and standoffish. "You considered going, didn't you?"

"Of course, I did. Still *am* considering it. Chace, I could end this tonight."

Chace's eyebrows wrinkle, and his eyes light up with fear. He feels even more distant from me. "You could *die*!"

"Yeah, I get that. So I'm not going, okay? At least not alone. I'll call Detective Lina and see how she wants to handle this."

All the times I thought about how things would be between me and Chace after we got together, none of the scenarios were like this. And I don't even mean losing Sonny and Isaac and the crap with Jake. Our relationship is tense, and I'm scared we're not strong enough to get through this without unintentionally hurting each other. I'm holding on to him by a thread. I can feel my old ways creeping back in. I want to put walls up and hide, so I need this to work.

There is so much loss and pain in our house; we need to foster the good so it doesn't turn sour.

"Chace," I whisper.

He's sitting close to me, but there may as well be an eight-foot wall between us. How did we get so far from where we were last night?

"What if they want to set a trap?" he asks.

"I think they will. It's our best chance. Jake has proved he's excellent at hide-and-seek, so we need to take advantage of him reaching out."

"They'll want you to walk into that building on your own."

"Yeah, but they would be there too," I say.

"Not close enough. Don't agree to that."

Okay, being bossy just stopped being cute.

"You can't tell me what to do," I tell Chace.

"I think I just did."

Closing my eyes, I grit my teeth so I don't say anything I'll regret. Arguing with Chace is new, and I don't like it.

"Lylah, I'm trying to protect you here."

When I open my eyes, I wish I hadn't. Chace looks at me, eyes glossy with tears.

"I can't lose you," he admits, his voice barely above a whisper.

"You won't." I reach out and squeeze his hand.

He dips his head in a curt nod. His jaw is still tight and shoulders bunched. *Seriously, why can't I be a mind reader?*

Chace watches me as I let go of him and dial Detective Lina. I work to keep myself composed as I tell her everything I just told Chace.

"I'm on my way, Lylah. Do not reply to his message," the detective says.

I don't intend to.

I hang up and give Chace a smile. "She's coming. God, this could all be over soon. I want to be able to leave the house alone. I want to feel safe when I go to sleep."

Chace's posture softens. He reaches out and covers my hand with his. "Let's hope they can finish this."

"You don't sound confident."

"It's hard to be confident after…everything."

"Are you okay, Chace?"

He sighs like the weight of the world is on his shoulders. "I don't know how to say it or if I even want to."

I place my hand on his tense shoulder, feeling the muscles bunch up with stress. I'd give anything to make him feel better about this whole thing. "You can talk to me."

Licking his lips, he shifts in his seat.

My heart starts to race. "Chace, you're kind of scaring me here."

One side of his mouth curls up. He reaches up and squeezes my hand that still rests on his shoulder. "Sorry. Sonny and Isaac... I have other friends here, but not like them. I can't get my head around the fact that they're gone, and they're not coming back. Isaac and I made a pact shortly after Sonny died to protect you, Charlotte, and Sienna. I'm the last guy, and that responsibility feels overwhelming. I hate being helpless and weak, and I *hate* Jake for that as much as I hate him for murdering our friends. I miss my friends."

He takes my hand, removing it from his shoulder but not letting go.

"Hey, protecting us isn't your job. If something happens to any of us, it won't be your fault. Just like it's not your fault that Sonny and Isaac are dead. You can't put that on yourself, Chace. No wonder you look like you're going to have a mental breakdown."

His eyebrows knit together. "I do?"

"Yeah, kind of. Don't get me wrong, you still look cute, but—"

"Wait," he interrupts. "Cute? Puppies are cute, babe."

With a laugh, I shake my head. "Sorry. Handsome, then. Is that better?"

He turns up his nose and wrinkles it. "My grandmother calls me handsome. You can go with *smokin' hot.*"

"Oh, I bet I can," I tease. "Anyway, my point is, focus on helping the police do their job. Like, no sneaking out, and support them if they think using me as bait will catch him."

"That's a big ask, Lylah. Shoving you under the nose of a murderer is too dangerous."

"Maybe, but you know it's the best chance of catching him…even if you won't admit it."

He pulls me into his arm and buries his face in my neck. He knows I'm right.

"I can't lose you," he whispers.

"I'm not going anywhere."

And I'm not. Jake won't hurt me. I'm tired of being scared and feeling weak. I'm ready to face him.

I'm ready to fight.

23

'm meeting Jake in five hours.

I've gone over the plan a million times in my head and Detective Lina and her colleagues have run through the events. The police got ahold of the floor plans for the building.

Limbo was a popular club when it was open, and I've been dozens of times before, so I know where the exits and bathrooms are. Lina and her team have formulated a plan in which I'll go in through the back fire exit door. It's closest to the bar, so it should put a physical barrier between Jake and me.

That's hoping the building hasn't been gutted or ransacked.

Detective Lina would have preferred more time—she wanted to check out the space first—but there is no time, and Jake is probably watching. They have plans of the building from the last renovation. But we don't know what's in there right now.

Sienna and Charlotte were against the idea of me meeting Jake too, but after Detective Lina explained that the police would be right there, they backed down a little. Sienna volunteered to go with me and claw Jake's eyes out, but I have to go alone. Jake has to think I'm following his rules.

The police will have cameras and will be hiding, waiting to take out Jake should he pose a threat to me before he's arrested.

This can work. This will work. It has to.

I'm sitting at the coffee shop by myself—sort of. I have two cops sitting at the table behind me. The house was suffocating, and I needed the only other place besides home that offers me comfort. The police kept reviewing the plan for tonight. Chace, Sienna, and Charlotte were hovering, repeatedly asking if I was sure I wanted to go through with it.

I had to get out, even for just an hour. The coffee house is closing in fifteen minutes, so I'll have to go home soon.

With one hand, I rub my necklace, and with the other, I take a sip of my lukewarm latte. Different outcomes of meeting Jake spin in my mind. Things could go horribly wrong, and I could be killed. Jake might not want to talk. He might take one look at me and shoot me in the head. But I have to believe that he wants more than that. Surely he wants to explain or gloat about what he's done.

"Lylah?"

The deep voice makes me jump. "God, Zak, you scared me!"

Chuckling, he sits down. "Sorry, I didn't mean to."

The cops watch us intently, but they know Zak.

"I thought you would have gone home by now."

He shakes his head. "Sarah's back with friends. Dad and I won't leave yet. We can't. Not until Jake has been stopped."

"You're not responsible for his actions. No one would blame you for wanting to get back to your life."

"No. I can't leave knowing you and your friends are at risk because of *my* brother." He puts his hands on the table and leans back into the chair. "I want to be here. If he shows his face, I want to be close. If only he would answer his phone to talk to me. I'm sure I could persuade him to turn himself in."

"Do you really think he would listen to you?"

Zak takes a deep breath full of uncertainty. "Well, I used to think he'd listen to me. When we were younger, he followed me around everywhere, hanging on my every word. Now I have no idea who he even is. The things he's done… He's not the person I thought he was. This Jake isn't my brother."

"I'm so sorry, Zak. I don't know what I would do if I was in your position."

"I hate it. I hate *him*. He's ruined our lives. Everyone looks at us like we're holding the fucking knife alongside Jake. My dad hardly leaves his hotel room because he can't face the persecution. The media are practically camped outside, wanting statements and interviews, and people on the streets hurl abuse about how he failed as a father."

I never really thought about how it must be for Jake's family, but they're victims too. I hate that people see them as guilty by association.

Zak continues, "I haven't been to the station for a couple of days, so I'm almost afraid to ask this, but are there any new developments?" His eyes look tired. This is taking a toll on him.

I bite my lip. How much should I disclose? "Yeah."

He arches his dark eyebrow, but he lets out a defeated breath. "Go on."

I relay the series of events as gently as I can.

"What?" Zak spits, his chest puffing. "He killed a cop? You're telling me my brother has *killed* a cop?"

Zak drops his arms to his lap, like his body has lost the strength to support itself.

"Lylah," he breathes. "I'm so sorry. I don't even know where to begin."

"He's getting desperate. And impatient. But Valentine's Day is tomorrow. We'll soon find out what he has planned."

Tomorrow is the anniversary of my parents' death too. I've barely had time to dwell on that.

"Maybe I should make a last-ditch effort to get a hold of him? I don't know…"

"I don't think he's going to listen to you, Zak."

"Yeah," he says solemnly.

I don't mention Jake's text. He's not going to listen to Zak if I handed over the number it came from and let Zak try getting through to him. I'm absolutely terrified knowing that Jake has nothing to lose. He's already cut his family out of his life in favor of murder.

He's going to take this all the way.

"Lylah, you okay?" Zak asks.

"Sorry. My brain was miles away."

"What's going on?"

I really can't tell you.

I tap my finger against my mug. "You know…"

"You can talk to me. If you want to rage about Jake, you can. Nothing you can say is going to be new to me. I've thought it all too."

I sigh. "I wish none of this had ever happened."

"Yeah, me too."

We sit in awkward silence for a few moments.

Then I say, "Looks like they're getting ready to close." I nod toward the barista, who is starting to clean the machines. "We should go."

"Would you like me to walk you home, or are you covered?"

"The officers will get me home, so I'm fine. But thank you."

Zak stands. "Please take care of yourself, Lylah. And remember, if you do want to talk, I'm here."

"Thanks, Zak. You too."

With a fleeting smile, he leaves, and the officers get out of their seats. I follow suit, leaving a tip by my mug.

"Almost showtime, huh?" I say.

The newest cop, Officer Harrison, I think, nods. "We'll keep you safe, Lylah."

Let's hope.

●　　●　　●

I blow out a deep breath and stare at the building. I have to walk a little way up before I can head down an alleyway leading out the back. *Has it always been this big?* Although I know I'm not alone, I feel like I am. Dozens of police officers are…somewhere watching, along with Detective Lina and Detective Alexander, who I can see.

It would be comforting if I could see the officers too, but obviously if I could, then so could Jake.

Pinned to my hoodie is a broach. It's pretty, I guess, a black jeweled butterfly with its wings out wide. The design doesn't matter though, it's what's hidden inside that counts. The police couldn't get in to scope the place out, they couldn't have officers hiding inside, they couldn't set up cameras because this is Jake's chosen location, and he could be watching. But they could have a camera on me.

Each step I take is being watched by a team in a van, parked on the side of the road. Detective Lina is watching too, on a phone.

Limbo is at the end of a strip of clubs and bars. The street is always packed in the evenings, and tonight is no different. Hundreds of students mill around, walking from one to club to another, getting fresh air, talking, laughing. A group of girls cackle as they pass me, waiting to get into one of the clubs, clearly enjoying their night out. I used to be like them, carefree, drunk, and obnoxiously loud. They have no idea how lucky they are.

Jake chose this location well. Not only is it familiar, but the crowded sidewalks and shadows from low lights will provide cover for him to blend into the throngs of people as he enters and exits the abandoned building.

I turn down the long alleyway. There are fewer smokers around the back. The rear door to Limbo is set back from the building next door, so hopefully no one sees me go in. Not that anyone is paying any attention to me.

I pinch my necklace between my fingers for luck, and I can feel the bulletproof vest underneath my thick winter coat. Detective Lina advised me to wear it as a precautionary measure, and I wasn't going to turn it down.

Who knows what Jake's end game is.

He could be watching from somewhere, so I don't hesitate. Twisting the handle, I push. Jake has unlocked it for me. I slip through the door and walk into the dark.

The heavy door slams shut behind me, and my pulse skyrockets. It's almost pitch black in here, the only light coming from the illuminated *Limbo* sign spanning the side wall. My eyes flick around the open space. I am alone. And although there is a lot of outside noise, I can't hear anything but my racing pulse.

"J-Jake?" I stammer.

I take another step into the room. The bar is in front of me, slightly to the left. Lina told me to get behind it, but there's an overturned table blocking my way.

Is Jake behind there?

I take three more slow steps, but my shoe slides, and my foot almost slips out from underneath me. I catch myself on the bar, but my heart thuds so hard it hurts. In the dim light, I can't see what's slick on the floor. My phone has a flashlight, but I'm almost too scared to know.

With my hands shaking so much I can practically hear my bones rattling, I pull my phone from my pocket and push the flashlight icon. I hold my breath and angle the beam downward.

No.

I recoil, slapping my hand over my mouth, but it does nothing to muffle my scream.

It looks like a lump of meat, but I know better. It's a heart, and it's only when I realize what it is that the smell hits me. Metallic overtakes the old stench of beer.

On the floor right above the heart, right below me, I can just make out the words, spelled in blood this time instead of magazine cutouts:

YOUR HEART IS MINE.

I turn on my heel and sprint to the door. With my phone still in my hand, I slam my forearms against the emergency bar on the fire door and practically fall out of the building.

Detective Lina is there in an instant, gripping my shoulders. She saw it too, she was watching. There's a loud bang, and footsteps echo as the officers storm the place, but I am hardly aware of what's happening around me. It's like I have tunnel vision.

I shake my head. "Jake's not there." Squeezing my fingers around my phone, I stutter, "I-It was a heart."

Detective Lina doesn't say anything because she already knows. She closes her eyes for a beat and takes a calming breath. When she opens them again, she looks angry. "Let's get you in the car."

Lina ushers me past the throngs of drunk people who are now paying *a lot* of attention to us. I tilt my head down, looking away from the many phone cameras aimed in our direction. Being shared all over social media doesn't bother me right now though; I almost stepped on my friend's heart.

My chest heaves with thick sobs that shake my body. *This won't end until we're all dead.* I curl into Detective Lina, who has us power walking toward a car around the corner. Another officer starts crowd control, telling people to go inside.

Detective Lina opens the door for me, and I slide in the back. She climbs in next to me as Detective Alexander seems to appear out of nowhere, getting behind the wheel.

"Don't you need to take care of the crime scene?" I ask, wiping my eyes with my free hand.

I wish I could un-see that blood, that note. Jake left that heart on the floor like it means nothing.

My stomach rolls, threatening to bring up my dinner and everything else I've eaten today.

"My job right now is to stay with you. We don't know where Jake is or why this was his plan tonight. My team will handle the scene."

That sounds like she thinks Jake has another plan. His *real* plan for tonight. She doesn't want to leave me alone.

I look down at my phone as Detective Alexander makes a hasty exit from the parking lot. The flashlight is still on, and it's still on silent. I didn't want it going off while I was meeting Jake. I go to switch the light off, and that's when I see the text, almost dropping my phone. "He's sent me a message," I say, my voice hitching as I struggle to get control.

I knew you would betray me.

I hand Detective Lina the phone. She purses her lips.

"Why?" I wail. "Why did he do that?"

Both Lina and Alexander stay silent, but they exchange a look in the mirror.

"What aren't you telling me? I think I have a right to know."

Lina puts her hand over mine. "We think he was distracting us."

My face falls. "He wanted us out of the way so he could get to who he wanted next?" *How could we be so stupid? Charlotte, Sienna, and Chace are at home, waiting for us to get back with good news that Jake has been caught!*

"We need to get to the house. Call them! Detective Lina, I need my phone. I need to call Chace," I ramble, my voice getting higher and more desperate, trying to grab the phone back from her.

"Calm down, Lylah," she says.

"Don't tell me what to do! If Jake has gone after them, he has a massive head start while we were messing around in an empty club!"

"Lylah, we thought about this. We figured it might be a possibility. There are four officers at the house. Don't worry, they'll be fine."

"Shut up! Stop telling me we will be fine. We won't! We aren't! Nothing is fine! Everyone is dying, and you can't stop the killer. We're all going to die!"

Oh my God, I can't breathe.

My chest is tight, lungs screaming, begging for oxygen. My hand slams against the door handle, and I grip it tight, trying to steady myself.

I gasp, but it's no use. I'm not getting any air.

I'm going to die like this.

Lina drops my phone and grabs my upper arms roughly. "Lylah, look at me. Concentrate on me. Breathe. Take a breath in. And out."

I'm trying.

My eyes sting with tears that roll freely down my cheeks. I tear at my coat, unbuttoning it, trying to get my lungs to work. *Is this what suffocating is like?*

"Shh, Lylah, keep your eyes on me. Deep breath in. I know it's hard.

Come on, deep breath in." Her voice is firm, filled with authority, but also soft.

I stare at her, focusing on her dark-brown eyes. I follow her instructions.

"Now out," she says.

I exhale.

"Repeat, Lylah. Keep watching me, keep breathing."

It starts to work. I take a few more big gulps of air and the aching in my chest stops.

"There, that's better. Are you okay now?" Lina asks.

With wide eyes, I nod. But I'm not okay. "What…?"

Oh God, it happened again. I'm losing it.

"You had a panic attack."

Yes, I did.

I press my lips together. I don't want her to know how many panic attacks I've had over the past couple of years. "Oh."

"Just try to stay calm. We'll be home soon." Lina lets go of me, and I sit back in the seat.

I haven't had a full panic attack in over a year. I thought I was past this. I thought I was mentally strong enough to calm myself down before I had an attack. My hands find each other, and I grip them together, trying to stop myself shaking.

Why can't I stay better? I have to be strong. There is no time for me to fall apart here.

My heart is still going a million miles an hour. Shouldn't I feel better now that I can breathe again? I'm through it, but I can't shake the feeling of fear, uncertainty, and the knowledge that my life is so wildly out of my control.

Closing my eyes, I count my breathing. In for five seconds. Out for five seconds. I concentrate on my lungs inflating and deflating until I can feel my heart slowing to its normal rate.

I *have* to stay calm. We're on our way home, and my friends will be fine. Jake won't have gotten in. I pray that my friends are okay. Jake will be against four cops. Two outside the house and two inside. My friends are probably safer than anyone else in the neighborhood. Jake is smart and strong, but he's not smart or strong enough to take on four officers.

I open my eyes. The house is just around the corner. As soon as I collapse in Chace's arms, I'll be fine.

24

Tuesday
February 13

Detective Alexander screeches to a halt outside the house. The police car parked out front is empty.

Oh God, no.

"What's going on?" I ask, but the detectives are already out of the car and running to the front door, hands on weapons.

I can't move. My body has seized up, muscles locked in place.

They're all dead. I know it. I can't go in and see that.

We had everything in place. This plan should have worked, but Jake was smarter, and now my friends are dead. I should never have gone to that club. I close my eyes and bend over, laying my chest on my legs.

I've lost everyone.

I wait for the searing pain to come, but there's nothing but vast darkness, which leaves me hollow. If it wasn't for Chace, Sonny,

Isaac, Sienna, and Charlotte, I wouldn't have gotten this far through school. They've been my family, and now they're gone.

Someone hammers on the window. I don't move. I don't want to face reality. I want to stay huddled here forever.

"Lylah!"

Chace?

I sit up, gripping the door handle with one hand and the passenger seat's headrest with the other. In the streetlight, perfect green eyes stare back at me through the window. He's here. He's okay.

Then where is Jake?

Frowning like he's a bit scared of me, Chace opens the car door and crouches down. "Are you okay?"

Oh God, he's alive!

I launch myself at him. Burying my head in his neck, I burst into tears. It's like an overflowing river I can no longer control. I sob, clinging to him like he's the only thing holding me together.

"Jesus, it's okay, Lylah," he says, wrapping his strong arms around me. He kisses the side of my head and stands us both up. "You're okay."

It's not me I was worried about. "I thought... Chace, I was so scared," I sob, pulling back so I can see him and make sure he's definitely all right. I run my hands over his face, making sure he's really here.

"Detective Lina told us what happened at the club. He won't get you, Lylah, I promise."

But I'm not so certain. He left a message. A message with a heart. A human heart from one of my friends. I avert my eyes, ashamed that I almost stepped on it.

Cops run from the house, and Detective Lina is behind them, on the phone.

"What's happening?" I ask.

Chace steps to the side, now on high alert. "Have you found him?"

Detective Alexander stops in front of us. "Chace, do you know where Charlotte is?"

The color drains from his face. Chace turns white. "She was in her room."

No.

"He's got her, hasn't he?" I ask out loud, trembling.

"What the hell!" Chace roars. "How is that possible with all officers around?"

"The back door was open," the detective says.

If Jake had gone out the back with Charlotte, the only place that the police are unable to park right outside because of the pedestrian zone, he could have made her jump the wall where it's not visible from the road where the police car was parked.

"We locked all the doors!" Chace snaps. "The locks have been changed! How is he doing this? How is he getting inside?"

"What if he messaged her?" I ask. "They're friends on Facebook. Maybe she left voluntarily."

"She wouldn't do that," Chace replies.

"I did. And she might have if she was blackmailed. Think about it, if he contacted her, she would know that tonight was a setup. This was the plan all along. He wanted to get to one of us, and he chose Charlotte."

Chace frowns. "Then why not just message her? Why contact you?"

"It's getting harder to get to us with the added security. But by diverting our attention…" I trail off. "He's sick. He probably got pleasure leaving that heart and threat for me to find."

I reach into the car and grab my phone from the floor of the car where it dropped.

"What are you two still doing out here?" Detective Lina says, shouting from the other side of the car. "You both need to get back inside. *Now*."

I unlock my phone. "No. I need to message Jake and try to get Charlotte back."

"No, you need to leave this to us."

Because that's been going brilliantly so far.

I ignore the detective and tap a message to Jake.

Don't hurt her. What do we have do to make you stop?

"Lylah, stop. Don't send that message," Detective Alexander steps toward me, but Chace blocks him with his shoulder.

"Not happening, buddy," Chace says.

"Lylah, Chace, inside now," Detective Lina snaps. "I'm going to need to see the message you sent."

I zip past the car and shove my phone into her hand, not stopping to see her reaction before I march into the house. She can read it all she wants. If Jake is willing to text me, we should be taking advantage of that. Nothing else has worked so far.

Detective Lina calls after me, her voice angry and disappointed, but I continue into the house. Unzipping my coat, I throw it on the sofa and rip off the Velcro on the bulletproof vest. I barge into the living room, dump the vest on the floor, and sit down in a huff. Sienna is alone on the chair, twirling her hair around her finger and staring into space.

Detective Lina follows us inside and folds her arms. Chace flies in behind her, pushing past her to sit beside me. Besides the two detectives, there is one other officer in this room. He stayed behind when the other three left to search for Jake and Charlotte.

"Say whatever you want, Detective, but someone has to do something." I reach out for my phone, and she drops it in my open hand.

She shakes her head. "We'll just have to deal with whatever happens next."

She's probably annoyed that I got in there and contacted him first. I don't care anymore. We've played it how the police want this whole time. Now Charlotte is missing. Something has to change.

My phone beeps, and I drop it into my lap like it's as hot as lava. The room falls silent.

"It's not going to explode, Lylah," Chace says quietly. "Look at what it says."

Charlotte's already dead. You shouldn't have turned me down.

"No," I whisper, rereading the message again and again. I see the words, but they don't seem real. Charlotte. He killed Charlotte. And he's trying to justify it! Charlotte is *dead*. But what does he mean by turning him down? Is he referring to when I denied his kiss last year or the fact that I didn't follow his orders to meet him alone tonight? I am numb. "When did Charlotte go to her room?" I ask my friends, passing the phone to Detective Lina, my voice breaking with emotion.

"What did it say, Lylah?" Chace asks.

"When?" I demand.

We've only been gone thirty minutes. Is that long enough to lure her out of the house, take her somewhere, and kill her? Maybe he's baiting me.

"Right after you left. She didn't want to wait up with us. We were tense, so she didn't want to hang out with us here in the living room. She wanted to go to her room, to her own space," Sienna explains. "Why? What did Jake say?"

Jake had thirty minutes. "He can't be far. He must have gotten Char out of the house right after I left." I pause, and Sienna looks at me expectantly. "Jake said she's already dead." My voice is hoarse, barely working as I stammer the words, still not believing them.

Sienna's face pales. "No."

"We don't know that's true. He's never told us before. He likes planting the seed, threatening, and leaving his victim's fate to be found," Chace says.

"Charlotte got a text before she went to her room," Sienna squeals. "Was that him? Could we have stopped this?"

Detective Lina shakes her head. "This is no one's fault."

Despite her insistence, I'm feeling pretty responsible right now. If I'd gone alone to the club like he asked, Charlotte...would probably still be with Jake. He never believed I would go alone, did he?

"Do we believe him?" I ask the detective.

She shrugs. "I want to say no. The timing is incredibly tight."

"You want to say no, but you're not actually saying it," Chace points out. "There's a difference." He pauses. "We should reply to him. Demand proof. I don't believe him, but I've underestimated him before."

I've had enough of seeing proof.

Detective Lina holds up her hands, my phone now being examined by Detective Alexander. "We need to take a step back and think this through."

"If there's a chance that Charlotte is still alive, we don't have much time. We need to act! Now!" I exclaim. "Detective Lina, come on!"

The two detectives make eye contact and have some sort of silent conversation. She nods at him, then turns to me. "You are not to send any messages that we haven't authorized. We need to get him to believe that he's won. He has to think we know there's no way we can get close to him. Feed his ego."

I nod. That I can do, even if it leaves a nasty taste in my mouth. I know what I need to send.

You're the one who holds all the power. I get that. The police can't end this. Only you can. Tell me how.

I show the detectives what I've typed, and when I get a curt nod, I hit send.

"Do you think he'll reply?" Chace asks.

"It's hard to tell," Detective Alexander says. "Some killers can't help themselves and others have more self-control over the impulse."

"So time will tell which type of psycho Jake is," I say.

Detective Lina gives me a sad smile. "Yes."

We wait. Minutes feel like hours. I can tell Jake has read the message, but he hasn't replied.

What is he thinking?

My lip is raw where I'm tugging it with my teeth.

I'll let you know.

My breath catches at his message.

"*I'll let you know* is all he's written," I say. "What does that mean? When will he let me know? And what will he let me know? What if he really has killed Charlotte?"

Detective Lina takes the phone.

"He's telling you he's in charge, Lylah. I expect he'll make contact again, but he'll make us wait," Detective Alexander explains. "That means if he hasn't already killed Charlotte like he claims, he's likely to keep her alive. She's his pawn."

"She's a person, not a pawn!" Sienna snaps.

She's our person, and I close my eyes, wishing and willing with all my might that she doesn't get killed.

25

Wednesday
February 14

walk with a cop into the town, away from the university. We've
parked at the end of a lot beside a corner cordoned off with tape
and cones for roadwork on the asphalt. It's a frosty morning but the
crisp air is refreshing. There are fewer students around, so I'm not
getting as many stares. I mean, a lot of people still know me because
of the damn media, but the farther from home I am, the less people
seem to ogle.

It's been a full day since Charlotte vanished, and so far, we've heard
nothing. Detective Alexander seems to think Jake's playing the long
game; he's patient, so he can keep Charlotte without harming her.
I don't care what anyone says, Charlotte is alive until I have proof
otherwise. I have to believe that.

I just have to wait for him to make his next move.

Zak called me this morning after seeing footage of me leaving the club, upset after my failed meet-up with Jake. People and their smartphones suck! They're so quick to take a video of something juicy without a single thought of the person on the other side of the lens. The last thing I need is to go viral. I'm hoping I can go unnoticed today—well, as much as one can be unnoticed with constant police protection. Detective Alexander and two police officers he'd called in for additional protection are with me now. I'm not sure if I feel safer with them. Jake has a way of getting what he wants no matter the obstacle.

Besides, it's only right that Zak knows what's going on with Charlotte. So despite Detective Lina's recommendation to stay home, I'm meeting him. With three cops with me for protection, of course.

Riley doesn't like me seeing Zak. To Riley, Zak is guilty by association. But I managed to convince him to stay behind.

Chace wasn't thrilled about me going either, but he's at home with a terrified Sienna, who is convinced she's next.

Maybe that's why I feel a bit safer: I'm pretty sure he's saving me for last.

And today is Valentine's Day.

Today is the day.

The day that has so much tragic history for me and, if I'm right, promises a tragic present.

Zak doesn't know the town as well as I do, so we're meeting in a small Starbucks instead of somewhere more remote.

I spot him as soon as I walk through the door. He's in the far corner, tapping his cup and looking around. I can tell he's uncomfortable from his body language. He watches people like he's trying to figure out if they're talking about him. It's a feeling I know all too well.

It's still early, so it hasn't been open long, but there are a few people in here already. Couples starting their day with a coffee, cuddled up and in love.

Did Mom and Dad plan to share coffee together at the hotel before venturing out? Before they were killed?

As I approach, he gives me a smile that doesn't reach his eyes.

I take a seat, and he pushes a drink in front of me. I take a sip. A latte. "Thank you."

"You're welcome. How are you?"

Blowing out a breath, I reply, "I don't know. Jake has Charlotte. The detectives won't let me text him again."

His back stiffens. "You're in contact with him?"

"Um…" I shift in my seat. *Damn it.* The cops are out of earshot, but they watch us like hawks. "Yes. God, I'm sorry, Zak. If I thought it would have done any good I would have told you sooner, I promise. I knew I should have messaged you after what happened yesterday. You have a right to know what is happening with your brother."

He rubs his palms over his face and groans. "Why didn't the damn cops tell me?" He drops his hands and looks up. "I want to know everything, Lylah. This isn't just about you and your friends. He tried to jump me too. And he's my brother."

"I remember," I say gently, then recount last night's events. There is a tiny red line on the side of his head from Jake's attack. He should know everything. "Okay. So I texted him again, asking him to let Charlotte go. To end all this. But he said she's... He said that's she's already dead," I finish.

"My God, this keeps getting worse."

It does. Right at the start of this, I was sure the cops would have Jake by now. But I feel like we're in a dark tunnel, and it just keeps getting longer.

"Yeah. I'm holding on to hope though. If Jake had killed her like he said, he would have left her body somewhere for us to find. That's what happened before. And there hasn't been a body, so I think that she's still alive somewhere. I have to think that."

Zak shakes his head sadly. "I can't believe the killer is the same person I grew up with. I keep thinking back over our childhood and trying to remember any clue that Jake could be capable of murder. Anything that could have alerted me to this so I could have stopped it before it started."

"There's nothing you could have done. It's not like he told you what he was going to do, Zak. How could you possibly have known?"

"My dad, sister, and I have lived with him for our whole lives— how could we *not* know, Lylah? I knew that he liked you a lot more than you liked him, and he was angry about the kiss, but there was nothing to suggest he would want revenge."

"How angry was he? When it happened, I told him I didn't think of him like that, and he seemed disappointed, but not homicidal."

"He came home at Easter, so a couple months after that happened. We were out one night, and he got drunk. I don't remember a lot of that night. I wasn't exactly sober. But he was rambling about how you didn't know what you were missing...or you didn't know how good you two would be together until it was too late. I didn't think much of it at the time, but he obviously wasn't over it then. If I thought for a second *too late* meant he was going to kill anyone in the future, I would have spoken up. I would have told someone. I would have stopped him. I know there's a lot of shit out there about how me and Sarah are in on it, but that's not true. She can't even be here she's so upset."

"Zak, you don't have to explain. Did Jake say anything else about us?"

"Not that I can remember," he answers. "I've spoken to everyone else who he might have had contact with, and they can't remember anything he said that would have caused concern either."

I take a sip of my latte. "I keep thinking back to the day he left. I was in their dorm, hanging out with Sienna and Isaac. Jake packed up his room and although we usually talked, he barely looked at me. At the time, I figured he was too busy to have a real conversation, but now..."

Now I examine everything that happened with Jake.

"Hindsight, I guess ," Zak says.

I give him a smile that seems to relax him a bit more. Chace and Sienna still won't talk to him, and he is right—a large portion of the student body seems to think he's in on it. I've seen the comments on Facebook, heard the rumors circulating. Just like they think me and Chace somehow cheated on Jake.

Speculation and frivolous gossip can ruin lives.

"Detective Lina doesn't want any of us to contact Jake."

He lifts his eyebrow. "And what do you think?"

"I think we have to try to get through to him. It's the only chance we have of getting him to stop."

"There's nothing I want to say to him, ever again actually, but if it could help, I would try." He leans in. "I've tried contacting him. Does he have a new number?"

I nod. "It came from a number I didn't recognize." His eyes flick to the officers behind me. They're talking among themselves and watching the general area.

"I'll text it to you. Detective Lina said we have to make Jake feel like he's already won. He has to think we know there's nothing we can do to stop him, that he's smarter than us and in control."

Zak scowls. "We have to pretend he's a criminal mastermind and we're beneath him?"

"Criminal mastermind is pretty accurate actually," I mutter. "It's part of the game, Zak."

"Game?" His voice is clipped, angry.

"To him! I'm really not explaining this well, am I?"

His face softens and he holds up his hands. "Sorry. This is all so... overwhelming. I understand what you're saying, but I'm not going to pretend he's some hero."

"I hated it too. But if it leads to his capture, keeps Charlotte safe, it's worth it," I tell him.

"Is there anything I can do?" Zak puts his head in his hands. "I feel so useless."

"We all feel like that, so you're not alone. Jake has all of the power, so I doubt there's anything we *can* do. Anytime we've tried to make a move, it's backfired. I know the cops are working to find him and hopefully they'll get a breakthrough, but I'm not holding my breath. I don't think we'll find him before he wants us to."

My phone rings on the table. Zak and I both look at it.

You're with him.

"What the… How does he know that?" Zak asks.

Detective Alexander must have heard the incoming text, as he pulls over a chair and sits. "What's happening?"

I slide the phone to him and exchange a look with Zak. His dark eyes are wide. "He can see us," he murmurs.

Detective Alexander shouts to the other cops, who run outside to scan the street while he calls in backup from the station. "Don't move," he says. He tells the manager to shut the café and get everyone out. One flash of his badge has everyone jumping into action. Quickly, people sprint out to the street and away from the store.

"What do we do?" I ask.

"Let's get you home, Lylah. Zak, you'll be escorted to where you're staying too."

Zak stands. "He followed us here. I don't need an escort anywhere. Next time my brother comes for me, I'll be ready. I can take care of this myself."

"Don't be stupid, Zak, he's dangerous," I say.

Zak's eyes narrow so that they look almost black. "I'm ready for Jake."

I get it. I'm tired of hiding and being afraid too. So why prolong it? If we can draw him out, then great. But that doesn't mean we should be reckless.

"It's basically suicide to turn away protection, Zak," I tell him softly. "Too many people have been lost. Please don't make it easy for Jake to add to the body count."

"Lylah's right, Zak," Detective Alexander says. "Let us get you both home safely."

We leave the café as more cops arrive to survey the scene and search for Jake. One of the cops who came with us moves to escort Zak.

Zak grabs my wrist hard as we're about to part ways. He leans in. "Watch yourself, Lylah."

Frowning, I nod. "Yeah. You too."

He drops my wrist and stalks off with the cop, who has to practically jog to keep up with Zak's long, angry strides.

"Lylah?" Detective Alexander asks. "Are you okay?"

I rub my wrist where Zak gripped it. "I think so. Let's get out of here. Knowing Jake could be watching gives me the creeps."

Detective Alexander starts to walk. For a second, I can't move. I have to force my legs into action. The street is long, and we could only get a parking space in the lot at the end.

"What do you think Jake would do if we locked ourselves in the house and didn't come out?" I ask.

It's about the only thing we haven't tried yet, and that's because we don't want him to have that power over us.

The detective glances at me out of the corner of his eye. "I think he would kill Charlotte. Then after a few more days of no contact, not seeing any of you, he would become enraged. I think he'd come after you. Or innocent bystanders. It's not something I would recommend."

"What *would* you recommend? I can't take much more of this."

"We'll get him, Lylah."

"Have you had other murderers who have been this hard to find?"

He nods. "Of course."

"How many?"

His lip twitches but his eyes are solemn. "A few."

My next question, I don't voice: *How many have gotten away?*

We pass the last shop and round the corner into the parking lot. A crowd has gathered around the police car in the far corner. The police car we arrived in.

Oh, God. What is it? Then a beat later, my stomach falls. *Charlotte.*

Detective Alexander looks at the cop with us, and before they can hold me back, I run.

"Lylah!" Detective Alexander bellows.

My feet hit the concrete so hard that pain shoots up my shins.

Charlotte.

In the background I hear sirens. Whatever's happened, someone has already called it in. There are people standing in front of the car, blocking my view. But the closer I get, the more horror I see.

Blood. Blood everywhere. Blood is smeared on the hood and dripping onto the ground. I stop dead in my tracks. I know what I'm about to see, so do I really want to go farther?

I've seen two of my friends' mutilated bodies already. I don't know that I can bear to see another's.

Detective Alexander catches up and growls, "Wait here!"

I plant my feet, my heart racing. I am light-headed.

The detective and the cop quickly disperse the crowd, but it's too late. Everyone has a phone in their hand videoing and snapping photos of the gruesome scene. As people filter to the side of the parking lot, where they've been instructed to wait to give statements, my friend comes into view.

Charlotte is starfished on the hood of the car, limbs stretched out wide. Her chest is cut open, but it seems more brutal than Sonny and Isaac's—her shirt is cut up and her breasts are on show.

The gash runs from her throat down past her belly button.

How much hate and physical power does it take to do something like that?

I turn away as my stomach rolls with revulsion. I slap my fist over my mouth. Bile burns the back of my throat, and I blink away the tears that fill my eyes.

Charlotte is dead because of me. I set up Jake. And he knew.

A cop I don't recognize wraps a blanket around my shoulders. I hadn't realized that I was shivering. He tells me to stay where I am. I sit on the pavement with the thick, itchy blanket wrapped around me. Lights from emergency vehicles flash around me.

The ground is freezing; cold seeps through my clothes and turns my butt and legs numb. I am so cold, and I am so alone. Everyone ignores me in the flurry of activity. I just sit there in shock.

It took every ounce of self-control not to shout at the cops when they started taking dozens of photos of Charlotte. They have to, I understand that, but it's so undignified with her bra cut open too. Charlotte never even wore low-cut tops, so she would hate so many people seeing her. Seeing her like this.

"Lylah!" Chace shouts.

My body leaps, startled that he's here. How did he get here? I push myself to my feet. Chace closes in, and I stumble the final few steps toward him.

"She's dead," I sob, falling into his chest and clinging to him. My body is trembling.

"Thank God you're okay," he mumbles. His arms are too tight, but I don't tell him to loosen them because I need him. "I was so scared when I saw."

Saw?

"What do you mean?" I ask, pulling back to look at him.

"There's footage and photos on Facebook," he says quietly.

"Are you serious? Charlotte is…" I can't finish my sentence.

Charlotte is dead and half naked, and people have posted it online for everyone to see. Now her body will be on the internet forever, this way forever, and my heart aches for her. What if her family sees that picture before they hear the news from the police? Even if they weren't close, that would be such a cruel way to find out that your daughter is dead.

Finally, Charlotte's body is covered and zipped into a dark bag.

I cry. "That means Jake can see this too. He can see his handiwork and reactions on fucking Facebook! She was violated!"

"Shh," Chace shushes, pressing his forehead against mine. "We'll get him, Lylah. I promise you."

And I cry harder. I know we will…because I'm going to make a deal with the devil.

26

Wednesday
February 14

We're there in that parking lot for an hour. Charlotte was taken away, and Detective Lina took my statement, but I could tell her nothing new. She had driven Chace to the scene after he refused to stay put. Other officers were left at the house with Sienna.

Detective Lina said someone was on their way to find Charlotte's family and tell them the news. They might know already. I haven't checked any social media because I can't bear to see those images, but I know by now she would have been identified. People may have even tagged her.

The whole thing is sick.

After we're taken back to the house, Chace follows me to my room, watching me like he's sure I'm going to shatter into a million pieces. We left a stunned Sienna in the living room with a cop answering her thousand questions as best he can.

A door slams. "Where is she?" Riley shouts from downstairs.

Chace and I look at each other. I should have known my brother would be here after today's events. He must have seen the news online. Or on television. It's everywhere at this point.

Riley's footsteps hammer up the stairs.

"Good luck," Chace says, backing out of the room to give me some time to talk to my brother.

Seconds later, Riley fills the room with his broad frame. "You're coming home with me right now."

I shake my head, filled with confidence. "No, I'm not."

"Are you shitting me, Lylah? You stay here, and you could *die*! It's too dangerous to stay here."

With him standing right there, glaring at me, my steely response falters. "No, Riley. You…you remember what Lina said. Jake will follow us. There is no way I'm—I can't put anyone else in danger."

"Oh, come on. They won't be in any danger. He's not going to go after the neighbors."

"You don't know that!" I shout back. "None of us knows what he'll do next, but we do know he has no morals and no compassion. He doesn't care who he hurts, don't you see that?!"

Riley sighs, closing his eyes. "I feel like I'm failing, Lylah. Ever since you moved here you've been distant, and I'm worried about you. I really don't care about 'getting my life back,' like you've said in the past. Family comes first. Always."

"I like it here. I like being on my own, Riley. When I lived at home, I was so reliant on you. We've always been close, and I love that," I tell him quickly. "But I think we were too dependent on each other. When Mom and Dad died, we formed our own little family, which was so great. But I found it hard to function without you. I want us to always have each other's back, but being *so* dependent on each other is not healthy. And right now, I need to be here—for the investigation and for my friends."

Riley frowns. "Lylah, we're siblings, we're supposed to be there for each other."

"Of course, we are, but we're also supposed to be able to live normal lives. I used to practically hyperventilate if you left the house without me," I finish quietly.

It was a really dark time. Back then, all I could think when he walked out the door was that he was going to get in an accident and never come back. Just like our parents.

But until now, I didn't realize how much Riley relied on me too. He took on the role as dad, and he's still doing it. Couple that with the situation now and him promising our parents to always take care of me, and it's easy to see how he's starting to unravel.

But I don't know how to fix this.

Riley straightens his back. "Okay, no more talking about that. I'm going to make some food. You need to eat. Then we'll put something on TV."

Despite not wanting to rely too heavily on my brother, I feel my heart warm. That actually sounds perfect, like the good parts of our old times living together as a family.

Riley spends the whole day being my shadow. It's actually nice to have him with me again, but after he follows me around like I'm going to break for hours and hours, I'm exhausted.

He's cooked and made sure I've eaten lunch and dinner. He's tried to keep my mind off everything by putting on movies and telling me about the home improvements he's planning.

Soon it fades into night—a little early for bed—but I can't hold off any longer. I need sleep and, honestly, I just want to be alone for a while now. I fake a yawn and stand up. Riley gets to his feet and turns the TV off.

"I'm really tired, Riley" I say. "It's been a stressful day."

"Yeah, of course. You coming home then?"

I cut him a look and grit my teeth. "We'll deal with that later, but for now I'm staying here." I'm not going at all, even if I made it sound like it's a possibility, but I need him to back down for a while.

"You're coming home."

I narrow my eyes. "This *is* my home."

Riley's hand flies out and slams into the wall beside him.

Gasping, I jump back. "What the hell was that?" I snap.

"Whether you like it or not, you're coming home!" Turning, he thunders out of the room, his stomps driving home his irritation.

How dare he demand I leave with him! He's not actually my father, and I'm a damn adult now! I need to be here for the investigation, and no matter what Riley says, I will not be leaving.

A moment later, Chace is by my side. "What happened?" he asks softly. He must have been listening from his room, because it didn't take him long to get back here.

"He's impossible! I'm not going anywhere with him."

"You don't have to. Let's stay here together. I really need to curl up with you and forget today."

That sounds perfect, though neither of us will likely be able to forget anything.

"Okay," I reply. I grab my pajamas and phone so I can go to the bathroom to change. I leave Chace in my room, knowing he'll be stripping and getting into my bed.

I lock the bathroom door behind me and set my clothes down on the side of the sink. With a deep breath, I type a message to Jake: You and me. Let's finish this.

His reply is almost instant. 5A Baker Street. 11 PM.

He doesn't tell me to come alone. He knows I will this time. And I know Baker Street—it's a shady part on the outskirts of town. There are rows of tiny houses, most of which are empty and vandalized. There's talk of demolishing the old houses and rebuilding that part of town.

Makes sense him being there, I suppose. If anyone were even around to see him, they wouldn't look twice.

I get changed, leaving my clothes stuffed in the bathroom cabinet so I can put them on later, and go back to the bedroom. Chace is lying in my bed with his hands behind his head. The call to forget everything and just cuddle with him is strong. I don't *want* to face Jake, but I know I have to go through with this. Or this will never end.

"Come here, you," he says.

I waste no time in filling his request. Slipping beneath the covers, I snuggle up to Chace and close my eyes. I don't want to think about what could happen tonight. The chance I won't come back crosses my mind, but I push it away.

Chace's lips brush against the top of my head. "I feel like I should say *happy Valentine's Day*, but I'm guessing you're not too concerned about that."

My heart beats faster, but I'm not entirely sure if it's in a good way.

When I don't reply, and silence stretches out in front of us, Chace sighs. "I'm sorry. I know this day isn't great for you anyway...for either of us."

"It's okay. I only wish we were a normal couple. I wish we could have had coffee together this morning and be at some fancy restaurant right now. This day is just awful. I'm sorry."

I feel his lips smile against my head. "We can do that on any of the other three hundred and sixty-four days of the year."

Closing my eyes, I sink further into his embrace and whisper, "Thank you."

"So, how are you doing?" he asks, steering the conversation to where he really wants it to be. But I'm not totally sure if he's asking about my parents or the Jake situation.

I sigh. "Honestly, I don't know. You?"

"I'm ready to leave. Take out cash, train hop randomly until we're confident Jake isn't behind us. Lay low until he's found."

His plan is appealing. I'd be a liar if I said it wasn't, but there are too many variables. What if he *does* find us? What if he gets angry that we've gone missing and kills more people? What if he goes after our families?

Sighing, he adds, "I know we can't."

"Can we not talk about Jake anymore, please?"

"Sure. Sleep, Lylah, it's been a long, shitty day."

That it has. I can't fall asleep though. I'm waiting for everyone else to drift off, and then I have to get out without the cops seeing. After Chace and I snuck out, and Charlotte too, they've been tighter on security around the back, parking the cop car in the pedestrian zone so they're closer, so it's probably going to be easier to sneak out the front now.

I kiss Chace's chest, feeling his heart thumping beneath my lips, and move next to him, making sure his arm isn't holding me, so it will be easier to get away later, after he's asleep. Chace turns on his side and runs his fingertip along my jaw.

"Good night, beautiful."

God, I've waited so long to hear him say something like that to me. In the midst of all this chaos, I'm so grateful to Chace for making me feel happiness. I've missed it.

We stare at each other in silence; no words are needed. I feel so light here with him, like we're the only people in the world.

I savor every second.

Chace's eyelids start to become heavy. His blinks grow long. When he doesn't open his eyes, I start to count. It shouldn't take too long for him to fall into a deep sleep. We're all exhausted.

I never realized how peaceful it is to watch someone fall asleep. Or how tired it makes you. Stifling a yawn, I shift slowly out of bed and head to the bathroom.

My hands shake as I change back into my jeans and sweater. This has to be the dumbest thing I've ever done. *Meet up with a killer, Lylah. Excellent idea.*

I creep out of the bathroom and down the stairs. The house is cloaked in darkness, which I was counting on. Outside is also super dark since the trees shield the streetlights.

Whipping my coat off the peg by the door, I slip it on and slowly unlock and open the front door. I step outside, sticking to the wall, and slither along. If I stay at the side, I'll be able to watch the cop from the front gate and make a run for it when he looks away. We're not far from the corner, so all I have to do is sprint there and hope he doesn't look back until I'm gone.

It all seems great…in theory.

Crouching down, I hold my breath to prevent it from fogging and giving myself away. Gripping the ice-cold metal gate, I peer around the side. The cop is sitting in the car, looking out at the road.

No time to second-guess. I've purposefully not allowed myself to think about what I'm doing so I can't talk myself out of it. I run. I shove myself to my feet the way sprinters do and fly down the path.

My footsteps aren't heavy, but they sound deafening to my ears.

Once I'm around the corner, I pause for a second.

Baker Street is about a fifteen-minute walk if you cut through a housing division. It's even colder than I anticipated.

Ignoring everything around me, which isn't much at almost eleven at night in the suburbs, I focus on the task at hand. If I wasn't scared that I would stick out if I used a light, I would use the flashlight on my phone. But I don't want to draw attention to myself. I should probably think of some plan, but I have no idea what I'm walking into or what Jake wants from me. I *do* know that I'm going to play along with whatever *he's* got planned. He liked me once, so maybe I can exploit that to get him to turn himself in.

Who knows.

It might all fall apart, but I have to do something; I can't sit back while my friends die.

And I'll die before I let anything happen to another one of them—or worse, my brother.

When I turn on to Baker Street, the magnitude of what I'm doing hits me. A chill runs down my spine.

I take a breath as I walk past the first house.

You can do this. Be strong.

I focus on the pure hatred I feel for Jake. I've spent every second trying to expel the images of Sonny, Isaac, and Charlotte from my mind, but right now, I welcome them. They will give me the strength I need to do this.

There it is. A silver number five with the letter *A* on a blue door, tilted to the side like some of the screws have come loose.

This is the house.

He's inside, waiting for me.

Wetting my dry lips, I pad slowly down the path up to the front door. My stomach may burn with anger and the desire to make him pay, but I'm still petrified. I clench my fists so he won't be able to see them tremble.

When I approach the door, it's open, only by an inch, but it's clear this is for me—an invitation to enter. I step through, and my eyes, which are already acclimated to the dark, slide everywhere, searching for Jake. The hallway is narrow. I press my lips together and try to breathe quietly through my nose.

Jake doesn't mess around. When he gives an order, he wants it followed to his specifications. I learned that the hard way. It cost Charlotte her life. I'm in love with Chace, Sienna is my best friend, and I cannot lose my brother. There is no way I'm risking any of their lives to protect my own. Jake has to be stopped. Tonight, I walked into the lion's den knowingly, willingly, and I'll face the consequences without any doubt or regret.

At the end of the hall, there is another door. It is closed, but light seeps around the ill-fitting frame. I step forward and reach for the knob. My fingers twitch the closer I get.

It's such a strange feeling to walk to your death. Doing something you know is going to get you killed is quite possibly the dumbest thing a person can do. Yet here I am.

I place my hand over the round door handle and twist. It's cold and sends a shiver down my spine. Though the shiver could just be from my terror.

"Jake?" I call as I push open the door.

My eyes widen, and I suck in a gulp of air.

The small room is filled with photos of me. Candid photos spanning a year. Maybe more. Some of my clothes are strewn around the room. A scarf I thought I lost at a party hangs off an armchair. On a coffee table at the side of the room is a large bowl full of hair clips, jewelry, and a few knickknacks I've collected over the years.

Stacked in the corner of the room is a large pile of magazines that once were read by me.

I have a lot of stuff, but even so, how did I not notice that any of this was missing?

Behind the table stands a man in a hoodie. The man who's been torturing my friends and me. He stole their lives. He won't steal any more.

He lifts his hood to stare me in the eyes.

My breath catches.

"Riley?" I whisper.

27

R iley smiles. It's not sinister. He doesn't look pleased with himself. He doesn't look victorious. He doesn't look evil. He looks normal, like he's smiling at me over the dinner table.

"What's going on?" My eyes dart around the room, taking in the scene again, and it makes my brain hurt. Why is he wearing that hoodie? "How did you know I was here? Where's Jake?"

How on earth did Riley find me?

Deep inside, I think I know what's going on, but my mind is rejecting what my eyes are seeing.

"Riley, where is Jake?" I repeat.

"Jake is gone."

I shake my head. "Gone? What do you mean he's gone?"

"He's dead," Riley says, matter-of-factly. "You should have heard him, Lylah. Every time I came to visit you, he was always going on about you like he thought you were interested in him. Like you were in love with him. It had to end."

I freeze and my face drains of blood.

No.

No, there's some mistake.

Riley...this can't be right.

My brother can't be a...a *killer.*

"Riley, what are you saying?" I mutter. Pinching the bridge of my nose, I try to process the meaning of his words. "I need you to be more specific, because none of this makes sense. I don't understand."

"I can explain everything, sis. I promise."

I lower my hand. "Tell me what you've done, Riley." The realization of what's happening begins to sink in.

"You needed me again."

If I wasn't so stunned I could have fallen over.

"You've done all of...this because you wanted me to need you again?"

Eyes the same shade as mine glower. "You left me, Lylah. Everyone leaves me. We were supposed to be there for each other. We said we would always stay close, and then you moved away!" His voice gets louder, and his chest puffs with rage.

"Riley," I say, holding up my hands. "I moved away to go to school! I thought you were happy for me. You agreed it would be the fresh start I needed."

"I was supposed to be *part* of that fresh start! You told me you'd be home on holidays and some weekends, but your visits got less frequent."

"So you killed my friends because I don't come home as much?" I screech, throwing my hands up. "Why didn't you tell me how you were feeling? And how could you have killed these people? That's not normal, Riley! You *killed* people! What's wrong with you?"

He frowns. He fucking frowns like he has no idea what I'm talking about. "I just needed you home, Lylah. But you wanted to stay…for *them*. So I eliminated that obstacle for you."

"I didn't stay for them; I stayed for me," I say softly. "Oh my God, I can't believe what I'm hearing. Tell me this isn't real. Please tell me there's been some mistake and you're not responsible for all of this." As I start to put the pieces together, I realize something else. "Shit, *you* grabbed me! In the alleyway. That was you!"

I can't breathe. I'm going to pass out. My vision blurs, and I claw at my chest, trying to get my lungs to inflate again.

"Lylah!" Riley shouts.

He moves toward me, but I leap back.

I shove my hand out, my palm facing him. "Don't! Do *not* come near me."

"I'm not going to hurt you."

"You already have. They were my *friends*, Riley. They were *people*. How could you? The things you did to them… How *could* you?"

His eyebrows furrow in anger. "They had your heart, and you had theirs. I saw how you were with them, laughing and joking. You spent all of your time with five virtual strangers, and you couldn't leave them to visit your own brother."

"You *cut out* their hearts out because we all cared for each other?" I repeat the sentence in my head, trying to get it to make sense.

"It was difficult, but I practiced."

"What?" I whisper, his words winding around me. He *practiced*?

"Pigs."

"You cut open pigs?"

He stares at me, his eyes searching for something. Forgiveness? Acceptance? I don't know what, but he won't find them from me.

"I've been working out. I'm stronger than I've ever been. The size of the pigs on the Daveys' farm isn't too far off the average weight of a person. I can keep us safe. I can make sure no one comes between our family again."

Daveys' farm is just down the road from our place back home. Growing up we would always help the Daveys whenever one of the pigs escaped. It was thrilling to chase a pig down the road as a kid. We thought it was brilliant.

The pigs' hearts. The ones Riley stuck to a noticeboard and sent in a box to make us think it was our friends' hearts.

No.

Why?

"What the hell happened to you? When did you decide to do this? I was home at Christmas, Riley!"

"You forced my hand, Lylah."

Bullshit. There may be instances when I've taken the blame when I shouldn't have, but I won't take responsibility for this. He can't seriously justify everything he's done.

"How long have you been planning this?" I demand.

"I started to think about solutions for my problem when I came to see you in November. That's when you told me you weren't coming home for the anniversary of our parents' death. But see? Now we're together."

"What the hell! I told you I wasn't sure if I felt *strong* enough to be at home with…with all of those memories. You said for me to stay!" I shouted.

"Because I was worried about you. But that got me thinking about how much your friends have changed you. My *sister* would want to be with her family during emotional times. My *sister* wouldn't miss a birthday or anniversary. Can't you see it, Lylah? You're getting cold and detached here. Your friends kept you from me. I knew that I had to get you out of here."

He takes a step closer, and I tense. Riley has always been my safety net, but now, he's shattered that. I am alone.

"I know it's going to be hard, but I'll get you help, and we'll make our family better. We can go home now."

"You really are insane if you think I'm going anywhere with you. How can you not see that you're the one who needs help? This isn't how you get someone to do what you want. If you were struggling without me, you should have told me. You talk to a therapist! You don't kill people!"

Riley looks astonished. "This isn't about me. You're the one who needs me. I helped you. I can't believe you can't see it."

My mind races. *He is sick, unstable. I'm so out of my league trying to get out of this. What do I do? If I go to the cops, will they simply throw him in prison? He's obviously not well. He needs treatment. Therapy. Something.* I am so angry at him, but he's still my brother. I can't just abandon him. My mind is spinning, trying to take in this revelation and figure out what to do. I need to keep him talking.

"Riley, what happened to Jake?"

"The pigs weren't my only practice. The pigs were key. They helped me hone my craft…and dispose of the evidence."

Frowning, I shake my head. "What? I don't under…"

Oh.

His human practice was Jake.

"You…you fed Jake to the pigs after you killed him?"

The corner of his mouth ticks up in a smirk, and I don't recognize my brother. I'm staring at a stranger. This boy used to bring injured birds home to nurse them back to health. That boy is not the one standing in front of me.

"Jake was so obsessed with you," Riley continued. "He came to see me after he dropped out of college. He said that he couldn't be around you after you rejected him. He tried to get over you, but then he saw how you would look at Chace… He came to see me to tell me that he couldn't be my friend either. And to tell me that I should watch out for you. That Chace was a player and would break your heart."

"Wait, Jake came to see you?"

"We were friends too, Lylah."

Riley had visited me at school more than any of my housemates' family members, but I didn't know he was forging his own friendships with my friends.

"Jake was texting me when he dropped out of school, so I invited him out for the weekend."

Thinking back, I remember that Jake packed his stuff and left the weekend after Riley had come to visit. There was a special event on campus, so we had all hung out together.

"What happened?" I ask, terrified of what Riley would tell me.

"Jake got drunk and poured his heart out. The guy was in love with you and hated Chace," Riley said with disgust. "He said he couldn't be around you and not be with you. Jake knew that you wouldn't give up Chace for him, and he could see what I see—that you are willing to give up the people who truly care about you for people you won't see again after graduation."

"You don't get to decide who I care about, Riley! They're *my* friends!" I run my hand over my face.

"Your friends aren't good people."

I shake my head. "What are you talking about? The people you killed were good people! You don't know them, and you've proved that you don't know me."

I'm at a total loss. Detective Lina said the killer would be unstable, but this is way more than I anticipated. This is my brother, but I don't know him at all. I wish knew how to talk to him. He thinks I'm to blame for his actions, so what do I say to get through to him?

"You've killed six people, Riley."

He dips his head in a curt nod. "For you."

Anger burns in my stomach, but I realize I can't say anything in response.

He continues. "After you moved here, you weren't interested in spending time with me anymore. Every time I visited, you were preoccupied with your so-called friends. I tried so hard to get you to spend more time with me. I asked you to go to come home in January, but you were having a girls' night! It was always one thing or another. I got tired of your excuses."

Riley was always an open book to me. Sometimes I knew what he was going to say before he did. We could practically complete each other's sentences. But this person, this evil human in front of me isn't my brother. "You look like you have a lot of questions, Lylah," he says suddenly. "And you look scared. Why are you afraid?"

Duh!

I try to keep my voice calm and even. "You confessed to murder, Riley. You killed my friends. You're telling me you did all these horrific things, and you expect me to be grateful? I'm heartbroken for the people who have died. The people who have died at your hand. How could I not be scared of you?"

"But I haven't hurt *you*." He reaches for me, and every nerve in my body screams at me to run. But running is too risky. He's too fast for me. "I would never hurt *you*. You're my sister."

With my palms sweating and heart hammering, I grab hold of every ounce of courage I have and step forward, meeting him halfway.

"I believe you, Riley," I whisper. "You've always taken care of me." The words I am saying disgust me. What I want is to scream at him. To hit him. To rewind time and undo this mess. "Will you tell me how the rest of it happened? I know why, but not *how*."

"I knew I had to come for you. Jake was ranting about how much closer to Chace you were when he left. Every second you spent with your friends, you were drifting further from our family—from me. It was only a matter of time before you and Chace got together, and I couldn't stand it. You would follow him, move away after school, and would never give a shit about me again. The thought of you and him makes so angry and so disgusted, I wanted to put my hands around his neck and squeeze." His hands ball into fists and press against the side of his thighs.

I squirm, frowning at his words. "When did you arrive?"

"Two days before I killed Sonny," he says simply. "But I have been back and forth since the new year."

His words are a punch to the stomach. He's been watching us—me—for more than a month. I press my lips together and breathe through my nose.

"Why Sonny first?"

Well, second, I guess, after Jake.

"He was cocky, always had been. I had to get rid of him first or he would have shouted his mouth off about what I was doing. I knew the police would make you keep quiet about aspects of my mission, but Sonny would have told everyone too soon about what was happening. Nothing would have been secret. I wanted people to know when I was ready, and he would have taken that away from me."

"You killed Charlotte and left her exposed in a public place! How could you do that to her? To *anyone*?"

He tilts his head. "Lylah, you disobeyed my terms. There are always consequences."

I still didn't understand. I pressed him. "How did you get into our house?"

"Lylah." He looks up to the ceiling, smirking and shaking his head like he can't believe how stupid my very valid question is. Somehow he was getting into my house. "I made a copy of your key when you visited at Christmas."

My lungs deflated. I'd misplaced them for an entire morning. Riley had found them behind the end table in the hallway. God, I'd looked there too, but he said I must not have looked properly.

He took them because he was planning to stalk me and kill my friends.

"What about after we changed the locks?"

"That was annoying. I knew I couldn't get to your key again. But thankfully I have a friend with…questionable morals who was only too happy to show me how to pick a lock. I wish I'd gone to him from the start; it was much more exhilarating to get in that way."

Oh my God. "How frequently were you in the house?"

"Only when I needed to be."

And how often was that?

"Right," I say, still in shock at his latest confession.

"I just wanted you to come home. When you refused, I knew I had to get rid of the barriers, the people who were keeping you here. Sonny, Isaac, Charlotte, Chace. They were all stopping you."

"But not Sienna? She's my best friend. And Jake had already left school! What about the cop? What did he do? He had a *family*! And Nora—she was completely innocent!"

Riley sighs in frustration, like the reasons he killed these people are obvious, and I'm just not getting it. He has always been very smart. I used to envy his mind. Not anymore. I don't want to be anything like him.

"Please, I need answers," I beg. *And I need to figure out how to call for help or get out of here.*

"Sienna wouldn't hold you back. She's always told you to go back home when I've asked you to visit in front of your friends. She was the only one who encouraged you to spend time with your family."

My head is spinning.

"Nora," he says, narrowing his eyes. "She spent the night with me when I visited at Halloween. We were both drunk, and I confessed how I felt about you never coming home, how I hated your friends. I didn't think she'd remember, but she mentioned it in the morning. I apologized for venting to her, and she agreed not to tell you. But when I arrived back in town this month, she caught me watching the house and put two and two together. I didn't want to hurt her, but I had to. She would have figured out it was me and turned me in before I could finish my work."

"You and Nora were...together?" I know that's not the detail I should focus on, but I never would have imagined them together. She was quiet and reserved, and he's always been loud and outgoing. Was that why she was trying to befriend me? She liked my brother and was trying to reconnect with him?

He rolls his eyes, and I get a glimpse of the big brother I knew. "She'd messed up some assignment or something and came to The Bar to get drunk. I was angry because you'd ditched spending time with me, yet again, for a dinner with Charlotte."

I remembered that. Char got one bad grade and was stressing over it, so I took her out.

"The cop caught me when I was trying to leave a note. He looked like he was asleep in his car, but he wasn't. He started to come after me, so I had to act fast. Thankfully I'd perfected my technique."

Technique. That's what he calls murder and mutilation.

I look away and close my eyes. What the hell would our parents think?

"What's the rest of your plan?" I whisper, looking at him, scared to hear the answer.

"You go back to the house and pack. We tell the cops that you're coming home with me. I'll come back and finish the job. The police will still suspect Jake…but they'll never find him. It's all tied up."

Oh my God, you're crazy.

"Riley, you need help."

"We'll help each other. It's what we've done since Mom and Dad died, and it's what we need to do again." He smiles at me, and tucks a piece of hair behind my ear. I hold my ground, knowing I can't back down, even though I want to recoil.

"Wait—what do you mean *finish the job*?"

"Chace." Riley smirks. "You won't be free until you cut ties with him. So I'm going to sever the hold he has on you."

My lungs empty. "No. No, Riley, you can't. Please."

"It has to be done. Do you think he'll let you leave? He'll follow you, Lylah. Once he's gone, this will all be over. How can you not see that?"

I shake my head, my eyes filling with tears. My heart aches in the worst way. We haven't been a couple for long, but my feelings for him run deep. We've been friends long before we were together. I have to protect Chace.

"Riley, I'll tell Chace I don't love him," I plead. "I'll explain that I was looking for a replacement, someone to take care of me, and that my feelings got muddled. That I was upset about our friends' deaths, and that I need my space to move on. He won't come looking for me if he knows there's no chance of us being together."

Riley's eyes, now void of humanity, stare straight through me. "No." He tilts his head to the side and grins. "I'm going to kill him and serve you his heart."

28

Wednesday
February 14

My ears are ringing. Riley's words are alien. He doesn't speak like that. Hell, he doesn't even think like that.

I open my mouth, but nothing comes out.

Riley smiles sweetly, and I get a glimpse of my brother again.

How ill is he? What's wrong with my brother?

He folds his arms. "Why are you still standing there? We need to get you back to the house so you can pack. I already have my things together. I'm ready."

What?

He's planning to kill Chace, and he expects me to go along with it, simply going home to pack and leaving him to his business? His *murder* business?

Somehow, I need to find a way to talk to this terrifying version of my brother. If I can do that, maybe I can talk him down. Maybe I can get him into police custody, where he won't harm anyone else—or himself.

"Riley, you're my brother, and I love you, but what you're doing, what you've done, is *wrong*. It's time to do the right thing. I'll stand by you, and I'll fight to get you the best help out there, but I won't protect you for what you've done, and I won't let you hurt anyone else."

"Family. First," he growls. "A person's heart belongs to their family, *not* their friends. When did you forget that? They had your heart, so I took theirs from them."

He bends over and lifts the lid on a wooden box on the table.

I crumble. Gagging, I almost sink to the ground. "No! No, Riley!"

Four hearts.

Sonny, Nora, Isaac, Charlotte.

The cop had his when they found his body, and Jake's was fed to pigs.

The hearts are dark, almost black, and squashed together. Who's is who's? Does Riley even know? Does he even care?

My stomach lurches.

"Oh God, you kept them." Pressing my palm to my mouth, I avert my tear-filled eyes and try to focus as my mind short-circuits. The smell is so rotten and vile that I retch. "How could you do that? You cut their hearts out and kept them." The words don't make sense even as I speak them out loud.

Why has he kept them? Are they trophies? How sick is he to put their hearts in a box?

"Calm down, Lylah. They are organs. They can't hurt you." He lets go of the lid and it slams shut.

I'm not worried about them hurting me! I'm worried about you hurting me—hurting Chace! I want to scream.

"I know this is a bit of shock, and I'm sorry that it's information overload. I had to tell you everything so you understand how much I love you, so we can move forward. You understand that, right? We've always understood each other, haven't we?" He looks deep into my eyes, and I don't recognize the person staring at me.

Rearing back, I almost choke. He killed my friends and cut out their hearts because he thinks I love my friends more than him.

Clenching my hands behind my back, I take a deep breath and know what I have to do. I reply in a whisper, "Yes, I understand. I do know you better than anyone, so I know you didn't mean this."

His eyes tighten. I've said the wrong thing. I keep talking. "You put me first so many times—you always put me first—of course you did all this for me. You are my brother. You always take care of me."

He scoffs, and his posture hardens. "When you used to cry so much you could barely breathe, who was there for you? When you couldn't leave the house, who stayed in with you? When you cried yourself to sleep, who sat in your room with you? It was *me*, Lylah. All of it was *me*. Remember that."

How long has Riley been sick? We lost our parents, and then I moved away. I was so messed up after their deaths, and Riley spent the whole time trying to make things better for me that I don't think ever grieved. Maybe when I moved away, he finally realized how much he'd lost.

Has he been slowly unraveling since the day I left? I was so consumed with keeping myself in a good place, I didn't notice his struggles. He knew if I was having a hard day just from looking at me, and I had no idea how low he sunk.

How could I not have known?

"Riley, I'm so sorry I didn't see what's been going on. I should have. This is my fault too, and I'll help you put it right."

I'm partly responsible for the monster he has become, and that guilt practically swallows me whole.

"You couldn't see it. Your *friends* brainwashed you into thinking you're better off here. They don't know you, and they don't know what you've been through. I do."

"I think we should call Detective Lina now," I say softly.

"That's not part of the plan, Lylah!" he snaps.

"I can't let you hurt anyone else."

Riley's chest puffs out his chest. I purposefully didn't mention Chace by name, but Riley knows what I mean.

He tilts his head to the side. "You think you love him."

I know I love him.

"How I feel about Chace has nothing to do with us. Riley, a person can have different relationships. You have friends outside of our family too."

"Yes, but they're not more important than family."

"Of course not, but that doesn't mean you can't have both. Why does it have to be all or nothing?"

We're not going to get anywhere here. I'm not sure he's even capable of seeing the situation from another perspective.

"I'll come home with you, Riley, but you have to stop this now. Leave Chace alone."

His frame looms huge in this small room. Every time I say something he doesn't like, it feels as if he grows larger and more ominous.

"You'll betray me. You'll come back for him. I have to get rid of the temptation for you."

"No, I won't. I promise." If it means Chace would be safe, I would stay away. "This day is already horrible, Riley. There are enough hurtful memories for us to carry for the rest of our lives. Our parents died two years ago today. Let's not make it any worse. We can reunite our family permanently—me and you against the world."

It's hard to believe that two years ago we became orphans. Riley was so caring and attentive. And now this.

He drops his eyes as I mention our parents. It's like talking about them has gotten through to him. Maybe the brother I knew is not totally lost. His eyes flash, and then he's gone again.

"I'll finish this, Lylah, and then we'll go home."

"You're not hurting him!" I snap. "Let's just go. I'll leave my stuff behind and that can be that."

His mouth splays in a wide grin. "I've missed my bossy baby sister. But you don't understand. The end has already begun."

My heart misses a beat. "What? What do you mean?"

Reaching into his pocket, he pulls out his phone. "Chace is on his way."

I step closer to him to try to grab the phone, as if by reflex. "No! Riley, no, please. Get what you need, and we'll go. Right now."

"No."

"Oh my God!" My voice is so loud, I don't recognize it. I shake my trembling hands. "You can't do this."

"You really do love him," he mutters, turning up his nose. "Mom and Dad would hate who you've become."

His words are excruciating. He may as well have taken a knife to my heart.

There is no reasoning with him. I have to intercept Chace. Turning, I head toward the door, but Riley grabs my wrist before I get to the hallway.

"Don't touch me!" I spin around. "What the hell happened to you, Riley? How is this you? How have you become this?"

"Lylah!" Chace shouts my name from outside, and my heart drops.

"Riley, please don't do this."

The front door slams open against the wall.

Chace stands in the doorway. His wide eyes are fixed on Riley, surprise on his face. "Riley?" he says, bewildered. His eyes flick to me for answers.

"Because of you, I lost my sister. You need to pay."

"You haven't lost me." I step closer to Riley, moving my body in between him and Chace. "Let Chace leave, and then we'll go."

"There's no way you're going anywhere with him," Chace spits as he realizes what's happening.

"Stay out of this." Riley waves his hand, and the light from the room glints off something he's holding.

A knife.

"Riley, no," I say, raising my hands in surrender. "Let's talk about this."

"We'll talk when we get home, Lylah. I need to deal with your *boyfriend*."

Deal with him. How did my life come to this?

Chace isn't having it. "I'd like to see you try, man. We may have been scared of you when you were jumping out at us from the shadows, but I see you now. I won't let you hurt Lylah."

"Don't even say her name!" Riley shouts. "You know nothing about us, about our life or our family. What do you even know about her past? You think you know her? You don't." Riley's hand tightens around the handle of the long blade, his knuckles turning white.

"That's enough, Riley!" I desperately plead. "Just stop. We all need to calm down and sort this out."

"That's what I'm trying to do," he replies, raising the knife.

"Put that down, and listen to me," I say firmly. "There is no going back if you do this."

"Do you think there is any going back after everything else he's done?" Chace asks, and I want to throttle him. He is not helping the situation. "The cops are going to arrest him. And I'm going to take you home. Sienna is losing her mind with worry."

Riley's eyes darken. "How does Sienna know Lylah is here?"

Chace takes a step forward, and that's when I hear cars outside screech to a halt. Lights flash outside. Chace told the cops. Doors open and footsteps thud toward us. We barely have time to react before the police storm the room.

Riley is the first to move. He grabs my arm with his free hand and wrenches me against his chest as he pulls me backward into the room.

My back presses against his chest. Something sharp press against my neck.

The blade.

I freeze. Riley has the knife against my neck.

My own brother has a knife to my throat.

The first face I recognize is Detective Lina's as I frantically scan the room. She looks calm and in control. She must have trained for these situations. I wish I had some of her steadiness. My heartbeat screams in my ears.

Around her are five other officers and Detective Alexander. Three guns are pointing at my brother. I can see the small black hole where a bullet will fire from if the trigger is pulled.

My heart thumps heavily.

Detective Lina speaks. "Riley, I know you don't want to hurt your sister, so put down the knife, and we can talk."

"Talk," he spits. "You don't want to talk. Back away all of you, or I'll shove this through her fucking neck!"

I'm shaking. I feel my body rattle in Riley's arms. He wouldn't actually do that, would he? People are capable of unspeakable terrors when they are cornered, but Riley has always been my protector. Could he do that to me? *Would* he do that to me?

"Riley...please," I whisper.

"Shut up, Lylah. Just shut up!" His arm tightens, and metal digs into my skin to the point of pain. His breathing is heavy and ragged with rage. He acts like a wounded animal lashing out.

"Okay, okay." Detective Lina raises her hands higher while Chace stares at me in horror. "We'll back up a little. But I know you don't want to do this. I know how much you love your sister. She's all you've got."

I squeeze my eyes shut. I don't have a brother anymore. He died the second he killed Jake.

Detective Lina keeps her expression calm, like this is just another day in the office. "You don't have to do this, Riley. You have options."

"Like going to prison. I don't think so."

"Riley, think about this!" I beg. I would try to squirm away, but his grip is too tight. With the blade to my neck, there is no room to struggle.

"I'm not going to prison. I'm not going to prison. I'm not going to prison," Riley chants. His voice is low and controlled. It doesn't sound like him, and a shiver runs through my body.

I look at the detective who seems to be working out her next move. We all knew that the killer was a psychopath, but I think this is more than any of us anticipated.

"I'm not going to prison!" Riley bellows. Spit flies from his mouth and wets my cheek. Suddenly, his arm moves quickly and the knife leaves my neck.

I twist in his arms, hoping the distraction will be enough for me to slip away. But Riley snaps his arm forward and a blinding pain shoots through my body.

He's plunged the knife into my stomach.

Screaming, I stumble backward, holding the hilt of the blade that is sticking out of my stomach.

What do I do?

"Lylah!" Chace jumps forward to catch me as I stagger, and Detective Lina runs toward the door at the back of the hallway. Riley is gone.

He's stabbed me. And left me here to bleed.

I can't even process what's going on right now.

Everything around me moves in slow motion. Chace's mouth is moving, but I can't hear what he is saying. Another cop crouches beside me but I can't focus on him either.

I'm cold. Really, really cold.

Am I dying?

My legs turn to jelly, and I slump to the floor. Chace and the cop don't leave my side. The police officer holds the knife still, but he's not removing it.

Chace takes my cheeks in his hands, his touch feather light. I open my mouth to tell him I love him. But I'm not sure if the words come out. All I can hear is my pulse working overtime, thrumming in my ears.

The world is getting dark, as if someone is dimming the lights. I blink hard, but it doesn't help.

Why is everyone so far away?

I'm falling.

My eyes close, and I know this is it.

My brother has killed me.

EPILOGUE

One year later…
February 14

I t's Valentine's Day. Again. Obviously, I like the holiday even less this year, despite the fact that Chace and I are deliriously happy together.

We're a couple, but we've agreed we aren't celebrating the holiday. I don't think we'll ever celebrate it, and I don't think Chace is too upset about that.

After I got out of the hospital, Chace, Sienna, and I rented a smaller place together. After our friends died, none of us could face getting new housemates or staying in a home we all once loved but that had brought so much heartache. Yeah, Sienna is stuck as a third wheel a lot, but she doesn't seem to mind.

It's a long road to recovery, again, and although I still have a lot of bad days, and I haven't weaned off my anxiety medication fully yet, I'm doing better. I still can't sleep through the night, waking in cold sweats, expecting Riley to be standing over me. I can't get through a full lecture without thinking about what happened on campus. I can't close my eyes without seeing the wrong end of a gun. But having Chace beside me, supporting me, is some comfort.

So there might still be plenty of things I can't do, but I can go on dates with Chace and not constantly look over my shoulder.

He's safety.

When we graduate, Chace and I plan on moving far away from here. I would have left already, but Chace and Sienna made me realize that running won't help. And I want my degree. I've worked hard for it. If I drop out, it will be my fault, not Riley's. And I won't let him take anything from me ever again.

"Do you guys want to come out with us tonight?" Sienna asks.

"No thanks," I reply a little too quickly. She gets it though. "Where are you going?" I ask her, trying to move past the moment.

"Nathan is taking me out to dinner, then to a club. I initially said no, but he convinced me. It's time to build some new memories," she says.

"Sienna, go and have a great night."

"Thanks, Lylah. Last year was the worst time of my life, but I finally feel like I'm coming through the other side of the tunnel."

Does the tunnel have an end? I feel like I'm constantly running toward it, only to find the tunnel stretches out again. I barely ever get a glimpse of light.

"That's great, Sienna," Chace replies, sensing my unease.

I'm happy for her. I truly am. But every time I hear how well someone is doing, it reminds me how much I have struggled.

"I'll see you guys later then," Sienna says. "I'm going shopping to find shoes to go with my dress."

"Don't you already own all of the shoes in the world?" I tease.

She playfully gives me the finger and heads toward the door. "The mail is on the side table, by the way. I didn't see anything that looks like a response from the film festival you submitted to, but you never know," she shouts back at us. Then the front door slams. I can't help but breathe a sigh of relief that she's gone. Some days it is so hard to be around people who are happy.

Chace look at me tenderly. "Are you okay?"

I run my finger along my stomach. My scar is just above my hipbone. It's about an inch long and has healed well. But it's a constant physical reminder of what's happened.

"I just want to get through today."

Leaning his forehead against mine, Chace pulls my hand away from my scar. "Tell me what you need."

"A big order of Chinese takeout and a movie."

Smiling, he presses his lips against mine. "Done. You pick the movie; I'll grab the mail and order our food."

Chace walks to the front door with his phone in his hand, and I go through to the living room. I'm never going to celebrate this day. I didn't want to after it took my parents, and I certainly don't want to after everything that happened with Riley.

My brother was caught half a mile from Baker Street. He's receiving the help he needs in a high-security psychiatric hospital, and this morning he was being transferred to another facility to continue his treatment. I can't bring myself to visit him yet, but his new hospital is closer, so when I'm ready it will be easier. My therapist agrees that it is still too soon. I may have healed physically, but emotionally, I still have a long way to go before I can face him again.

Zak has been to visit Riley; he had a lot of questions about Jake. He asked if I wanted to know about their conversations, but I don't. Zak's family still hates us—Sarah especially—but Zak has forgiven me, and, somehow, he's forgiven Riley too. I'm so thankful for that. He's stronger than I am, and he's become a good friend to us all. And after losing so many friends, I need to hold on to the ones I have.

I can hear Chace placing an order for our favorite dishes as I curl up on the sofa. I switch on the TV and scroll through what's streaming. Romantic or scary movies are completely out of the question, so I scroll through the list of action titles.

Chace slowly shuffles into the room. I look up and my heart plummets at his pale, somber expression.

"What is it?" I whisper.

Beside me on the sofa, my phone flashes with Detective Lina's name. In the hallway, I hear the landline ring too.

He holds out his hand. In it is a cream envelope. My name is printed neatly on the front. No address or stamp. Hand delivered.

My mobile stops ringing, and Chace's starts.

No.

I take the envelope and pull out the note inside.

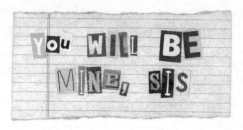

ACKNOWLEDGMENTS

As always, there are a few people I need to thank.

My husband, Joseph, without whom I wouldn't be able to achieve half of what I somehow manage to get done. Thank you for being my rock, for cheering me on, and for making sure I have time and peace to write.

My boys, Ashton and Remy, you two are absolutely everything. I hope you know how proud I am of you both and how much I love your love of books. But no, Ash, you can't read any of Mummy's just yet!

Kirsty and Zoë, two of my favorite people in the book world. Thank you for your support encouragement in the form of words and GIFs!

And my editor, Annette. This schedule has been a little full on, so thank you so much for everything you've done to make it as easy as possible for me.

ABOUT THE AUTHOR

UK native Natasha Preston grew up in small villages and towns. She discovered her love of writing when she stumbled across an amateur writing site and uploaded her first story and hasn't looked back since. She enjoys writing NA romance, thrillers, gritty YA, and the occasional serial killer thriller.

For more, visit Natasha at natashapreston.com or find her on Facebook, Twitter @natashavpreston, or Instagram @natashapreston5.

Ready for another heart-pounding read
from Natasha Preston?

SEE IF YOU CAN
ESCAPE *THE CELLAR*

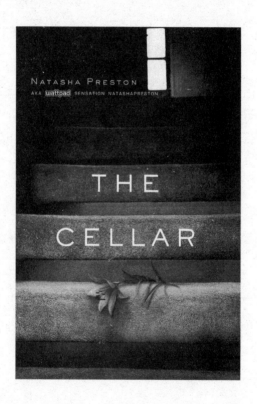

I

SUMMER

Saturday, July 24th (Present)

Looking out my bedroom window, I'm faced with yet another dull English summer day. The heavy clouds made it look way too dark for July, but not even that was going to faze me. Tonight I was going to celebrate the end of the school year at a gig by a school band, and I was determined to have some fun.

"Hey, what time are you leaving?" Lewis asked. He let himself into my room—as usual—and sat down on the bed. We'd been together over a year, so we were more than comfortable with each other now. Sometimes I missed the time when Lewis didn't tell me he was getting off the phone because he needed to pee or when he would pick up his dirty underwear *before* I came over. My mum was right: the longer you were with a man, the grosser they became. Still, I wouldn't change him. You're supposed to accept someone you love for who they were, so I accepted his messiness.

I shrugged and studied my reflection in the mirror. My hair was boring, flat, and never looked right. I couldn't even pull off the messy look. No matter how "easy" the steps to the perfect bedhead look were in a magazine, I never could make it work. "In a minute. Do I look okay?"

Apparently the most attractive thing was confidence. But what did you do if you weren't confident? That couldn't be faked without it being obvious. I wasn't model pretty or *Playboy* sexy, and I didn't have bucket loads of confidence. Basically, I was screwed and downright lucky that Lewis was so blind.

He smirked and rolled his eyes—his *here she goes again* look. It used to annoy him at first, but now I think it just amused him. "You know I can see you in the mirror, right?" I said, glaring at his reflection.

"You look beautiful. As always," he replied. "Are you sure you don't want me to drop you off tonight?"

I sighed. *This again.* The club where the gig was being held was barely a two-minute walk from my house. It was a walk that I had done so many times I could make it there blindfolded. "No thanks. I'm fine walking. What time are you leaving?"

He shrugged and pursed his lips. I loved it when he did that. "Whenever your lazy brother's ready. Are you sure? We can give you a lift on the way."

"It's fine, seriously! I'm leaving right now, and if you're waiting for Henry to get ready, you'll be a while."

"You shouldn't walk alone at night, Sum."

I sighed again, deeper, and slammed my brush down on the wooden dresser. "Lewis, I've been walking around on my own for *years*. I used to walk to and from school every day, and I'll do it again next year. These"—I slapped my legs for emphasis—"work perfectly fine."

His eyes trailed down to my legs and lit up. "Hmm, I can see that."

Grinning, I pushed him back on the bed and sat on his lap. "Can you take your overprotective boyfriend hat off and kiss me?" Lewis chuckled, and his blue eyes lit up as his lips met mine.

Even after eighteen months, his kisses still made my heart skip a beat. I started liking him when I was eleven. He would come home with Henry after football practice every week while his mum was at work. I thought it was just a silly crush—like the one I also had on Usher at the time—and didn't think anything of it. But when he still gave me butterflies four years later, I knew it had to be something more.

"You two are disgusting." I jumped back at the sound of my brother's deep, annoying voice.

I rolled my eyes. "Shut up, Henry."

"Shut up, Summer," he shot back.

"It's impossible to believe you're eighteen."

"Shut up, Summer," he repeated.

"Whatever. I'm going," I said and pushed myself off Lewis. I gave him one last kiss and slipped out of the room.

"Idiot," Henry muttered. *Immature idiot*, I thought. We did get along—sometimes—and he was the best big brother I could ask for, but he drove me crazy. I had no doubt we would bicker until we died.

"Summer, are you now leaving?" Mum called from the kitchen. *No, I'm walking out the door for fun!*

"Yeah."

"Sweetheart, be careful," Dad said.

"I will. Bye," I replied quickly and walked out the door before they could stop me. They still treated me like I was in elementary school and couldn't go out alone. Our town was probably—actually definitely—the most boring place on earth; nothing even remotely interesting ever happened.

The most excitement we'd ever had was two years ago when old Mrs. Hellmann—yeah, like the mayonnaise—went missing and was found hours later wondering the sheep field looking for her late husband. The whole town was looking for her. I still remember the buzz of something finally happening.

I started walking along the familiar pavement toward the pathway next to the graveyard. That was the only part of walking alone that I didn't like. Graveyards. They were scary—fact—and especially when you were alone. I subtly glanced around while I walked along the footpath. I felt uneasy, even after passing the graveyard. We had moved to this neighborhood when I was five, and I had always felt safe here. My childhood had been spent playing out in the street with my friends, and as I got older, I hung out at the park or club. I knew this town and the people in it like the back of my hand, but the graveyard *always* creeped me out.

I pulled my jacket tightly around myself and picked up the pace. The club was almost in view, just around the next corner. I glanced over my shoulder again and gasped as a dark figure stepped out from behind a hedge.

"Sorry, dear, did I frighten you?"

I sighed in relief as old Harold Dane came into view. I shook my head. "I'm fine."

He lifted up a heavy-looking black bag and threw it into his garbage can with a deep grunt as if he had been lifting weights. His skinny frame was covered in wrinkled, saggy skin. He looked like he'd snap in half if he bent over. "Are you going to the disco?"

I grinned at choice of word. *Disco*. Ha! That's probably what they called it back when he was a teenager. "Yep. I'm meeting my friends there."

"Well, you have a good night, but watch your drinks. You don't know what the boys today slip in pretty young girls' drinks," he warned, shaking his head as if it were the scandal of the year and every teenage boy was out to date-rape everyone.

Laughing, I raised my hand and waved. "I'll be careful. Night."

"Good night, dear."

The club was visible from Harold's house, and I relaxed as I approached the entrance. My family and Lewis had made me jumpy; it was ridiculous. As I got to the door, my friend Kerri grabbed my arm from beside me, making me jump. She laughed, her eyes alight with humor. *Hilarious*. "Sorry. Have you seen Rachel?"

My heart slowed to its normal pace as my brain processed my friend's face and not the face of the *Scream* dude or Freddy Kruger. "Not seen anyone. Just got here."

"Damn it. She ran off after another argument with the idiot, and her phone's turned off!" Ah, the idiot. Rachel had a very on/off relationship with her boyfriend, Jack. I never understood that—if you pissed each other off 90 percent of the time, then just call it a day. "We should find her."

Why? I had hoped for a fun evening with friends, not chasing after a girl who should have just dumped her loser boyfriend's arse already. Sighing, I resigned myself to the inevitable. "Okay, which direction did she go?"

Kerri gave me a flat look. "If I knew that, Summer…"

Rolling my eyes, I pulled her hand, and we started walking back toward the road. "Fine. I'll go left, you go right." Kerri saluted and marched off to the right. I laughed at her and then went my way. Rachel had better be close.

I walked across the middle of the playing field near the club, heading toward the gate at the back to see if she had taken the short-cut through to her house. The air turned colder, and I rubbed my arms. Kerri said Rachel's phone was off, but I tried calling it anyway and, of course, it went straight to voice mail. If she didn't want to speak to anyone, then why were we trying to find her?

I left an awkward message on her phone—I hated leaving messages—and walked through the gate toward the skate ramp at the back of the park. The clouds shifted, creating a gray swirling effect across the sky. It looked moody, creepy but pretty at the same times. A light, cool breeze whipped across my face, making my light honey-blond hair—according to hairdresser wannabe Rachel—blow in my face and a shudder ripple through my body.

"Lily?" a deep voice called from behind me. I didn't recognize it. I spun around and backed up as a tall, dark-haired man stepped into view. My stomach dropped. Had he been hiding between the trees? What the heck? He was close enough that I could see the satisfied grin on his face and neat hair not affected by the wind. How much hairspray must he have used? If I weren't freaked out, I would have asked what product he used because my hair never played fair. "Lily," he repeated.

"No. Sorry." Gulping, I took another step back and scanned the area in the vain hope that one of my friends would be nearby. "I'm not Lily," I mumbled, straightening my back and looking up at him in an attempt to appear confident. He towered over me, glaring down at me with creepily dark eyes.

He shook his head. "No. You are Lily."

"I'm *Summer*. You have the wrong person." *You utter freak!*

I could hear my pulse crashing in my ears. How stupid to give him my real name. He continued to stare at me, smiling. It made me feel sick. Why did he think I was Lily? I hoped that I just looked like his daughter or something and he wasn't some crazy weirdo.

I took another step back and searched around to find a place that I could escape if needed. The park was big, and I was still near the back, just in front of the trees. There was no way anyone would be able to see me from here. That thought alone made my eyes sting. Why did I come here alone? I wanted to scream at myself for being so stupid.

"You are Lily," he repeated.

Before I could blink, he threw his arms forward and grabbed me. I tried to shout, but he clasped his hand over my mouth, muffling my screams. What the heck was he doing? I thrashed my arms, frantically trying to get out of his grip. *Oh God, he's going to kill me.* Tears poured from my eyes. My heart raced. My fingertips tingled and my stomach knotted with fear. *I'm going to die. He's going to kill me.*

The Lily man pulled me toward him with such force the air left my lungs in a rush as I slammed against him. He spun me around so my back pressed tightly against his chest. And with his hand sealed over my mouth and nose, I struggled to breathe. I couldn't move, and

I didn't know if it was because he had such a strong iron grip or if I was too stunned. He had me, and he could do whatever he wanted because I couldn't bloody move a muscle.

He pushed me through the gate at the back of the park and then through the field. I tried again to scream for help, but against his palm, I hardly made a sound. He whispered "Lily" over and over while he dragged me toward a white van. I watched trees pass me by and birds fly over us, landing on branches. Everything carried on as normal. Oh God, I needed to get away now. I dug my feet into the ground and screamed so hard that my throat instantly started to hurt. It was useless, though; no one was around to hear me but the birds.

He tugged his arm back, pressing it into my stomach. I cried out in pain. As soon as he let go to open the van's back door, I screamed for help. "Shut up!" he shouted as he pushed me inside the vehicle. My head smashed into the side of the van while I struggled.

"Please let me go. Please. I'm *not* Lily. Please."

━━━━━━━━━━ **#getbooklit** ━━━━━━━━━━

Your hub for the hottest young adult books!

Visit us online and sign up for our
newsletter at FIREreads.com

 @sourcebooksfire

 sourcebooksfire

 firereads.tumblr.com